PARADX

FORGED IN

BLOOD

A Historical Murder Mystery

MARY FRANCES FISHER

Cambron Press

United States

Copyright © 2016 Mary Frances Fisher
All rights reserved.

Published in the United States of America
Cambron Press, an imprint of Cambron Publishing Group LLC
Bigfork, Montana

Fisher, Mary Frances
Paradox Forged in Blood; novel/Mary Frances Fisher
ISBN-10: 0996507647
ISBN-13: 978-0996507646

Cover design by Potterton House Author Services
Cover imagie of mansion is reprinted with express permission of Special Collections, Cleveland State University. All other cover images from Shutterstock.

PRINTED IN THE UNITED STATES OF AMERICA

DEDICATION

For my parents, Frank and Ellen, whose unconditional love gave me the strength to overcome life's adversities. And for my son and best friend, Sean Francis Patrick. In times of fear and doubt, your support and encouragement can be summed up in four beautiful words: "Mom, you've got this." You are my rock and strength—for this, you have my undying love.

TABLE OF CHARACTERS

O'MALLEY FAMILY

Parents	Michael & Mary
Children	Ellen Grace (b. 1916)
	Margaret (b. 1917)
	Mayme (b. 1920
	Patrick (b. 1921)
	William (b. 1923
	Veronica (b. 1925)
	James (b. 1928)
	Thomas (b. 1930)

SHERIDAN FAMILY

Parents	Louis & Marianne
Children	Edward (b. 1919)
	Timothy (b. 1922)
	Bridget (b. 1939)
Staff	Alice Webber—Housekeeper
	Clifford H. Smith—Butler
	Sara B. Smith—Cook
	Sadie Leibowitz—Temporary Cook

O'RILEY FAMILY

Parents	Bob and Evelyn
Child	Joseph (b. 1916)

LEIBOWITZ FAMILY

Parents	Benjamin & Rachel

Children	Sadie (b. 1924)
	Gretl (b. 1924)
Extended Family	Elsa (Benjamin's sister) and Asher Goldstein
	Children: Miles & Aaron
	Alona and Albert Leibowitz (Benjamin's brother)

KAUFMANN FAMILY

Parents	Dietrich & Clara
Child	Eric (b. 1920)

MUELLER FAMILY

Parents	Karl & Eva
Children	Kurt (b. 1909)
	Stephen (b. 1920)

FRANK & ELLEN O'MALLEY SZABO'S FAMILY

Children	James Francis
	Thomas Michael
	Eileen Marie
	Mary Frances (the author)
Grandchildren	Sean
	Colleen
	Madie
Great-grandchild	Chris

AUTHOR'S NOTE

This story is based on true events and stories passed down from the author's family. Events surrounding World War II are factual based on numerous books, documentaries, and research. Certain experiences and fictional characters have been added for creative purposes and entertainment value.

PROLOGUE

ELLEN O'MALLEY SZABO thought to herself, for perhaps the hundredth time today, why couldn't the past stay where it belonged? It held such power over the present and impacted the lives of many, including her own. Ellen knew her well-kept secret of more than 40 years would be revealed, and with it, her complicit actions leading to murder. Yes, the past would wreak havoc on so many people including her family, who believed her to be a saint. Just the thought of their disappointment would be heartbreaking. But Ellen had to put her feelings aside and act normally as she sat upstairs in her bedroom waiting for the "surprise" birthday party being prepared downstairs.

Despite her advancing years, Ellen had an energy that belied her age and an irrepressible laugh and charm, which made others long to be around her. Today her children and grandchildren prepared for her long-awaited seventieth birthday party. As the giggles and suppressed laughter wafted upstairs, she imagined the decorations, food preparations, and last-minute gift wrapping.

Recently widowed when her beloved Frank died in his sleep, Ellen's adjustment was difficult following forty-two years of marriage. At the beginning of each day, she awoke with a smile on her face, ready for the day's adventures. But her happiness quickly disappeared when she reached over to Frank's side of the bed—a cruel reminder he was gone. Their children used to call them "the dynamic duo," always on the go and eager to explore a new town or event. Many days, she found it difficult to get out of bed as tears rolled down her face at the prospect of facing another day alone. She knew her four children were concerned, but they had their own lives to lead. Their festive attempts to cheer their mother with a birthday feast following her devastating loss did bring a smile to her face.

How she could go on when a piece of her soul died as Frank took his last breath? They had so many plans and a love that grew stronger with each passing day, firmly believing they had all the time in the world. But time, a fleeting, heartless commodity, steals away your dreams and leaves you in a waking nightmare until your body succumbs to sleep. In her dreams, she was free to be in Frank's arms once again as they danced the night away and laughed with abandon.

As Ellen got up to retrieve the newspaper from her dresser, the reflection staring back at the mirror was a complete stranger. Furrows creased her forehead and deep lines appeared on her cheeks. When did I look so old? Surely the lines weren't there yesterday. With a heavy sigh, Ellen sat in her favorite rocking chair and picked up the newspaper.

With trepidation, she glanced at the headline story in *The Cleveland NorthShore Post.* She felt the past dragging her back into its cold and unforgiving clutches. One moment in a lifetime of moments changed her life forever, and she harbored a secret for more than forty-five years, even from her beloved Frank.

Despite her plan to catch a quick nap before partaking in today's festivities, the anxiety generated by recent events refused to dull the pain or provide any release. Hoping in vain to find answers she instinctively knew weren't there, Ellen reread the editorial that changed her life.

The Cleveland NorthShore Post

Saturday	June 7, 1986	60¢

Cold Case Unit Reopens 1939 Murder of Cleveland Socialite with Receipt of Missing Evidence

Cleveland, Ohio. Forty-seven years ago on December 23, 1939, socialites Louis and Marianne Sheridan attended a party leaving three people at home: Alice Webber, the housekeeper; Bridget, the Sheridan's seven-month-old daughter; and Ellen O'Malley, the nanny.

A neighbor heard a loud scream about 9:00 p.m. and called the police. Cleveland detectives Frank Szabo and Kevin Collins found the Sheridans' front door open and two bodies lying in a heap inside the foyer. Although Marianne was alive, her husband had sustained a fatal gunshot wound.

Mrs. Sheridan remembered a sense of great alarm at the sight of a burglar, dressed in black from head to toe, lunging toward her husband. Prior to losing consciousness, and after her husband pulled off the murderer's dark, transparent mask, she heard a loud explosion. Her last recollection of the intruder was a vague impression of red hair.

The housekeeper, feverish all day, had retired to her bedroom around 7:00 p.m. Ms. Webber did not awaken until she heard the commotion and saw the Sheridans lying on the floor. She was unable to provide any useful facts about the case.

When Detective Szabo questioned the nanny, Ms. O'Malley stated she had heard a noise downstairs at approximately 8:30 p.m. Following a cursory check of the first floor, she assumed the racket was caused by the howling wind and the trees banging against the house. Ms. O'Malley returned upstairs where she remained until Bridget fell into a deep sleep. As she exited the nursery, she heard Mrs. Sheridan's scream.

Ms. O'Malley stifled a cry as she looked over the balcony. The Sheridans were slumped together on the floor with an ever-growing red pool of blood spreading around Mr. Sheridan. His eyes remained open in a death stare. As she ran downstairs, Ms. O'Malley briefly saw a red-haired man dressed in black running out the front door.

When she reached the foot of the stairs, Ms. O'Malley heard Mrs. Sheridan moan softly. Ms. O'Malley ran into the downstairs bathroom in search of smelling salts to revive Mrs. Sheridan. Without realizing it, Ms. O'Malley knelt in the sticky red pool on the floor as she administered aid to Mrs. Sheridan.

A thorough search of the home and grounds did not reveal the mask or murder weapon. Despite a canvas of the neighborhood and mounting fear from nearby residents along Millionaire's Row, the only available clue was a description of the getaway car. Despite heavy political pressure for a speedy resolution, the case closed in late 1941 without an arrest. The police file attributed the robbery to a series of similar heists in the area, although this was the first time violence had occurred.

Two days ago, Cleveland police received a package wrapped in the 1939 newspaper account of the murder. The anonymous submission contained a small handgun covered with a dried substance (believed to be blood), a mask, and a sheet of paper with the cryptic handwritten message *Forgive Me.*

Through the use of enhanced imaging techniques, forensic pathologists conducted RFLP testing—the latest tool used by forensic pathologists in identifying the genetic coding of an individual. Future installments, including police and witness interviews, will be posted when available as this strange tale with a mysterious twist unfolds.

Byline: Chris Hooker

THE MURDER OF Louis Sheridan forever fractured time for Ellen into events characterized as "before" or "after" the homicide. Even to this day, the painful memories engulfed a surreal quality with gory details that failed to diminish or bow to the passage of time.

She realized introspection of her motives on the unfortunate December night (when Ellen was twenty-three years old) would be fundamental in understanding her actions. She knew placing them in their proper context may dispel the uneasy sensation continuing to resonate in her life. However, to fully understand her behavior, Ellen had to examine events leading up to the

Sheridan murder—including the painful memories of her brother's abduction, the Great Depression, and frightening encounters with Nazis in America.

In times of extreme stress, sleep (or relaxation when sleep was illusive) had been her link to sanity. Anesthetizing her guilt-ridden conscience, Ellen sat back and allowed her mind to journey back in time to the very beginning—as her memories unfolded like a sepia-toned movie on a projector running of its own accord.

PART ONE

Humble Beginnings with Crosses to Bear

(1916–1939)

ONE

1916–1934
Cleveland, Ohio

LEGEND HAS IT that Ellen Grace O'Malley's ear-piercing entrance into the world on June 7, 1916, was heard by anyone within a three-block radius of the modest home at 3104 Carroll Avenue. The oldest of eight first-generation Irish Americans born to Michael and Mary O'Malley, Ellen grew up in a culturally diverse neighborhood known as Ohio City, located in the heart of Cleveland. Ohio City was often referred to as Whiskey Island based on Irish immigrants with a fondness for homemade whiskey. Although it was also known as Irish Town, a strong contingent of Germans settled nearby. The Cleveland Irish stood firm and proud against surrounding prejudice and rising acrimony. In their fierce determination to immerse the family into an American lifestyle, Ellen's parents rarely spoke Gaelic. However, they bestowed upon their children the Irish traditions and folklore as well as a profound faith.

The O'Malley home became the favorite meeting place for the neighborhood kids. Painted a soft lemon yellow offset by black shutters and flower boxes bursting with a spectrum of warm colors, a feeling of contentment was bestowed on anyone who entered. Without consciously realizing it, the cozy atmosphere provided by select family photos artfully displayed, handmade afghans, needlepoint with comforting messages, fresh flowers, and their most prized possession—a dome-shaped radio—became a beacon of serenity to all.

The much-loved front porch served as the nightly gathering place for family and friends. The sweet fragrance of lilacs that graced the small front yard coupled with the sound of birds chirping provided a safe haven for Ellen and her siblings.

In keeping with the times and dictated by narrow lots, extensions to a home loomed upward. Lying on the grass and looking at the roof, Ellen believed her home stretched up into the heavens.

The first floor consisted of a parlor (rarely used except for company), the living room, four small bedrooms, and the kitchen. Ellen's father built cabinets in the kitchen, complete with leaded-glass doors, which proudly displayed her mother's cherished dishes from Ireland.

The second story housed two bedrooms set apart from the attic. The full basement contained a coal chute and steps leading to the cellar doors opening outward to the backyard.

The neighborhood teemed with children and loud proclamations of "Ollie Ollie Oxen Free" could be heard during games of hide and seek.

By unspoken rule, stints inside the home, including meals and bathroom breaks, were kept short during a game or you risked the chance of being replaced. Your team depended on you.

"It's my turn to pitch."

"Nuh-uh. You pitched two days ago."

"*Please*! Besides, it's my ball. Maybe I'll take it home

where—"

"Okay, okay. For Pete's sake, don't get in a lather. We were just jokin'."

While the boys played ball, the girls played make-believe.

"I want to be the princess today. You can be my maids."

"I'm tired of this game. I heard my mom talk about a sugar daddy. We could pretend we're puttin' on the Ritz, like the society pages. And our daddies would give us lots of candy."

The girls giggled with delight as visions of unlimited chocolate and cotton candy made their mouths water in anticipation.

"Gee, that's a swell idea. Let's go home and get some sheets for fancy dresses. I have a box of broken lockets and shiny trinkets we can use for jewelry."

"Then we can meet at Ellen's house."

"With our flowing gowns, we can take turns standing on the cement block by the curb as we wait for the arrival of our fancy carriages. That way, our gowns won't drag on the ground."

"Whoopee! I can't wait! Then we can parade past the boys to—"

"Now why'd ya wanna spoil a good time hangin' around a buncha dumb boys?"

As the children debated the pros and cons about sports' careers and glamorous ambitions, their parents toiled to put food on the table and provide the loving comfort synonymous with home.

Ellen's sister, Marge, one year her junior, was a natural beauty with shoulder-length chestnut hair, forming waves around her heart-shaped face. Mayme was next in line, three years after Marge, and she possessed an artistic temperament prone to tantrums and theatrical posturing. When she wanted to make a point, Mayme shook her pixie-style brown hair and stared a person down with green eyes so large everyone thought they would bulge right out of her head. At the age of ten, Mayme began to stage plays for the family's enjoyment.

"Oh Romeo, Romeo, wherefa art thou?" She thought her dramatic presentation more than made up for performance deficiencies in diction and enunciation. Mayme practiced with her eyes closed in front of her siblings, trying to impress them with her acting skills. But when she opened her eyes to an empty room, giggling could be heard from her retreating audience. Following her creative reverie, Mayme stormed out of the room in search of a new audience.

The birth of Patrick Michael O'Malley in 1921, the first male to ensure the O'Malley name would carry on for generations, was a source of immense pride for his father.

Peeking into his handmade bassinet, Ellen marveled at Patrick's sky-blue eyes, dimples, and unruly mop of curly red hair. With his sweet temperament, it was easy to understand why he became a family favorite.

In her beautiful lilting voice, Mary sang her favorite Irish lullaby as she rocked her cherished son to sleep. Ellen reverently stood next to Patrick and reveled in the melodious sounds of "Magic O'er the Land." To christen the special occasion, Ellen brought in her mother's sewing kit and watched as she embroidered the initials *PMO* for Patrick Michael O'Malley on his blue baby blanket—a special honor for the newest member of the family.

Despite their newfound bliss, tragedy loomed on the horizon. The O'Malley family, and Ellen in particular, would soon face the harsh reality of life's fleeting joy morphing into despair, forever changed by evil.

TWO

A T SIX YEARS old, asleep in her trundle bed, Ellen awoke to an irrepressible urge for a glass of water. But she was *so* tired and didn't want to move, especially when she heard gentle snoring from Marge. Ellen fought the yearning until it grew stronger with each passing moment, as though someone continually nudged her to get up. Still sleepy, Ellen traipsed down the hall and passed by her baby brother's door. She saw her father standing over his crib and smiled to herself.

Ellen quietly entered the room but was shocked to discover the man was smaller than her father and smelled as though he hadn't bathed in weeks. Afraid to confront a stranger, Ellen slowly backed away and ran into her own room. Curiosity won out and she peeked from her doorway to see the man carrying Patrick wrapped in his blue baby blanket. The stranger was making strange cooing noises and handled her brother with the same gentleness as her own father. Ellen wasn't sure what to make of it, but it didn't appear he would harm Patrick.

After the man cleared the hallway, Ellen headed for her parents' bedroom. The door was locked and Ellen could hear strange sounds coming from within. The children had been warned not to enter their room if the door was locked. Unsure of her next step, and fearful of being reprimanded at disobeying her parents, Ellen returned to her room and decided to tell her parents in the morning. She buried herself under the covers.

When daylight arrived, Ellen prayed she made the right decision but awoke to a nightmare. Her mother's screams could only mean one thing—Patrick was gone. Frantically, they searched the entire house and found the cellar door ajar. Ellen kept quiet as she recalled what had transpired during the night and realized her mistake. Despite a search by the entire neighborhood, Patrick's whereabouts remained a mystery.

Ellen retreated to the cellar and fought the guilt that consumed her like a fire, refusing to be extinguished. Oblivious to the passage of time, Ellen placed her head on bent knees with eyes firmly shut as she attempted to make herself as small as possible. She sat in the deathly silence, far removed from the anxiety and fear emanating in the rooms above. When nighttime arrived and Ellen could not be found, her parents frantically searched their home.

"Ellen, me darling. Where are ye?" cried an anxious Mary O'Malley.

Hearing the concern in her mother's voice and realizing she was sitting in the dark, Ellen became afraid and called out, "Ma, I hid in the cellar."

Mary ran to the cellar and scooped up her weeping child.

"Whatever could ye be thinkin', me darlin?"

But Ellen refused to answer.

Ellen heard her mother's cries night after night while pacing the floors.

"Mary, me love," said Michael O'Malley. "Please come back

ta bed. Ye know we'll be searchin' tomorrow. All the neighborhood are makin' trips to St. Patrick's Church, each prayin' for Patrick's safe return."

During this time, without realizing it, Ellen picked up the mantle of guilt—a recurring role she played throughout her life.

Ellen didn't know what to do. What if the man returned and hurt her entire family? The dilemma of telling the truth or protecting her family became too great, and Ellen had difficulty eating and sleeping. Although she wrestled with her ever-growing anxiety over the next few weeks, Ellen didn't know how much longer she could withhold the truth from her parents. Almost three weeks to the day after the kidnapping, Ellen divulged the events surrounding Patrick's abduction to her parents.

"I, I s-s-saw . . ." Ellen stammered as her body shook with fear. In a low voice she continued. ". . . Wh-what happened to P-P-Patrick."

Following her declaration, Ellen saw hope in her mother's face for the first time since Patrick was taken.

"Ellen, me dearest. Why haven't ye mentioned this before?" her mother asked in a tremulous voice.

"Because your door was locked and you told us never to bother you." Her parents exchanged guilty glances as Ellen wept until it reached a heartbreaking sound that defined the extensive burden she carried in solitude.

Mary cradled Ellen in her lap to soothe her and said, "Darlin', ye are not to blame. But, child, we need to know—whatever did ye see?"

"It was dark, and at first, I thought it was Da bending over Patrick. When I realized it wasn't, I ran back to my room where I peeked out and saw him carrying Patrick wrapped in his blue blanket. But the man was a stranger in our home when it was dark outside. Although he seemed gentle and comforted Patrick, something felt wrong. I wasn't sure what to do so I stayed in bed and didn't tell anyone. I'm so sorry." Ellen tried to be brave, but her chin quivered as tears continued to flow down her cheeks.

Mary comforted her oldest child.

"Me darlin, we know the tellin' is hard, but we need to know all of it. Can ye help us?"

Ellen nodded, and for the first time thought she could shed some of her deep-seated shame.

"Sweetheart, did ye see what he looked like?" her father asked in a voice cracking with anxiety and dread.

"He was very pale, shorter than Da, with greasy hair and smelled real bad."

Mary held her daughter until she cried herself to sleep. Mary laid her daughter down, gently covered her with a blanket, and kissed her forehead. Mary's heart was filled with grief and anger from her own loss and the malevolence that stole her child's innocence at such a tender age.

The following day, Ellen's parents returned to the Cleveland Police Station with their daughter's account, but the vague information failed to yield any leads and the case remained unsolved.

Several weeks later, Ellen was placing garbage into the bin behind their home when she found a newspaper article wrapped around fish bones and dug it from the trash. The man in the photo stared back at her with sinister eyes. Without realizing it, Ellen placed it in her pocket and silently trudged back into her home as panic consumed her. Mary found her daughter shaking in a chair with her small hands clenched into fists as Ellen stared blankly ahead. Mary wrapped her oldest child, clearly traumatized, in a blanket and carried her onto the porch swing. She held Ellen close and stroked her hair while slowly rocking.

Over the next three days, Ellen remained mute and refused to eat. When her father could no longer bear his child's suffering, he took her gently in his arms and whispered in her ear. Ellen's wracking sobs, held at bay as she bore her guilt in silence, were finally released. Ellen unclenched her fists to reveal an article torn from the newspaper about traffic fatalities. It featured a picture of the latest victim, a hit-and-run casualty around the time of Patrick's abduction. She looked into her father's eyes until he understood. Carefully looking at the man's features, Michael saw the similarities in Ellen's prior description.

"Ellen, me darlin, was this the man who took Patrick?"

Ellen put her head down in shame and whispered, "Yes, Da."

Armed with the newspaper photograph, Michael raced up to the police station where he breathlessly told his story to the officer on duty. "Officer Mulligan, me name is Michael O'Malley and I have here a picture of the cowardly man who took our dear Patrick. Me oldest child saw it in a paper and says it was he."

"Mr. O'Malley, this is good news. It's our first lead and we'll track down this man and his family to get to the bottom of this." He added, "You go on home now and let us do our job." When Michael hesitated, Officer Mulligan said compassionately, "I have children, too, Mr. O'Malley. You have my word we will do our best."

"But, Officer, surely . . ." Michael couldn't finish his sentence as rage and helplessness choked any semblance of conscious thought. Instead, Michael put his head down, thanked the kind man, and returned home.

The next two days felt like a year as the O'Malleys waited to hear from Officer Mulligan, someone they trusted to keep his word. The family greeted the officer within seconds of his knock, and as he looked at the young children, he asked, "Mr. and Mrs. O'Malley, perhaps we could have a word in private?"

"Children, run upstairs and play." They trudged up the stairs as it became apparent the kind officer did not bring Patrick home—surely, an ominous sign.

Entering the parlor, Officer Mulligan recommended Michael and Mary sit down before he reported his findings. Mary slumped into the nearest chair as Michael, too upset to relax, stood behind his wife in support.

"Now, Officer, what did ye find out?" Michael's voice was unsteady as he prepared for the unthinkable.

"We tracked down the accident report and identified the man in the photo as George Reams. He was survived by his wife, Dora. We went to their home and attempted to interview her, but it wasn't possible."

"What do ye mean, it's not possible? By God, if I have the doin' of it, I will make her talk."

Mary patted her husband's arm and said, "Michael, let the man speak."

"Dora Reams has not uttered a word, eaten, or moved since the untimely demise of her husband. We searched the home but didn't find any evidence of a baby. We interviewed the neighbors, and they confirmed the couple never had any children. From the neighbors' brief conversations with George, Dora became a recluse when she discovered she could not have any children. The mere sight of a little one sent her into a severe depression. We've done all we can, but there isn't much to go on. I wish I had better news, but all I have are the facts and they're a sorry lot at that."

Mary rose and escorted Officer Mulligan to the door before collapsing in her husband's arms. Their tears mingled as they realized the finality of Patrick's absence from the O'Malley home. With their hopes raised so high, they were crestfallen when their only lead failed to locate the light of their life.

The children were gathered at the top of the stairs and Ellen called down tentatively, "May we come downstairs now?"

Brushing away tear-stained cheeks, Mary and Michael shared a look—each drawing strength from the other—before they responded. "Yes, me darlin'. We need to speak with ye."

While Ellen and her sisters sat in the parlor across from their parents, the news Patrick may never return home started a fresh round of crying. To their credit, neither Michael nor Mary shed a tear as they consoled their children. Ellen, however, buried the combined guilt and sense of loss deep in her heart.

THREE

BEREFT FROM THE loss of her baby, Mary experienced a profound pain piercing her soul. She exuded a palpable air of quiet desperation kept hidden from her family as she valiantly attempted to resume her daily tasks. Mary had witnessed her parents' plight from the Potato Famine and discovered fortitude resonated from a reservoir deep within the soul, and in times of despair, was lovingly tapped to protect others. Mary drew upon that strength to care for her loved ones, just as her parents had protected their children.

Despite her young age, Ellen knew there was something different about her mother since Patrick's disappearance. Mary rarely smiled or laughed anymore. Ellen stayed close by her mother's side, helped with chores, and did everything she could to make her mother happy like telling silly jokes and making funny faces, but nothing worked. As she continued to help without complaint, Ellen prayed with a child's intensity for her mother's condition to improve.

"Ma, can I dress Mayme? Or go to the store?"

"Ah, me darlin' Ellen. What would I do without ye?"

But hearing those words filled Ellen with renewed hope and confidence. Perhaps she *could* atone for the remorse trapped

in her heart. Being a good Catholic, Ellen had been taught guilt
ᵃ way of life. She was unfortunate to learn this lesson as a
ᵇhild but it would become a persistent theme in her life.

time, and with the chore of caring for her lively brood,
neanor gradually improved, and she even managed
ᵒme of her former gaiety. The following year
ᵗngs when Mary discovered she was expecting
ᵈlen marveled at her mother's ability to
oᵥ   ᵗches. William made his grand entrance
on J   ᵗned the household upside-down. Once
again,   led the air.

"DO NOT   ᵉ!" The stern nurse admonished the
children as   from the bedroom and placed a
bundle on the   ᵗₕₑn table. The children gazed inquisitively at
the mysterious heap. Their mother had told them a miracle was
coming but none of the children thought about another baby
since William was a recent addition to their growing family. In
the past, babies seemed to appear like magic. Perhaps this
strange mass on the table was their long-awaited surprise.

Of course, the instant the nurse walked away, they
scampered over to get a closer look—even two-year-old William
waddled over to the table, curious about the excitement. Their
Irish setter Ennis ran with boundless energy around the table,
determined to fulfill her role of protecting the little ones from
harm.

"Why, it's a doll!" said Marge. But when the doll moved, she
squealed, "It's a *bay*-by."

Marge's playful emphasis piqued the other children's
attention and desire to see the new addition.

"Let's go tell Ma. Won't *she* be surprised."

Their mother's pregnancy had been hidden under flowing, long dresses and, as was the custom at the time, children didn't know about their mother being in a "delicate way." In hindsight, Ellen realized her mother's embarrassment about the upcoming "miracle" was her attempt at modesty before curious minds inquired about where babies came from, a subject considered taboo in polite society.

Caught up in the fun, even the older siblings ran toward their mother's bedroom

As the children reached their parents' bedroom door, their father deftly sneaked in ahead of them to block the doorway. "Yer Ma's not feelin' well. Ye can't go in."

"But how will she know about the surprise?"

"Boy baby? Like me?" asked William with a cautious grin as he pointed to himself. When he found out it was a girl, William was inconsolable and threw himself onto the floor, pounding his little fists as he screamed. "Me want boy baby." His father picked him up and rubbed his back while his small son sobbed.

Finally, his deluge of tears dried up, although it would be weeks before William ventured near the newest addition to the household. But the comical events surrounding Veronica's birth remained folklore in the O'Malley family for years to come.

Following Veronica's birth, William finally got his wish when James made his debut three years later. With every new addition contributing to the O'Malley lineage, the household rang with laughter.

But despite easy laughter and competitive spirits, the O'Malleys remained protective of one another, especially after the loss of their beloved Patrick. Together they faced times of hardship when Irish immigrants battled discrimination just as the Germans and Italians had before them. Each group of immigrants brought customs, food, and accents from their homeland to America. But to those already established and working hard to adapt as real Americans, they looked down upon foreign ways as inferior and their malcontent would later become a breeding ground for prejudice and bigotry.

FOUR

W HEN JAMES O'MALLEY was a few months old, everyone was excited about St. Patrick's Diamond Jubilee celebration scheduled for October 24–26, 1928. The long banner advertising the event hung on the front church doors the entire month: *Homecoming with Games and Raffles.*

Ellen and Marge did extra household chores over three weeks for a well-earned ten cents that each could spend at the carnival, which promised a day of thrills filled with pony rides, Irish dancing, games, and other attractions. Finally, the opening day of the Jubilee Celebration arrived, and the sisters both received their hard-earned dime. *Gee, thought Ellen, we're rich.* The entire family attended the opening festivities on Friday evening with the youngest in tow.

"Ma, can Marge and I see the Irish dancers? Then ride the ponies? Then buy some cotton candy? Then—" Ellen took a breath when her mother interrupted her while laughing at her daughter's enthusiasm.

"All right, girls, but ye should be takin' care. The crowds are large and I don't want ye lost." At their mother's warning, Ellen and Marge laughed. They were so close to home, how could they get lost?

"We promise to stay together," they sang in unison and were off in a flash.

When Mayme realized she was being left behind, she began to cry. "Why can't I go with them? I'm almost eight."

Her mother recognized the signs of a tantrum in the works and said to her husband, "Michael, do ye think Mayme might be of age to see the jugglers?"

Mayme puffed up her chest and declared, "Of course I am. Let's go." A theatrical outburst was mercifully avoided.

The Irish dancing was wonderful but, with so many choices, Ellen and Marge couldn't decide on their next activity. When Ellen turned her back for a moment, Marge rushed over toward the ponies. As a crowd of people swarmed around Ellen to watch the colorfully clad dancers, she reached for Marge's hand but all she grabbed was empty air. Panic set in as she called out her sister's name and ran into the crowds milling about. Being a little over four feet didn't help, so she stepped onto an overturned box and called loudly for her sister but got no response.

"Looking for *her*?" a young boy asked, dragging a frightened but defiant Marge in tow. "I found her standing by the ponies and crying out for you when I heard your call."

"Golly gee, Marge! You shouldn't run off like that. You know what Ma said." Ellen hugged her sobbing sister and then turned to the young boy. "Thank you *so* much. I'm Ellen O'Malley, and this is Marge." With the introductions complete, Ellen looked closer at the scrawny young boy with flaming red hair. "You look familiar. Do you live nearby?"

"Yep. Family moved onto Carroll Avenue near your home last week. Name's Joseph O'Riley. My parents own the local bakery on West 25th Street."

"Pleased to meet you," Ellen said with a lady-like curtsy. "My parents were discussing the wonderful new bakery in town. I can't wait to sample the goodies. Just thinking about all the tasty treats . . ."

Ellen stopped as her mouth watered at the prospect. But when she brought herself back to the present, Ellen knew her parents wouldn't appreciate their being gone too long.

"I guess we better find our parents before they get worried. If you'll be attending St. Patrick's school, maybe I'll see you next week? I'm in the sixth grade."

"Me, too! That would be great. Being the new kid is never easy." Despite an easygoing smile complimented by a smattering of freckles on his face, Joseph exuded an underlying sadness. Ellen assumed he dreaded attending school as the new kid.

Ellen and Marge waved good-bye to their new friend and searched the crowds for their family. The sight of their parents made the sisters run into their parents' embrace. Michael and Mary exchanged surprised glances and smiled.

Ellen realized, despite her recently-acquired wealth of ten cents, it didn't compare to the richness of a loving family.

In the middle of Friday's festivities, Father Kenny took center stage to make an announcement. The crowd fell silent.

"To celebrate your wonderful generosity in reaching our goal of $5,000 for much-needed church and school renovations . . ."

The crowd murmured in assent.

". . . the entire parish will attend Cedar Point Amusement Park in Sandusky."

Thunderous applause rang out at the unexpected treat.

"That's very kind, Father. But how will we get there?" an older parishioner asked.

The clapping slowly died out as many realized travel obstacles prevented them from partaking in the merriment. Happiness drained from the crowd as quickly as flour through a sieve.

"I've a friend with a boat charter along Lake Erie. He agreed to take everyone to Sandusky for free."

The news was a wonderful surprise, since none of the parishioners could afford this extravagance.

Once again, the applause reached thunderous levels as the children, filled with ecstasy, ran unfettered, and their faces reflected pure bliss.

"Wow, an entire day of rides and thrills *plus* a boat trip!" Ellen said in her best grown-up voice as her siblings danced around their parents.

On Sunday afternoon following Mass, Fr. Kinney announced another surprise. The photographer, a member of St. Patrick's Parish, would take a picture of the entire parish to commemorate the wonderful weekend as his donation toward the new renovations.

Ellen wore her favorite dress and donned a cloche hat similar to those on display in the large downtown storefronts. Try as she might, her unruly curls popped out from beneath the brim of her form-fitting hat.

"Hurry up," Ellen said impatiently to her siblings lagging behind "We want to get a good spot in front."

Ellen pulled her family toward the O'Rileys so she could stand next to Joseph for the official picture. Ellen made introductions before being jostled about to accommodate the large turnout.

Within a month, each family received a copy of the precious photograph. Ellen became enchanted by the proud display of family and friends.

"Ma, can I keep this picture? I promise to take real good care of it."

"Of course ye will, me darlin'. It's yers for the askin'."

Over the years, the portrait would become Ellen's most cherished and haunting possession—a glaring reminder of Patrick's absence but a talisman of hope in her never-ending quest to find her baby brother.

She always remembered Patrick in her nightly prayers and updated her mental images as though he grew up beside her. Many times she spotted him in a crowd, but rushing to greet him, she would be disappointed when a stranger looked back. By the next day, hope would return and she continued her surreptitious search for Patrick, never wavering in her conviction he was just around the next corner.

FIVE

ALTHOUGH ELLEN WOULDN'T understand until much later the effect of the 1929 Great Depression on the nation, she knew her parents did their best to weather financial challenges. Her father received sporadic government contracts assigned to the O'Malley Plumbing Company as Mary made certain to surround the family with love, laughter, and respect for one another. The birth of Thomas Michael in 1930 rounded out the O'Malley clan and gave rise to endless delight from his mischievous exploits. Veronica developed a love of the earth, and with her green thumb, provided many meals from her own vegetable and fruit gardens.

As the O'Malleys scraped by, they became aware of their less fortunate neighbors. Bob and Evelyn O'Riley's income from their bakery slowed with the sinking economy.

Other than economic problems, Ellen was unaware of the problems within the O'Riley's household until one bright Sunday morning when she walked onto their porch to see if Joseph could play. She loved going to the O'Rileys' home because, in times of prosperity, they shared Ellen's favorite comfort food—chocolate ice cream. It became their little secret for Ellen and Joseph to enjoy small bowls of ice cream while sitting outside under the tree, a lifelong memory conjured up whenever Ellen indulged in her favorite treat.

"I swear woman, if you don't get off my back, you'll be sorry. Every guy needs a drink once in a while. So leave me the hell alone."

Ellen cringed as she recognized Mr. O'Riley's voice.

"But Bob," his wife pleaded, "you drink too much."

Ellen flinched as she heard a loud slap and a muffled cry from Mrs. O'Riley.

Looking through the window, Ellen saw Joseph step in front of his mother. "Don't you dare hit her!"

His father's anger now focused on Joseph as he knocked him to the ground with one solid punch. "You lazy, good for nothin' brat. What do *you* know?"

Ellen slowly backed off the porch, covering her ears to the constant stream of muffled obscenities and muted cries of pain. She headed back to her home and attempted to block out the anger and grief she had witnessed but kept the O'Rileys in her nightly prayers, especially Joseph.

SIX

WHEN CHARLES LINDBERGH'S twenty-month-old baby was abducted on March 1, 1932, newspapers hailed it as "The Crime of the Century." Although the O'Malleys tried to block the event from their minds, all forms of news media—newspapers, newsreels, and radio—updated the story daily in all its gory details. Like moths drawn to a flame, they followed the sad story and prayed the Lindberghs would experience an outcome different from their own. Michael and Mary developed a strong kinship to the famous couple built upon the shared agony as they were forced to relive their own horrific loss ten years earlier. But hope and faith remained strong that Patrick, taken when he was fourteen months old, would one day be found.

Although the family rarely discussed Patrick's abduction, William was curious. At nine years old, he wanted to know more about the brother he never knew. "Da, did we receive a ransom note when Patrick was taken?"

"No, me son," his father said with a heavy spirit.

"Then why did someone steal him?"

Michael cleared his throat several times before he could reply. "Evil is always around us. We hav'ta believe that God has a plan for each of us, even when we canna' be makin sense of the thing." Michael, whose brogue always thickened in times of distress, didn't say aloud his faith was sorely shaken at the dark forces from which no one was immune.

At the conclusion of the Lindbergh tragedy, twelve ransom notes would be exchanged and $50,000 paid while state and federal agencies conducted an exhaustive search—all to no avail. The baby's badly decomposed body, discovered by accident two months later, revealed the epitome of malevolence. The forensic exam findings were consistent with the child's demise from a blow to the head shortly after the abduction.

To Ellen, it represented the very definition of evil by perpetuating hope for the family over two months in the pursuit of murderous greed. Despite the dissimilarities of the two abductions involving ransom demands and a nationwide search, a single outcome linked them irrevocably—neither baby returned home.

SEVEN

I N 1930, ELLEN and Joseph attended high school together
and remained friends. Ellen secretly had a crush on her
neighbor but would never admit it. All the girls in school
noticed his handsome and carefree appearance including his
fiery red hair and a full mustache, which he wore with great
pride. And, as many of his peers discovered, the grown-up
addition of facial hair won the hearts of many female
acquaintances. But Ellen's discerning nature was impressed by
the deferential treatment he accorded his mother through his
acts of kindness and willingness to help.

On a day when Joseph was particularly troubled and
withdrawn, Ellen finally approached the subject of abuse with
him as they sat together at the lunch table. Joseph reacted with
surprise when Ellen confronted Joseph but, with her kind and
gentle prodding, he admitted the frequent beatings at the hands
of an abusive father and husband. Ellen listened as the rage
poured from Joseph's heart, understanding it was cathartic and
required no response. She gave Joseph a hug and they never
spoke of it again.

Joseph's fate took many strange dips and turns. As he grew
older and stronger, his father's physical abuse stopped—once he

came face-to-face with Joseph's fists. Without an outlet to unburden his frustrations, Mr. O'Riley turned to gambling, often late into the night. During a routine poker game, Bob was certain the "Luck of the Irish" tapped him on the shoulder. Someone foolish enough to bet his new Ford V-8 lost his prized possession to Bob's straight flush. Unfortunately, Bob's drinking increased to celebrate his good fortune and turn of events.

On a particularly heavy night of drinking, Mr. O'Riley fell down a flight of stairs and died from a broken neck. At eighteen years old, Joseph became the man of the house and worked full-time at the bakery to support his mother. Joseph remained attentive to his mother's needs, lending a shoulder to cry on, running errands, and providing emotional support. Inwardly, he was happy the man who had caused so much heartache was forever gone from their lives. Outwardly, Joseph maintained his composure.

To support her friend, Ellen attended the wake for Bob, held in the O'Riley home. "Hi, Joseph. I'm sorry to hear about your da."

Joseph's demeanor of self-satisfaction and happiness within days of his father's death made Ellen recoil. Although she knew the source of his relief, Ellen couldn't understand being happy at the death of a parent, no matter what the underlying circumstances. When he saw her reaction, Joseph was eager to please Ellen and changed his inappropriate smile to a somber expression.

"When things settle down, why don't you come with us to the movie theater?"

"Thanks," Joseph said with a sad smile. "But I'm pretty busy taking care of my mom and helping out at the bakery."

Since the passing of her husband, Evelyn had become introverted and rarely left the house. As pressures mounted, Joseph began hanging out with a rough crowd who taught him easier ways to earn money. He knew his newfound career of petty thievery could land him in jail if caught. His doting mother believed her only child could do no wrong and failed to see the subtle changes in Joseph's behavior. He still remained conscientious and polite in her presence, readily willing to help with chores. She ignored rumors circulating the neighborhood.

"Just a buncha' hooligans. And Joseph, he is no' to be trusted. I don't want to see ye with 'im," said Mary to her oldest child.

But Ellen always found Joseph to be engaging, respectful, and thoroughly charming on the rare occasion they spent together. She decided her mother didn't know him very well. Ellen was convinced Joseph would outgrow his impulsive although somewhat criminal behavior. All he needed was to find a better group of friends. When Ellen befriended someone, she could look past their faults to a future filled with potential—if they were strong enough to change.

However, one evening, without a word to anyone, Joseph and his mother moved away. When the bank discovered the O'Rileys left town without paying their loan in full, they boarded up the property and placed a "For Sale" sign out front. Rumors, rampant in the neighborhood, yielded a general consensus that the family's hasty departure resulted from an inability to pay the mortgage. At first, Ellen was distressed to discover Joseph was no longer in her life until she realized perhaps he left so he could turn his life around. Although Ellen missed Joseph and often wondered what became of her friend, she was hopeful he would stay out of trouble and they would, one day, meet again.

For several weeks after his disappearance, Ellen kept a watchful eye on their former home—expecting Joseph to show up unexpectedly. Knowing the hardships Joseph suffered at the hands of his father and pressures to provide for his mother, Ellen hoped Joseph found some measure of peace and happiness.

EIGHT

1935–1936
Nazi Germany

A S MICHAEL AND Mary struggled to keep their family fed and a roof over their heads during the Great Depression, families in Europe, especially Nazi Germany, would consider this type of existence a safe haven compared to the complexities they faced daily.

"Gretl, as your older sister—" Sadie taunted her younger sister.

"I know, Sadie. Being a whole four minutes older surely makes you superior in every way but not this time."

Before Sadie knew what happened, Gretl ran and reached the Leibowitz home four minutes ahead of her sister. Gretl held up her father's stopwatch, borrowed for a school project, to prove she was an equal to her twin.

Whenever Sadie and Gretl became bored in school, they implemented a wonderful diversion to the delight of all; except, perhaps, their teachers. Before leaving home every day, their mother made certain each wore an item different from the other. This allowed the teachers to differentiate one girl from the other by a unique ribbon, sweater, or hair comb. However, the girls found a way to exploit this while amusing themselves.

"Sadie, can you please turn to page forty-two of your history book and respond to question number three on the blackboard?" The teacher turned her back to underline the proper question, a perfect opportunity for the grand switcheroo. The girls changed seats and swapped sweaters before their instructor turned around.

"I'm sorry, Miss Ackerman, but I'm Gretl."

The teacher looked at Gretl in confusion.

"But I thought Gretl wore a red sweater and sat closer to the window. I always make a point to note the difference in your appearances to tell you apart. Dear me. I'm sorry, child. I must be confused." Miss Ackerman shook her head.

"Now where was I? Oh yes, Gretl, can you answer question number . . ." She looked at the blackboard, giving the girls sufficient time to reverse their caper.

"Yes, Miss Ackerman, but I'm Sadie."

Giggles sprouted up from her students as Miss Ackerman realized she had been duped and joined in the laughter. Not everyone had Miss Ackerman's sense of humor, however. The girls' antics usually ended in a trip to the principal's office. The principal warned the girls that their parents would be contacted if another incident occurred. The rebuke stopped them from confusing teachers, but they still delighted in tricking their friends and classmates.

NINE

WHEN SADIE AND Gretl arrived home from school, they completed their chores and homework. But mealtime was filled with laughter as the girls regaled their parents with exaggerated accounts of successful pranks and the latest round of childish jokes. Every night as Benjamin and Rachel Leibowitz tucked their daughters into bed, they thanked God for enriching their lives *and* doubling their happiness. Sadie was wise enough to understand her close-knit family, bound by love and respect, more than compensated for wealth or material possessions they lacked.

The girls often begged to stay up late and hear the oft-told story of their parents' first meeting.

"It's late, so I'll tell you the short version. I left America on holiday and decided to visit Germany, among other countries. When I stopped at a restaurant for lunch, your mother was working as a waitress. I was enthralled by her beauty and gave her my order, in very poor German. But she graciously pretended not to notice. When she brought my food out, she tripped and I was covered with—"

"Wienerschnitzel!" The girls clapped their hands.

"Now, if you're especially good, tomorrow we'll continue

your English lessons. Besides German, it's always a good idea to have a second language. But for you both, it has a special meaning."

"Why, Papa?"

"So you can talk to your relatives when we go to America. You know my brother runs a clothing store. Perhaps he could make special outfits just for you. Wouldn't that be exciting?"

"Oh yes, Papa." Their father had shown them picture postcards from America and they couldn't wait to see the sights.

Sleep came quickly to the girls as they dreamed of the exciting voyage to America and meeting their extended family.

The next morning, the eleven-year-old girls said in unison, "Bye, Mama. Bye, Papa," as their parents headed into town on the back of a neighbor's truck. Sadie and Gretl thought they were in heaven, free at last from the watchful eyes of their parents! Their grandparents allowed them to roam, too tired to keep up with them, and the twins had every intention of exploiting their independence.

"Don't go too far," their grandmother said after them as they raced into the hills without a care in the world. The hours passed quickly, filled with games and laughter.

"Betcha Mama and Papa are having their own adventure," Sadie said with a false bravado as the sun began to set. She tried to reassure her younger sister while her own heart beat faster than she could remember. They were both worried their parents had yet to return.

"Maybe they went to a toy store and will bring us surprises," said Gretl.

When nighttime approached, the girls perched themselves on the front porch nervously awaiting their parents' return.

They had *always* arrived home before dark, since they never missed the nighttime ritual of telling their daughters a wonderful bedtime story.

"Perhaps the truck broke down," Sadie said, looking at her grandfather for reassurance.

"I'm sure you're right, Liebchen," he said, although his worried expression told another story.

"Girls, come in from the cold before you get sick," their grandmother said.

Sadie could tell she, too, was worried.

"Just a few minutes more, pleeease," said Gretl. "They should be home any minute."

With growing dread, Sadie and Gretl waited on the porch until they fell asleep. Neither felt their grandparents carry them in the house and place them into bed.

The girls awoke to an eerie silence.

"Gretl, wake up! I'm sure Mama and Papa have a wonderful tale to tell about buying supplies in town, perhaps even some toys for us."

Sadie and Gretl rushed into the kitchen, expecting to see their parents.

"Sadie, where could they be?"

"Maybe, they're putting away all the goodies they bought."

The girls ran from room to room until they reached the front porch. Their grandfather sat stoically on the porch swing as he stroked his wife's hair, her sobs muffled into his shoulder.

"Why them? What did they ever do to anyone?"

They saw the twins trying to hide behind the door, although neither of them had the strength or fortitude to tell their precious grandchildren the devastating news. Their parents were never coming home, they knew it was a chore to be done. And they had to be the ones to tell them.

"Hush, my love. It will be all right." But he knew nothing would ever be the same.

Sadie and Gretl crept back into the house but their grandfather called out in a voice filled with unmistakable sadness.

"Sadie, Gretl. Come here. We need to speak with you."

Slowly, the twins approached their grandparents huddled together on the porch. The sat up and the girls ran into their outstretched arms. "We have some very sad news about your parents. They . . ." He couldn't utter the unthinkable words out loud.

The twins fought back tears but their faces reflected a hint of optimism that their parents were still alive.

Always the pragmatic one, their grandmother spoke up when she saw their spark of expectation. She knew they were clinging to the possibility their parents were merely injured but would still return home. Placing a comforting hand on the head of each girl, she spoke through her pain. "I'm so sorry, my darlings. But your parents were killed in an accident yesterday in town."

"No, it can't be!"

"Surely they'll be home at any minute." Gretl paused between sobs. "Listen. There's the doorbell. I bet it's them now."

When the girls ran to the door, it was a neighbor bringing food. Soon the doorbell chimed constantly as a stream of friends stopped by with more food and words of sympathy. Although old enough to understand, the girls refused to acknowledge their parents were dead. It was easier to pretend their parents were still in town and hold onto misguided hope than accept their parents were never coming home.

But when their aunts and uncles arrived, the girls could no longer pretend. Their parents did not spend time with their brothers and sisters for as long as the girls could remember. A long-ago series of caustic arguments, whose details no one could recall, divided the family until all communication stopped and the siblings became estranged.

Knowing the animosity between their parents and the extended family, Sadie and Gretl exchanged worried glances. They thought, Why were they here and what did they want? Unspoken words were communicated between the twins through their bond of intuitiveness shared since birth. The sudden appearance of extended family confirmed their worst nightmare and crushed all hope. They could no longer pretend. Their wonderful, loving parents were gone. With empty hearts and fear of the unknown, the twins exchanged frightened looks and wondered what would become of them.

TEN

UNKNOWN TO THEIR aunts and uncles, Sadie and Gretl hid in the pantry storage as they listened to the adults' discussion.

"I read in the underground newspaper that, under Nazi rule, the truth is an inconvenient blur never to be confused with judgments meted out by Hitler's puppets. The only justice we can expect is *in*justice—and this is a perfect example."

"But, surely there were witnesses."

"Of course, but you know the punishment to anyone who speaks against the Nazis. Jews, under German hierarchy, are inconsequential and moral decency a thing of the past. They say justice is blind. Now she is deaf and crippled under Hitler."

Neighbors arrived throughout the day to express condolences but also to revel in the latest gossip about the last few minutes of Benjamin and Rachel's lives as each one embellished gruesome details with increased fervor as the sad story unfolded.

A neighbor said, "I heard Eric Kaufmann, a fifteen-year-old unlicensed driver, revved the Mercedes engine, ready to pounce as the other Hitler Youths in the car cheered and chanted—'Look at Eric go!'"

"Some of the bystanders heard the boys gloat, 'This is the best fun we've had all year,'" another neighbor chimed in. "Why they couldn't wait to tell their parents."

Anyone who had witnessed the disturbing events saw how much Eric enjoyed the attention. Bragging and provoking the Jewish couple was tantamount to providing his friends with a good show. He doggedly pursued the couple down the main thoroughfare. Onlookers gaped in horror and undisguised revulsion.

"Helmut, we should help that poor couple."

"Don't get involved or they may start chasing *us*. Can't you see they're wearing Hitler Youth uniforms?"

His wife nodded and remained mute as they continued to walk with their eyes cast downward, faces burning in shame.

"Eric, slow down," his friend in the front seat had yelled when he gazed at the speedometer and saw the downward slope quickly approaching.

"I'm trying, I'm trying!" Eric screamed in terror. His body shook and his sweat-stained hands kept sliding off the wheel. "Where is the brake? I can't remember which pedal to push." His voice rose in pitch as panic consumed him.

"Hit the brakes *now!*" said his friend as the car's occupants screamed and were thrust from side to side.

The car gained momentum. Attempting to reduce speed while maneuvering the recalcitrant wheel, Eric accidentally pushed the accelerator to the floor.

The couple died on impact as the youths heard the sickening sound of bones crushing, felt the car's uneven trek over the bodies, and realized in horror their prank had turned lethal. Panicked and frightened, they fled the scene, leaving poor

Benjamin and Rachel—still holding hands—as broken lumps of human flesh displayed in the town center.

Someone anonymously contacted the police. Within hours, encompassing a cursory investigation, the incident was declared the result of an accident. They cited the Leibowitz couple for carelessness by crossing in front of a passing car. No charges were brought against the youths, despite many witnesses who knew the truth and discussed events in hushed whispers.

"Did you see the 'accident'?"

"No, but I saw the *murders* as that lovely couple tried to outrun the car."

"With the final police ruling, the poor family has no recourse or hope of retaliation against the boys who wreaked such havoc."

After the "accident," the crowd disbursed, effectively dissuaded by the show of military strength when Gestapo forces appeared on the scene.

ELEVEN

THE TWINS REMAINED huddled in the pantry as they heard the ghastly details from snippets of conversations describing their parents' fate. But when they heard family members discussing *their* future, they opened the pantry door a crack and listened intently as their grief entered a new realm of despair.

"We all know their parents didn't have much money. Certainly not enough to support two growing children."

"Well, I can take Sadie but not both."

"It would be a shame to separate them, but we already have two growing boys."

"We would love to take them, but your father's arthritis is getting worse. And my sewing for wealthy Bavarian residents barely provides enough money for the two of us. I'm afraid we can't afford any additional mouths to feed," their grandmother said sadly.

The girls ran to their grandparents, begging to stay with them. All conversation ceased as they realized the girls had overheard the brutally honest assessments.

When everything was settled, both girls remained in their homeland separately with their German relatives and would not be forced to live with their American relatives. When the day arrived for the girls to separate, they hugged and sobbed until the adults pried them apart.

"Promise me you'll write every day," cried Gretl.

"Of course. And I'll think of you every night," said Sadie, who broke loose from her aunt's grip to hug her sister one more time.

They vowed that, no matter what it took, they would be reunited one day.

Sadie moved to Munich with Uncle Albert Leibowitz and Aunt Alona—their father's brother and his wife. Although she hadn't seen them since she was little, they welcomed her into their home with love and support. Their quaint cottage, nestled in the mountainside beside a flowing brook, displayed lovely flowerboxes and decorative shutters typical of many Bavarian homes. Gretl resided in Berlin with the Goldsteins—Aunt Elsa, who was her father's sister, Uncle Asher, and two cousins, Miles and Aaron.

In the beginning, Sadie and Gretl wrote to one another daily. But over time and given adjustments to their new lifestyle, the letters decreased to several times a week, then once a month, and eventually stopped completely. Acclimating to a life without their parents required sacrifice and it became painful for the siblings to communicate as they attempted to shed their former life and become part of other families. Yet, knowing they lived in the same country and would one day be reunited brought an inner peace written words could never convey.

TWELVE

URING THE FIRST year that Sadie lived with her aunt and
uncle in Munich, things settled into a new but
comfortable routine. One cool March afternoon, Sadie
watched her uncle shuffle his feet as he entered the kitchen, his
normally upright posture severely stooped. It appeared each
step forward became more difficult until he finally acquiesced
and sat heavily into a kitchen chair. Sadie's reaction to
impending tragedy, similar to events surrounding her parents'
death, kept her hidden in the next room filled with dread.

Alarmed, Alona asked, "Albert, is everything all right?"

"I've been fired without any reason. And this, after twenty
years of hard work without even missing one day. I've heard
rumors about cheap labor from newly constructed camps, but I
never thought they would replace *me*," said Albert. Ironically,
Albert was unaware the "cheap labor" force to which he
referred consisted of fellow Jews living in concentration camps.

"Oh, Albert. I wish I could find a job outside our home. But
you know I have no skills. Even if I was able to find a job, who
would take care of you and Sadie?"

Alona cried at the overwhelming crisis and her inability to
contribute to the family's coffers. Albert held her in his arms

and contemplated their bleak future.

After weeks of futile job searches, Albert complained as he sat in the kitchen with his head bent down in defeat. "No one's hiring, especially when they hear my name. Jews aren't even considered, despite their expertise. Alona, I don't know what to do."

Sadie desperately wanted to help her aunt and uncle but she was helpless. If her uncle couldn't find work, how could she?

Several days later, her uncle said, "Sadie, can you please come here? We need to discuss something important with you."

"Yes, Uncle Albert?"

"Several weeks ago, I lost my job to workers in a nearby factory. I haven't been able to find another job, so I cabled my brother in America and he found employment for me. We will be leaving Germany—"

"No!" Sadie said. "I'd never see Gretl. I'm not going—*ever!*" Arms folded in defiance, Sadie stamped her foot in a rare display of anger.

"I'm sorry, Sadie, but we have no choice. I can't get a job in Germany. They're not hiring Jews."

Sadie staged her own protest by remaining in her locked bedroom where she cried for days and refused to eat.

Eventually, hunger won out, and Sadie snuck into the kitchen late one night to find her aunt sitting alone at the table.

"Auntie, are you all right?" Sadie asked as she cautiously approached.

Her aunt tried to muffle the heart-wrenching sobs as she cradled her head in her arms. For the first time, Sadie realized how difficult the relocation would be for the entire family. She stood behind her aunt and rubbed her back until the sobbing eased. When Alona looked into the face of her young niece, the glance between them became an unspoken promise. Both would be brave throughout the move to ease the pressure placed upon Albert, who believed himself a failure, driven from the land he loved. Tearing himself away from Germany with its beautiful countryside, quaint customs, hardy beer, and wonderful friends, was a necessary sacrifice to provide for his family. But Albert never dreamed he would be forced to flee his birthright as a German and start all over in a new country.

THIRTEEN

1936
Immigration to America

IN 1936, THE Albert Leibowitz family migrated to Bridge Avenue in Cleveland, Ohio. But Sadie despaired that, being an entire world away, she would never see her precious Gretl again. Although they no longer wrote to one another, they remained in each other's heart. The weekly services at B'nai Israel, a temple located at West 25th and Lorain Avenue, became a familiar ritual that brought Sadie comfort as she recalled similar services in Germany.

"That's very good, Uncle. C-A-T spells cat."

Albert grinned at the encouragement from his young niece.

Shortly after settling in Cleveland, Sadie began tutoring her aunt and uncle in the language of their adopted country, a gift from her father's careful lessons. Doing something positive helped to alleviate the anxiety of leaving her sibling behind.

The bittersweet exercises reminded Sadie of the homeschooling lovingly taught by her father. Although her aunt and uncle never lost their accent, Sadie's small contribution helped her adopted parents gain the confidence of acceptance as they assimilated into their new homeland.

The days were drawing closer to the beginning of a new school year and an appointment was made with the head of St.

Patrick's School, despite misgivings about sending Sadie to a non-Jewish school.

"Father Kenny, we're Jewish and this is a Catholic institution. Won't our Sadie feel out of place?"

"Not at all. St. Patrick's School is attended by children of all faiths."

Sadie couldn't wait to be in a classroom filled with kids close to her age. It was decided, despite her age of twelve years, she would be placed in the sixth grade to compensate for her sporadic and limited education in Germany. Her aunt and uncle agreed to Sadie's attendance on a trial basis.

The first day of school filled her with trepidation and uncertainty. The principal kindly led Sadie to her classroom where the teacher introduced her, and she took her seat beside an adorable, talkative young girl.

"Hi, I'm Veronica O'Malley." When she noticed Sadie shaking, she added, "Don't worry. The teachers are really nice, and I'll introduce you to all my friends." At least, this got a tiny smile from her new classmate.

"My name is Sadie," she said as she stored her meager supplies in her desk.

Sadie soon discovered one indisputable fact: it was impossible not to like Veronica and her family. When Veronica introduced her to the entire O'Malley clan, they befriended the charming young waif with blond braids whose tragic tale induced a chilling malice that shocked their insular lives. As the oldest, Ellen was protective of their new friend. Facilitated by the encouragement and support doled out by the O'Malleys, Sadie, over time, made a relatively smooth transition to American life. But even being around her new friends couldn't diminish the desire to be with her twin sister once more.

Sadie developed a love of the cinema and performed odd jobs in the neighborhood to earn a precious nickel for an entire Saturday's entertainment in The Hippodrome Theater.

Sadie fondly recalled her first encounter with the wonderful theater and diligently added this milestone to a diary she hoped to share with her twin one day.

> The first time I entered The Hipp, as my friends call it, I read the plaque that said the theater could accommodate 4,500 people! Plants surrounded the Corinthian columns (don't know what that means, but they sure are pretty!) in the lobby and the vines extended to the top of each column. The spacious main staircase had the same marble floor in the lobby. Floral displays and a curved archway made me feel like a princess whenever I entered.

Not only did her new friends accompany Sadie to The Hipp, they even taught her the latest American slang including the term "gassers," which meant they were fun to be with and quick with a joke. Sadie couldn't wait to show off her newfound slang to her aunt and uncle.

At the breakfast table, Sadie casually said, "Boy, those O'Malley kids sure are gassers. We have such a blast together."

Albert and Alona gaped in astonishment at their young Sadie. "Perhaps the O'Malleys shouldn't eat so many beans, but it is not appropriate for you to make fun of them."

When she realized her aunt and uncle took the meaning of her expression literally, gales of laughter erupted from Sadie.

Although she enjoyed her life in America without the Nazis and their loathsome Hitler Youth, Sadie's cup of happiness remained half-full. Opening her blue eyes at the beginning of a new day, Sadie's heart filled with hope but disappointment reigned when her one wish remained unfulfilled—waking up next to her twin sister, Gretl. To make her dream a reality, Sadie began to pray for a miracle. Surely, God would listen if He wasn't too busy. Filled with optimism, Sadie was certain He would never let her down but to be safe, she sent a few daily reminders. Just in case. In the meantime, Sadie had the love and support of her wonderful friends, Veronica and Ellen O'Malley.

FOURTEEN

1936–1938
Nazis in America

ALTHOUGH LIFE IN Germany became intolerable for Jews, who were forced to wear a yellow star with its oppressive psychological demoralization and suffered physical abuse by Hitler's Brown Shirts, Sadie's small world in America revolved around becoming accustomed to school at St. Patrick's with her newfound friends. On a routine school day during recess, two unfamiliar boys taunted her on the playground.

"Her name's Leibowitz. Sounds Jewish, don't it?" the shorter boy sneered.

"Yeah, and we don't want any *Jews* in our neighborhood," the second boy said with a familiar accent.

Sadie's terror was palpable, and Ellen summoned her siblings to assist in the confrontation. They surrounded their tiny new friend who shook so fiercely her balance became unsteady.

"Go on and pick on someone your own size," said William O'Malley, in a voice he hoped would inspire fear. Instead, the two boys snickered and punched William in the face. As other children gathered around, the hooligans ran away laughing. Despite William's battered face, he never shed a tear, and the escapade earned him a trip to the nurses' office where he was promptly sent home once the bleeding stopped. William was later relieved to discover the two boys were banned from the school premises.

By the afternoon, after her protector had been sent home, Sadie stopped trembling although her lips quivered.

"What's wrong, Sadie? Did you know those nasty boys?" Veronica asked with concern in her voice.

"No, but they remind me of the Hitler Youth back in Germany."

Veronica scoffed and attempted to reassure her friend. "Don't be silly. You're a long way from Germany and we don't have anything like that in America. You're finally safe."

Despite encouragement and support from both Ellen and Veronica, Sadie believed Nazis were everywhere. She couldn't help but hope and pray Gretl had escaped their wrath in Germany.

FIFTEEN

SHORTLY AFTER THE bullying incident, Sadie skipped out the rear door of her home without noticing anything unusual as she reveled in the warm temperature of Indian summer on a beautiful afternoon. The trees burst into a spectrum of color and the balmy air brought a delightful respite from the cold winter looming ahead. As she rounded the corner, Sadie almost collided with two boys carrying a large box. They ignored her as they laughed at the stains on their shirts. Sadie overheard snippets of their conversation about pride in a bund.

"Silly boys. They don't even know how to pronounce the cake they're carrying. It's a Bundt cake," Sadie whispered in amusement.

Sadie forgot her near-collision and trooped over to the O'Malley home for their usual adventure. They went to The Hipp to see the latest Oliver and Hardy movie, *The Swiss Miss.* It was so funny, she laughed until she hiccupped, which sent her and the O'Malleys into fits and giggles. Thinking of them in ridiculous Swiss costumes posing as mousetrap salesmen in a country brimming with cheese made her laugh all over again as she returned to the O'Malley home with her friends. Sadie was surprised to find her aunt and uncle sitting in the kitchen and sensed trouble.

"Uncle, Auntie, what's wrong?" Sadie hugged them. When they didn't respond to her question or touch, she looked to Mrs. O'Malley for an answer.

"Darlin', someone painted a hateful symbol on the front of yer home."

"What symbol?"

The kitchen grew very quiet. When no one responded, Sadie *knew* and spoke the unthinkable. "How did the swastika follow us from Europe? Who would do this, and why?" Deafening silence greeted her.

On their way home, the Leibowitz family walked quickly and glanced over their shoulders in panic. Memories of unrestricted violence and brutality in Germany, thought to be in their past, were once again brought to the forefront. They expected the thugs responsible for defacing their home to emerge from the shadows, block their path, and whisk them away. They realized becoming an American citizen did *not* protect them for bigotry knew no boundaries.

ONE WEEK AFTER the last home was defaced, Father Kenny held a meeting at St. Patrick's Church to discuss the vitriolic act of hatred embodied in the painted swastika. Dozens who entered St. Patrick's Church passed by the Leibowitz home, and the abhorrent sight reinforced the necessity of the hastily arranged gathering. And, a show of support was deemed the Christian thing to do for neighbors frozen in panic and unable to act on their own in fear of retribution. Those who attended the meeting knew it was easier for the victims to live with the revolting symbol than risk something worse—perhaps a midnight abduction if rumors were true.

"This is the third home defaced with tha' detestable swastika. An' what do ye propose should be done?" asked an irate Mary of her neighbors. Her normally reserved manner and quiet demeanor would not stand for any type of intolerance. "After all, are we not all immigrants? If'n we don' stand together as one, these hooligans might be targetin' our homes next."

Everyone agreed. As a mob mentality surged to the forefront, Father Kenny's voice of reason prevailed. "I propose we show a force of support by breaking up into three groups. Each group will be assigned a home to cover the loathsome defacement with fresh paint."

Murmurs of assent spread through the crowd.

"Do ye know if the police were contacted?" asked Michael.

"No, they're afraid of causing any trouble, which is ironic since many are corrupt and others are German sympathizers," said Mrs. Patrice Campbell, who was always up-to-date on the latest gossip. "But I think fines and jail time would be appropriate, don't you?"

"That's right! We have to take control back!" said one of the parishioners to the gathering, as everyone nodded in agreement.

Father Kenny promised to discuss the matter with the police and recommend the perpetrators be appropriately punished if they persisted in mutilating any further homes. The group disbanded and resolved to prove this behavior would not be tolerated in their neighborhood.

A lone figure sat in the last pew of the church and listened to the discussion but kept his opinions to himself. With his head down and silently shuffling outside, he managed to exit the church without incurring unwanted attention. As he trudged home, his thoughts turned dark and he hoped his suspicions were unfounded.

Sixteen

EXPERIENCING MALICIOUS HATRED in their community was a foreign concept to Ellen, unaware of the plight her father faced when he first arrived in America. Signs posted in storefront windows offering employment to all but "Irish Need Not Apply" became a familiar and heartbreaking site. But each ethnic community faced similar discrimination, including Germans.

Until recent events, Ellen's years in grade school were filled with tolerance because she treated everyone as equals without distinction and regardless of their origins—lessons she learned from her parents. But not everyone was as fortunate when their lives were dictated by hatred, resentment, and failure. From her childhood friends, Ellen heard about the sad tale of the Mueller family and hardships they endured as German immigrants. Still, she was not privy to, nor could she fully understand, the extent of destitution they suffered as fate doled out adversity and misfortune in abundance.

AT THE AGE of eleven, Kurt Mueller's younger brother, Stephen, was born and within an hour, his mother died after giving birth. Their father went into a deep depression following his loss but continued working two jobs to support his family. This meant daytime care of the new infant fell to Kurt. By the time Kurt was twenty, their father lost both his jobs when the Depression gripped the nation, and he committed suicide, his lifeless body found by Kurt. Now orphans, Kurt tried to support himself and his nine-year-old brother but was unable to find work in the face of bigotry against his heritage.

Homeless and unemployed, both brothers deeply resented being treated as foreigners in their birth country. Despite his young age, Stephen resolved he would one day make a name for himself and avoid his father's path of destruction. With his brother, they joined the German American Bund (pronounced "Boond")—a league of German businessmen who assisted their countrymen in finding employment while promoting Nazi ideology and Germanic culture. Stephen's birthright as an American demanded he succeed. The Bund professed it and the recruiter reinforced it. In the waiting area, the brothers read a brochure stating there were Bund offices in every major city across America and boasted more than 200,000 members, including children.

"Why, strong and determined young men like you can do anything. If the stupid Americans fail to see your potential, it's their loss. You are entitled to the same opportunities everyone else has and we'll make sure you get it."

They felt ten feet tall, and as instructed, signed on the dotted line.

"Now swear to uphold the Third Reich and support the Fatherland."

Swearing allegiance to Hitler and joining the Bund accorded the brothers pride and self-respect, something denied them by their birth nation. Giving the new recruits a crisp Nazi salute, a gesture promptly returned by the brothers, they joined in pride and solidarity and loudly proclaimed, "Heil, Hitler!"

ATTENDING REGULAR SATURDAY Bund afternoon meetings, the time passed quickly for the Muellers. By the time he was sixteen, Stephen met a young man his age who recently immigrated to America. As Stephen introduced Eric Kaufmann to fellow Bund members, they treated him like royalty with his blond hair, blue eyes, and confidence of a Hitler Youth. Stephen was eager to help Eric adjust to America and together they forged a bond in perpetuating Nazi ideology as they supported the Führer.

"Come on, Eric. There's someone I want you to meet." Stephen propelled his friend toward a husky man, over ten years his senior. "This is my brother, Kurt, another proud member of the Bund."

Stephen Mueller idolized his older brother and emulated his every move. Burly and powerfully built, Kurt never backed down from a fight. Kurt's tough façade contrasted with Stephen's handsome appearance. Muscled, not buff, Stephen grew to appreciate and exploit his looks when he discovered it gave him an advantage with women.

Kurt's beefy hand gave Eric a firm, bone-crushing handshake. "Pleased to meet 'cha. And who might you be?"

Eric's grasp of English slang made him feel anxious and slightly awkward—feelings distinctly foreign to him.

"Name's Eric," he said with feigned nonchalance. "My family lived in Germany. Until recently."

"What happened, kid?"

"The decision made by my *parents*," he spat the last word, "did not include my input. They forced me from my homeland. Do you know what it's like to be betrayed by loved ones?"

"Sure, kid. I remember how much my life changed when my parents told me they were going to have another baby. I couldn't believe it. I told them I didn't want another sibling, but they tried to convince me everything would be great. It didn't turn out that way. I had to quit school—didn't mind that part—and couldn't play with my friends. I thought to myself, 'This baby better be worth it.' When Stephen here was born," Kurt tousled his brother's hair, "life became unbearable."

"Yeah, I bet Stephen was a real handful." Eric teased his new friend.

"Our Ma died shortly after Stephen was born. After the Depression, our Pa lost everything and committed suicide. So, yeah, kid, I know all about betrayal. My father took the easy way out, and I was forced to put the pieces back together alone."

"How did you survive?"

"It wasn't easy. No matter how hard I tried, I couldn't find work or permanent lodgings, and we were forced to live in Hooverville camps."

"What are those?"

"Makeshift tents, usually in parks or abandoned lots. But *genteel* society couldn't stand the sights or smells. In the early morning hours, cops rousted us from camp with threats of vagrancy and defacing property. But I knew the folks most offended by the camps were hypocrites. *They* had a roof over their heads, plenty of food, clean clothes, and a decent life. *They* lived the Great American Dream while we lived the Great American Nightmare. I became desperate until a friend told me about an organization known for placing Germans in good-paying jobs. I joined the Bund in the early 1930s when it was known as Friends of Germany. Figured this country owed me *something*. But the Bund has really taken hold. Have you seen the newsreel about the Bund at The Hipp?"

"Yep, saw it a couple of days ago. That's why I'm here."

"I couldn't believe at least twenty-five thousand members of the Third Reich reside in America. But I think the clip underestimated the number of members. We read in the official brochure there were really 200,000 loyal Bundists. But hearing they were willing to recognize twenty-five thousand members made us sit up a little straighter as we watched the film clip."

It never occurred to either of the Mueller brothers the brochure they read was based on inflated propaganda.

"We just got back from that rally."

"You were there?" Eric inquired with a tinge of jealousy. *His* parents would never have attended any Hitler Youth rallies or parades in which he was involved.

"Yep. We expected to see our faces on the big screen, but the camera moved too fast and everything was a blur."

"Did the Bund ever help you find jobs?"

"They found me a construction job and even found employment for Stephen on Millionaire's Row, despite his age. How ironic we worked on mansions after living in Hoovervilles. The way we figure it, with every success Hitler achieves, we cheer because we're finally on the winning side, taking what's rightfully ours. That's the American way!"

Eric laughed and said with pride, "Maybe living in America won't be so bad after all."

STEPHEN'S CAMARADERIE WITH Eric at local Bund gatherings grew into a tight-knit friendship of teenagers with similar interests and goals. Both were eager to attain inroads within the Bund hierarchy. They developed a special connection based on comparable ages and aspirations. Kurt thought he'd lose his mind if he heard one more story about Eric, Stephen's new idol.

Unfortunately, his lack of vigilance coincided with a gradual decline in Stephen's demeanor and attitude. Kurt failed to notice Stephen's impressionable mind-set as he became entrenched in the Bund's misguided ideology espoused by Eric.

When Kurt recognized the poisonous hostility embraced by his younger brother from the Bund in general, and Eric, in particular, he cursed the day they first met Eric or became involved in the Bund. He could now see it for what it really was—an organization to promote hatred and violence without regard to human life or morality. It reinforced Kurt's refusal to support anti-Semitism in thought, word, or deed. He still retained a sense of decency instilled by his parents, lessons that his younger brother didn't learn before their untimely demise.

SEVENTEEN

KURT ENTERED HIS home after leaving St. Patrick's Church
unable to dispel his nagging suspicion.

When Kurt walked in the door, Stephen said he heard
rumors about the meeting at St. Patrick's Church. Eager to earn
his brother's approval, he proudly proclaimed, "It took us a
while, but we found three Jewish families. Eric and I followed
them home from the synagogue over the past several weeks and
we sure taught them a lesson. We left ladders nearby, and using
a torch borrowed from the Bund, painted their homes at night."

Kurt stopped and asked, "What are you talking about?"

Stephen didn't notice the quiet anger building in his brother.
"We painted a huge swastika on the front porches, and if we
had enough time, on the side of their homes as well." He waited
for approval from his older brother. Stephen believed their
accomplishment would ensure status and fame within the
American Bund organization while earning Stephen long-
overdue respect from his older brother.

Furious, Kurt said, "You and Eric are both fools. Don't you
realize we could get arrested for that? I attended a town meeting
tonight, and the entire neighborhood was enraged. They
mentioned contacting the police and fines for vandalism. You

know we can't afford that."

"Why would you be arrested? Eric and I were the only ones brave enough to carry out the Bund's wishes."

Kurt responded with a sharp slap across Stephen's face. "Because I'm responsible for paying the bills, and if you went to jail, no one would hire me. It's tough enough to find work, but no one wants to get mixed up in family troubles, especially if they involve the law."

Stephen rubbed his cheek but his wounded ego couldn't acknowledge his brother was right.

"Don't tell anyone about this and don't do it again," Kurt said as he walked toward the kitchen. The events of the evening had decreased his usual appetite.

"I will if I want to!" Stephen said, ashamed of his brother. But when Kurt raised his fist, as he often did, to teach his younger brother a lesson, Stephen relented.

Stephen vowed to take another direction and independently achieve a life of affluence as he removed himself from his brother's prying eyes. Since his destiny coincided perfectly with ideologies professed by the Bund, he decided to find other ways to support the Bund, and hopefully earn sufficient wages on his own. That evening, he shed the infantile need to emulate his older brother. Stephen realized it was his responsibility to change his future—one that would make everybody notice him. Especially his brother.

EIGHTEEN

TAKING SOLACE IN his friendship with Eric, Stephen met him the next day and wanted to know everything about life in Germany, Stephen's new adoptive home.

Eric enjoyed reliving his glory days in Germany with Stephen.

Impressed with Eric's membership in the Nazi hierarchy, Stephen asked, "What did your parents think when you joined the Hitler Youth at age ten?"

"At first, they were proud and believed the organization would discipline me. What fools."

"What did your parents do?"

"Dietrich was a pharmacist who owned his own drugstore, which also sold medical supplies, and Clara worked at the register. They made a good living, as well they should, to support a prominent member of the Hitler Youth. At the age of fifteen, I was no longer a child. They should have respected that."

"Why do you call your parents by their names instead of Dad or Mom?"

"Because they're old and don't deserve any titles. In Germany, we were taught the elderly have little need for respect, unless they're members of the Nazi Party, of course."

"Well, what did you do?"

"Despite my humiliation and jeers from my friends, I continued to march. But my hard work and Aryan looks did not go unnoticed as the officers told me that I embodied the very definition of a true Nazi warrior. I held the place of honor during parades and nighttime rallies. Once the Führer actually patted my cheek! Following this epic event, high-ranking positions within the Nazi ranks would be a sure thing. I knew exceptional youths were being groomed for recruitment into the SS."

Noticing the quizzical look on Stephen's face, he explained, "The SS, which stands for Schutzstaffel, was the source of Hitler's power by enforcing his edicts as the Nazi's secret state police. It became my fundamental goal to join this elite organization."

"So, how did you end up in America?"

"When I was fifteen, shortly after I ran over a Jewish couple named Leibowitz, I started to keep a notebook of Jews and traitors to the Nazi cause, including the names of my parents. When they discovered my notebook and realized the Jews listed in my book had been deported to concentration camps, they made plans to immigrate to America when I let my guard down."

"What do you mean about letting your guard down?" As he looked at the startling transformation of Eric's normally handsome face into a mask of unbidden fury, Stephen felt an instant chill as he listened to Eric's narrative.

"My imbecile cousins told me the story of my parent's treachery. Deitrich and Clara secretly packed up their prized possessions as Christmas gifts and lugged them to the nearest postal station. They had to resort to devious methods because their actions were carefully scrutinized since they weren't Nazi loyalists. When a curious attendant noted the boxes were marked with the same address in America, Dietrich explained they contained early holiday gifts for his brother. The stupid clerk bought their story and sent the boxes overseas.

"Dietrich and Clark filled suitcases with clothes and personal belongings as they waited for an evening when I returned for a hot meal. Clara slipped a crushed-up sleeping draught into my hot chocolate, and when I fell into a deep sleep, they packed the rest of our belongings. My cousins were eager to tell me about my parents' plans, including their ridiculous statement, 'Then we began our trek toward freedom and our son's redemption.'"

"What happened when you woke up?"

"I didn't."

"Huh?"

"Because Dietrich was a pharmacist, he had an ample supply of sleeping pills for the long voyage and knew the right amount to knock me out without doing permanent damage. I later found out they used a wheelchair from their store to transport me and covered my legs with a blanket."

"But you had to wake up sometime. Couldn't you figure out what they did?"

"I underestimated their resourcefulness. Whenever I began to wake up, I didn't have the effort to talk and I didn't care at the time. My food contained crushed-up sleeping pills to ensure my drug-induced state throughout the trip. At times I felt lucid but had no control of my limbs. Clara fed me like a baby. My cousins were happy to share the vivid details with me. It was humiliating." Eric's fists balled up in anger but he continued his story. "It was like a nightmare that I couldn't wake up from."

"How did you learn the language? You can obviously speak English pretty well."

"When we arrived in America, my first impulse was to run away. But I had nowhere to go, no friends, and couldn't talk to anyone. I attended night classes to learn the new language and bided my time until I could devise an escape. Then I discovered a wonderful secret at The Hippodrome Theater that would circumvent Dietrich and Clara's plans."

"What did you see?"

"I was no longer alone as I watched newsreels of the German American Bund parading in Madison Square Garden, growing in popularity across America. I found the local branch and knew I was back home once again. And now that I've found you, we can carry out the Führer's wishes together in America."

Stephen beamed at being included in Eric's plans and knew his life would never again be the same.

NINETEEN

W ITH THE HATEFUL swastika violating the exterior of their home, Albert stayed home from work. Both he and Alona kept Sadie safely inside. Afraid of the repercussions by hidden forces responsible for upending their new life in America, once again the Leibowitz family felt threatened. They remained quiet and careful, too terrified to emerge from their home.

The weekend after the traumatic event, Albert opened the front door in response to loud voices and a thunderous sound of boots gathering on their front porch.

Alona and Albert told Sadie to wait upstairs.

"Albert, who is it?" Alona asked in a frightened voice, half hiding behind her husband.

"Uncle, Auntie, what is it? Can I come downstairs?"

"Oh, Sadie." Alona dabbed her eyes. "Come down and see for yourself." Her aunt and uncle hugged one another at the sight of their neighbors carrying paint supplies, scaffolds, and refreshments. Together, they painted over the large swastikas on the front porch and one side of their home.

Sadie laughed when she saw her friends and joined them as they attempted to help. Although the children managed to get underfoot, no one minded. Laughter joined chaos to create a congenial gathering of families and friends. Veronica gave Sadie a copy of their newspaper. She read the front page article of the afternoon newspaper, *The Cleveland NorthShore Post,* aloud to her aunt and uncle, which contained a statement issued by the police chief. When they heard his warning about further acts of vandalism resulting in hefty fines and imprisonment, their fright gradually subsided. The show of solidarity on that warm sunny day restored their faith in this new country. To the Leibowitz family, it became a hallmark event as they, too, shared in American pride.

DURING THE DAY'S festivities, Ellen couldn't forget the newsreel she'd seen at The Hipp about the German American Bund and the terror evoked by the images of Americans raising their hand in a Nazi salute and disparaging comments about Jews. Ellen was convinced the Bund was somehow behind these acts of terror, and determined to help her friend, Ellen asked Sadie if she saw anything unusual on the previous Saturday morning.

"Nah. Just a couple of dumb boys with stained shirts. They carried a heavy box."

"Any idea what was in the box?"

"I think it was a Bundt cake. They didn't know how to pronounce it but were sure proud of their 'bund.' Isn't that silly, Ellen? They were—" Sadie stopped mid-sentence when she noticed Ellen's pallor. "What's wrong?"

"Remember the Saturday when you had the flu and couldn't go with us to The Hipp?"

"Uh-huh."

"Well, in between pictures they showed a newsreel of the funny little German dictator with a strange mustache."

"Hitler," Sadie whispered.

"That's right. Anyway, he was screaming and gesturing to adoring crowds, although he struck me as nothing more than a bully. But the people were caught up in his frenzy as they showed torch-filled night rallies that inspired everyone to salute and scream 'Heil!'"

"He hates the Jews and we were lucky to escape his wrath. But what does that have to do with a cake?"

"The newsreel featured a rally in Madison Square Garden—it's in New York—and they boasted twenty-five thousand Americans joined the Nazi party."

Sadie's face drained of color when she repeated, "*Twenty-five thousand?*"

"That's right. But the important thing is the organization's name: The German American *Bund*. They claim to assist in job placement for German immigrants and have offices all around the country."

"Do you think those two boys were members of the Bund and I misunderstood their meaning? And maybe they painted the swastika?"

"Sure do. You mentioned stains on their shirts."

Sadie became very quiet as she realized the significance of what she had seen. "They were teasing each other about black stains ruining their shirts."

Ellen said decisively, "Well, I think we should tell your aunt and uncle."

"Oh, no, no, Ellen. Please don't. They looked familiar, but I can't place them. Besides, they know where we live, and if they remember passing me, they might return and do something worse." Sadie trembled at the thought of *American* Hitler Youths murdering them just as the German Hitler Youths killed her parents.

Ellen held Sadie until she stopped shaking and her tears subsided. "If you don't want me to, I promise I won't." Despite her unease at keeping a potentially dangerous secret, Ellen didn't want to upset her friend any further.

"Thank you, Ellen."

ELLEN DIDN'T MENTION to Sadie that the newsreel attempted to downplay anti-Semitic beliefs fostered by the Bund. Rallies showed picnic settings of bonhomie with American and Nazi flags prominently displayed side by side. The chilling footage had subconsciously made Ellen reach for her sweater as the horrifying images threatened life as she knew it. An ominous undertone had seeped into the theater as a subdued audience watched the cancerous growth develop in their homeland. Ellen could barely imagine the fear Sadie must feel, with Hitler's puppets taking up residence in America and invading her newfound security.

TWENTY

ELLEN'S SISTER MAYME, true to her childhood tantrums and theatrical posturing, decided to become an actress. Although none of the O'Malleys had been surprised at her decision, they couldn't believe seventeen-year-old Mayne had landed a part in the new play, *Victoria Regina*, at The Hanna Theater in 1937. The Hanna, a palatial theater centrally located in Cleveland on the corner of West 14th Street and Prospect Avenue, had become the most important theater for show business enthusiasts.

Mayme explained to her family the production revolved around a young Queen Victoria, portrayed by Helen Hayes, and her Prince Consort, played by Vincent Price. Mayme's role as Queen Victoria's maidservant may not have been the largest role, but her family believed she would be the best.

Finally, Mayme saw her childhood dreams coming true. She would see her name in lights—*big* lights! As the production evolved, Mayme became fascinated by the transformation of actors into different characters. Unseasoned performers, including Mayme, had a role model to teach them the basics and critique their performances.

"Mayme, this is Lawrence Talbot. He will play Lord

Melbourne, and I've assigned him to work with you since this is your first production," said the stage manager.

Mayme had to look up to see her new best friend and mentor in the theater. Extending her hand, Mayme said, "Pleased to meet you, Mr. Talbot."

"Call me Lawrence. Things move at a fast pace in the theater and you must keep up, Mayme, to learn everything you need to portray your character appropriately."

He coached her in the art of applying stage makeup, use of wigs, and accents. Mayme followed Lawrence everywhere he went as she absorbed his techniques, and Lawrence enjoyed the attention of his new sidekick.

Mayme had been so eager to learn her new profession, she overlooked Lawrence's movie star looks with large chartreuse eyes, a round face offset by dimples, slicked-back blond hair, and wire-rimmed glasses giving him a scholarly look. With a cultured and refined demeanor, Lawrence gave the impression of maturity to his protégé. Mayme would have been astounded to learn they were very close in age. Each time he entered a room, Lawrence exuded an air of supreme confidence, as if the world depended on his arrival.

"Lawrence, where did you learn so much about theater?" Mayme asked with an open expression of adoration.

He smiled at Mayme, whose eyes grew so wide they seemed to pop out of her head. "Years of experience and acting lessons in New York. You show real talent, Miss O'Malley, and should attend theater classes."

Mayme blushed and thought someday she would. In the meantime, she became proficient at the tools of her trade by mimicking his techniques.

"Maybe I should wear glasses, too. They give you an air of importance, and I need all the help I can get."

Lawrence smiled. "Mayme, these aren't props. With my poor vision, I'd probably fall off the stage without them."

The image of her idol tumbling into the audience made her laugh. Mayme said, "I'm so fortunate to have a terrific role model like you. Why, you even drove me home when I missed the last streetcar after a late rehearsal."

She whispered to herself, "What a guy!"

HER ENTIRE FAMILY arrived early for opening night and sat in their reserved fifth row seats. Despite feeling nervous, Mayme overcame her anxiety because this was her big chance to prove, in front of her family, that she belonged on the stage. She asked her family to specifically watch Lawrence. Mayme promised to introduce him, Helen Hayes, and Vincent Price to her family after the show.

During intermission, the O'Malleys gathered in the lobby and took turns sipping from the water fountain.

"Mayme looks pretty keen up there," James said nonchalantly, secretly awed by the sight of his older sister onstage with famous actors.

"I can't see a thing," Veronica said. "I'm sitting behind a lady with a huge hat."

"Me darlin', I'll change seats so ye can see."

Throughout the performance, Ellen kept a close eye on Lawrence. She certainly understood why Mayme was enthralled with this handsome young man. "So, what do you think of Lawrence? I think he's very convincing as Lord Melbourne."

"He's pretty cool. I can't wait for Mayme to introduce us."

Marge spoke loud enough for her brother to hear, "Wow, he really is the bee's knees."

"Huh?" said William in confusion.

"It means he's really handsome."

"Then why didn't ya say so? I think Mayme should continue her role at home. We could use a maidservant and we wouldn't have to pay her." William laughed at his own joke while everyone else rolled their eyes.

When the lights dimmed, they went back to their seats and sat spellbound throughout the performance until its exciting conclusion. Overcome with pride, the O'Malleys jumped up and applauded as the actors bowed onstage, especially when they caught sight of their beloved Mayme.

Mary couldn't stop smiling with an overwhelming sense of pride in her daughter's achievement. She congratulated Mayme at the stage door where all the actors congregated to meet friends and fans. Mayme's father gave her a small bouquet of flowers from their garden as he beamed with undisguised delight at her performance.

"So, what did you think?"

"Mayme, you were the bestest one up there," seven-year-old Thomas said as he hugged his sister.

Mayme, the center of attention as she gave out autographs to friends and neighbors, knew she had finally arrived. She turned around to her mother and said, "Ma, *this* is where I belong."

Out of the corner of her eye, Mayme saw Lawrence surrounded by several beautiful women wearing furs and diamonds.

"Yoo-hoo, Lawrence. Can you meet my family?"

"Wow, did you catch the jewelry on those dames?"

"William! Ye should be watchin yer tongue" his mother scolded. Behind her back, William comically stuck out his tongue and crossed his eyes to look at it.

Lawrence left his harem and politely bowed to the O'Malley clan. They, in turn, bowed to him, but knocked their heads with one another—clearly not a coordinated effort on their part. He laughed while they rubbed their sore heads and said, "Mayme shows real promise. I told her she would benefit from professional acting classes."

Mayme, star struck, radiated at the hard-won praise and nodded her head vigorously.

He turned and waved to his friends. "Well, I have several ladies waiting and they appear to be rather apprehensive. But, it has been my pleasure to meet you, and I hope you liked the performance."

Everyone nodded and murmured praise for his tremendous acting skills and stage presence. While Mayme attended to her adoring neighborhood fans, Lawrence hopped into a new 1937 Aston Martin 2-Litre C-type roadster. The crowd gasped as they stared at the luxury vehicle most dreamed about but none could afford. Laughing gleefully as he gunned the metallic-blue sporty vehicle, Lawrence's eyes sparkled as he saw their dropped jaws in the shiny gleam reflecting off the car. The sleek, space-age design emanated from the large polished mesh grille with long, curving fenders and a rounded trunk capped with a spare tire and glistening wheel rims garnished with silver spoke covers.

As James walked around the car, reverently touching the elongated glossy fenders, he said, "Wow! This car can go ninety miles per hour!"

After Lawrence drove off the dusty parking lot, Mayme said,

"See, I told you working in the theater could be profitable. If you're good, maybe I'll give you a ride in my new speedster when I make it big."

Mayme saw Helen Hayes and introduced her mother to the award-winning actress. Mary could not utter a sound as she met the famous actress.

As they walked home, everyone agreed Mayme's dream of becoming an actress seemed like a pretty great idea after all.

TWENTY-ONE

THE LANDMARK DAY in October 1938 when Ellen first became acquainted with the Sheridans started as any other Sunday.

"Ellen, yer ma is feelin poorly. I expect ye to take the children to Mass and keep 'em in line."

Ellen gulped as she realized the responsibility her father thrust on her shoulders. Out of the corner of her eye, she noticed her siblings performing victory dances and knew they would take full advantage of the situation. She had her work cut out for her.

During the short trek to mass, Ellen noticed the younger children had tucked books, toys, and a jump rope beneath their coats. She knew they planned on detouring to the park. Ellen had to agree it was a beautiful day but she didn't think God would understand the deviation. Although she loved her siblings dearly, Ellen knew the course her parents expected her to take.

"Walk in a straight line, and for heaven's sake, try to behave." Her words were ignored and Ellen could see the beginnings of a rebellion. She resorted to logic.

"I think everyone should decide for themselves about

attending Mass today," Ellen said.

Sensing an opening, her siblings nodded so hard she was afraid they'd all have migraines before the day was over.

However, before a vote could be taken, and she had no doubt what the decision would be, Ellen said, "Ma and Da expect us at Sunday Mass. So, it's *your* decision if you will enjoy Mass or not."

Speechless, except for occasional groans, they trudged along single file toward St. Patrick's where they sat on lumpy books, bulky toys, and a knotted rope for the duration of Mass. Once outside the church, they veered toward the park.

"You only have half an hour to play before dinner. Keep that in mind," but no one was paying attention as they headed toward the swings and slide.

"Excuse us, Miss—"

"Name's Ellen O'Malley. Just a second." She produced a whistle from her pocket and placed it to her lips. After taking a deep breath, the shrill sound rooted her siblings mid-stance. They knew Ellen would tell their parents if they didn't instantly obey her. "Remember, only thirty minutes." Turning back to the couple, she inquired, "Now, how can I help you?"

"Ellen, my name is Louis Sheridan and this is my wife, Marianne."

Ellen firmly shook their hands but maintained a curious expression on her face.

"My wife is expecting our third child next May. We believe the person to care for our baby must have a strong sense of responsibility equal to the task of lavishing love and discipline. We noticed you had full command of your siblings, especially during the long-winded sermon that sent many heads bobbing.

My wife and I would like to offer you the position as our nanny."

Ellen managed to maintain her composure but believed their offer was heaven-sent. Inwardly she laughed at the timely reflection.

"I'd love to," she responded before the shock constricted her vocal cords, making further speech incapable.

"Can you come to our home on Euclid Avenue in East Cleveland tomorrow at noon, and we can discuss this further? Here's our address," said Louis as he handed Ellen a card.

Ellen nodded mutely, wondering what happened to her voice. She gratefully accepted the information and shook Louis's hand. Finally able to talk, she managed to add, "I look forward to it."

TWENTY-TWO

ELLEN RAN INTO her home shouting, "Ma, Da, you'll never believe it—"

"Shhh, yer ma's tryin' ta sleep. What's all the yellin' about?"

Ellen explained her job offer and her father smiled as he hugged his oldest child. "Yer ma will be so proud. Of course, I am, too."

At the dinner table, Ellen explained her good fortune to the rest of her family. She could tell from the siblings' expressions they were relieved Ellen would be bossing around someone else's children.

Ellen awoke early the next day and selected her best frock— a simple mid-calf black dress with a rounded white collar, complimented by a plaid belt and sensible walking shoes. Crowded downtown streets bustled with people jostling one another, and streetcars side by side in opposite directions traversed the middle of the crowded thoroughfare. Double-decker buses and automobiles caused further congestion but contributed to Ellen's overall sense of exhilaration. She walked to a nearby Cleveland railway station and caught a streetcar to her destination.

Ellen arrived at 7525 Euclid Avenue and found herself in

the heart of Cleveland's famous Millionaire's Row, aptly named for the city's richest business tycoons who resided in comfort and style. The palatial mansions sat back from the widest streets Ellen had ever seen. Their front yards contained multiple shade trees and beautifully manicured lawns with statues artfully placed amidst flowering plants and fountains.

Ellen stared open-mouthed at the most elegant estate she had ever seen. Beyond a white picket fence, a long curving drive rose slightly to accommodate the bridge over a man-made lake. The main house looked like a picture from a fairy tale, complete with turrets and spires surrounded by spacious grounds. From the street, Ellen saw a lake complete with ducks and a rowboat lying on the bank.

A row boat in the backyard? What will they think of next? Ellen thought and gazed in wonder across the beautiful landscape artistically designed to inspire awe and appreciative glances from all who passed by.

Ellen rang the bell, as nervous as a child attending the first day of school, despite being twenty. A butler escorted her into the parlor. She wandered into the foyer where Ellen noticed an artist's rendition of the home as it appeared in the mid-1800s. Other than the barn being replaced by a garage, the property remained unchanged. However, the tranquility of her surroundings were interrupted and replaced by yelling and laughter.

"Give me back my shirt. Wait 'till I get ahold of you. You little brat!" A young adult shouted at a younger boy, running through the home swinging a shirt in the air.

When they saw Ellen, they both temporarily slowed their pace and their faces became flushed at being shirtless. The elder of the two breathlessly said, "Sorry, ma'am, I'm Edward. Catch you later after I wrangle my brother, Timothy, and get my shirt back." The chase was on and Timothy's laughter could be heard throughout the house. Ellen smiled, thinking of her own siblings' banter.

"Oh, dear. Those two are always at it. But they really do care about each other, despite today's performance." Mrs. Sheridan appeared in the doorway wearing a lovely blue dress that accented her rosy complexion. Her brown hair, styled in deep lush waves, framed her face. She extended her hand to Ellen.

"Not a problem. I'm used to it. Caring for my siblings without risking a major riot seems to be my specialty."

"Nineteen-year-old Edward was accepted into the U.S. Naval Academy in Annapolis, Maryland. Sixteen-year-old Timothy is still in high school and quite the prankster." A smile crossed Marianne's face. "Now, let's discuss your upcoming employment. I'd like you to start one month before the baby is due so you will be acquainted with the household staff and our routines. I have a feeling I may need your assistance, too, during my last month. You will, of course, be compensated for this time at $4.25 per week. This amount will include $1.25 for your weekly streetcar pass, if you find it agreeable."

Wow, Ellen thought. A veritable fortune! With as much composure as she could muster, Ellen said, "Yes, that would be terrific."

"Wonderful. I will have our housekeeper give you a tour of the home. We'd like you to stay for lunch, if it fits into your schedule."

What schedule? Ellen thought. Turn away free food? No chance. "That would be very nice. Thank you."

"Very good, Ellen. I expect our partnership will be long and fruitful."

When a slightly overweight woman entered the room, Marianne made the introductions. "Ellen, this is our housekeeper, Alice Webber. She will give you a tour of the house while the cook finishes our meal."

As Alice conducted the tour, Ellen noticed she was short, about five feet, with mousey-brown hair worn in a bun so tight it seemed to pull her entire face backward giving her a pinched, stern look. Ellen took pity on the homely lady. Her nose was large and her mouth formed a permanent, rigid line as if her immovable lips never had the energy to produce a smile.

"How long have you worked here, Alice?"

"More than eight years since I was twenty. Both my older sisters are also housekeepers. Seems I'm following in their footsteps."

Ellen wasn't sure how to respond to the implication Alice was doomed to a life of menial labor, so she reverted to a habit that always served her well. "You have the most beautiful eyes I've ever seen."

Alice blushed at the compliment as she blinked her large sapphire eyes surrounded by long, thick lashes. But despite her compliment, Ellen knew most men would not be attracted to the plain woman before her.

After the tour, Ellen returned to the dining room where Marianne waited. "I hope you enjoy the food."

"Thank you, ma'am. I'm sure I will."

"Ellen, we don't stand on formality in this home. Please call me Marianne."

"I will ma'—Marianne."

When Edward and Timothy joined the luncheon, Ellen marveled at the handsome and well-behaved gentlemen. Edward towered over his younger brother at six and a half feet and resembled his father with the same dark hair and blue eyes the color of cornflowers. Ellen could imagine girls lined up for miles for a chance to be seen with him; yet, he had an unassuming manner. But, to be fair, Timothy was equally handsome with unruly auburn hair, dimples, and devilish attitude. Yes, Ellen could easily envision girls vying for his attention, too.

During lunch, Ellen shared comical stories about her siblings and delighted Marianne with her no-nonsense approach to child care. And with that, Ellen secured her first real job.

TWENTY-THREE

L OUIS SHERIDAN KNEW he needed help.
Walking briskly to the telephone, he placed a call. "Is this Ellen O'Malley? This is Louis Sheridan."

"Yes, this is Ellen. How can I help, Mr. Sheridan?" Ellen thought, I hope they didn't change their mind about the job. It's still months away.

"Marianne is barely able to keep any food down or sleep through the night. This pregnancy is much different from her prior two. Although her doctor gives her intravenous fluids and B-12 shots for energy, they haven't helped very much. She is bedridden from sheer exhaustion and miserable at feeling so helpless but refuses to have a full-time nurse in the house. When I suggested it, Marianne said it would make her feel like an invalid and didn't want the subject brought up again. I know the two of you had a connection from your afternoon together a few months back. Do you think you could start work early and keep Marianne company? I think a woman's presence would greatly improve her despondency."

"Of course. Would you like me to start tomorrow?"

"How perfect! Thank you so much. For the first time in over a month, I can return to work knowing Marianne is in good hands. This may seem like a strange question, but I don't suppose you know of a chef who could start within the next week, do you? Our permanent chef is out on pregnancy leave and the ones we've interviewed just won't do."

"As a matter of fact I do. Her name's Sadie and she lives around the corner from me. Sadie is brilliant, and although she's only fourteen, she's taking a break from school. But she's a remarkable cook and could use the money."

"Only fourteen? I don't know—"

"I think you'd be pleased if you gave her a chance. News of her culinary skill has spread throughout the neighborhood, and she's been assisting many families in creating economical sumptuous meals. Sadie has a flair for creating delicious meals by combining leftover food with spices and seasonings."

"With such a remarkable recommendation, we'd be happy to give her a try. Do you think she could start next week?"

"I'm sure she can. If there's a conflict, I'll call you back." They said their good-byes and Ellen smiled to herself, happy that she was able to help Sadie and have a friend to share her new experience.

Twenty-Four

UNDER ELLEN'S CAPABLE guidance and careful monitoring, in addition to Sadie's delectable meals, Marianne's health and attitude improved. Ellen and Marianne became very close, and despite the age difference, looked upon one another as sisters. But there were times when Ellen, adept at reading people, knew Marianne's feeling of helplessness led to bouts of sadness. Ellen decided a diversion would allay Marianne's intermittent melancholy.

Over the past several months, they broached several subjects, many of them personal. Ellen knew a trip down memory lane would take her friend's mind off her current situation. "Marianne, how did the Sheridan fortune begin?" asked Ellen as she filled her water glass and sat down beside her.

"Louis's grandfather, Christopher Sheridan, founded Sheridan Clothing Mills in the mid-1800s. He adhered to a strict work ethic of putting in twelve hour days, six days a week, to personally oversee all aspects of his business. Christopher believed in treating employees like members of his family. He greeted each person by name, handed out a free turkey the day before Thanksgiving, and permitted days off for special occasions. A devoted and loyal workforce resulted with hundreds vying for a position following a rare vacancy.

"Christopher purchased land and built this estate in the late 1800s. His son died unexpectedly so he placed the Cleveland-based company in his grandson's capable hands when he retired. Louis expanded the company into three neighboring communities and within three years earned his first million. Louis's foresight in opening a clothing outlet store was so successful, he could have retired at a young age and lived a life of luxury. However, like his grandfather, the need to excel kept him hard at work. Despite the company's growing size, he continued to maintain the same personal touches renowned throughout the company."

"How did you two meet?"

Marianne's eyes sparkled with delight as she recalled their first encounter. "In January 1918, Louis attended a dinner party at the home of my brother, Jack. The Mulchrone and Sheridan boys had been friends since they were children, but I hadn't met Louis until that night. When Jack introduced me as his baby sister, Louis became tongue-tied and nervous. He blurted out I was the most beautiful women he had ever seen and compared me to Helen of Troy. Before then, Louis never had a problem communicating with *anyone*. He later revealed my soft-spoken elegant manner captivated him until he couldn't think straight. Louis believed I had the power to wrap any man around my finger." Marianne blushed at the fond memory.

"Well, he certainly was honest."

"What a nice thing to say, Ellen. Anyway, I resisted going out with Louis because I was taking care of our elderly mother. Jack insisted I needed to get out more and our mother agreed. However, that particular evening, my brother had to nudge Louis into arranging our first date.

"We decided to have dinner the following week, much to Jack's delight. However, at the last minute, my good old-fashioned Catholic guilt took over when our mother's health began to decline and I almost cancelled our date. When Jack heard that, he hired a full-time nurse to care for our mother and I convinced myself it was just one night. But one night turned into dozens when I experienced a feeling of exhilaration and happiness unlike anything I'd ever known before. Louis was kind and considerate, unaware heads turned whenever he entered a room." Marianne looked at the picture on her nightstand and smiled at Louis's handsome features—dark hair, neatly-trimmed full beard, pale blue eyes, and strong physique.

"Before I knew it, we were attending dinners and assorted social functions several times a week. Gradually I became involved in Louis's numerous charities and he came to rely on what he called my 'wise counsel.' Following our short courtship, we married at St. Patrick's church on October 17, 1918."

Alice knocked on Marianne's door as she brought in her evening meal and a newspaper for Ellen to read. Ellen's nightly routine involved surreptitious glances over the newspaper to make sure Marianne finished her meal before she bade her employer good night and made her trek home.

She knew Louis Sheridan normally didn't arrive home until late and was happy to help out in his absence. However, the current headline disgusted Ellen. The appalling ramification of thefts occurring while a grieving family attended a funeral was insufferable. She thought in anguish how anyone would be this callous to profit from someone else's grief. Ellen fervently hoped the thief would soon be captured and sentenced according to the heartache dispensed.

TWENTY-FIVE

WITH AN OVERINFLATED *ego, combined with delusions of grandeur, he referred to himself as the Mastermind. Today he woke up in a good mood. After reading yesterday's obituaries, he knew a home on Millionaire's Row would be vacant for several hours. He found it ironic that fancy folk refused to have wakes for their dead at home like normal people and instead used a funeral parlor close by.*

Don't they realize death ain't contagious? he asked himself. But, from his perspective, it was a fine practice and the obits became his calling card for new business opportunities.

After eating an early breakfast, he assembled items for the day's job, including a gun he purchased several weeks before. He preferred to keep the pistol unloaded. The mere threat of a weapon should be sufficient to win over reluctant "customers." At precisely 11:00 a.m., he hopped into his car and whistled a popular tune as he drove to the address listed in the paper. After a casual walk around the property to confirm its vacancy, he placed a dark mask over his head with holes cut out for his eyes, in case someone remained behind, and popped a screen from a back window, which landed him in a kitchen larger than his entire flat. Being an avid subscriber to the Robin Hood theory—at least, the part about the rich giving to the poor—he generously helped himself to the delicacies there for the taking. He continued to whistle as he strolled through the mansion and placed choice items in his large bag. As he approached the grand staircase, he heard the sound of people on the front porch.

He ran to the back of the home and let himself out through the window, quietly replacing the screen after he reached in to grab his tools and current stash. Casually strolling through the backyard, he crossed to the neighbor's yard and ambled down their driveway.

When he reached the sidewalk, he turned around and casually strolled through the neighborhood. He took perverse pleasure in watching the reactions of friends and neighbors, secure in the knowledge he had outwitted them all. He smiled at the sound of loud rumblings followed by a scream coming from the home of his latest "client."

"Where's the silver tea service?"

"My radio's gone!"

"Quick, call the police. We've been robbed!" Their loud, distraught voices could be heard through open windows.

Smiling to himself, he thought, "There goes the neighborhood."

TWENTY-SIX

WHEN MARIANNE ENTERED the seventh month of pregnancy, her depression increased when her physician relegated her to strict bedrest. Ellen convinced Edward and Timothy, while coercing Louis as he arrived home from work early, to have a family picture taken. Ellen knew having something positive to keep on Marianne's nightstand could work miracles when she started feeling down from exhaustion and being bedridden. However, to Ellen's surprise, the family included her in the photo, as well as Alice and Sadie, while the butler, Clifford, played photographer. When the picture was developed, Marianne presented Ellen, Alice, and Sadie with their own copies. The March 1939 photograph would become one of Ellen's most prized possessions for years to come.

Once again, Ellen sensed her friend's attitude would improve if she focused on her two favorite subjects.

"Marianne, did you ever consider a nanny for Edward or Timothy?"

"No, because my sons were such a delight and constant source of amusement, I didn't want to miss any of the fun. They were both loving children but distinctly unique. Edward bubbled with infectious laughter. With his quiet manner, he could get away with just about anything. And he pretty much did, too. Three years later, we were blessed with Timothy. Although he, too, had boundless energy, his personality was the exact opposite of his brother's—boisterous, loud, and daring.

"However, this pregnancy is much different. I don't have any energy, I'm much older now, and I feel useless lying in bed all day. Although I'm so happy you're here, Ellen. Time passes quickly when we're together."

Ellen could see Marianne grew tired from the lengthy conversation, so she fluffed her pillows and sat in a corner reading a book as her employer silently nodded off to sleep.

TWENTY-SEVEN

MARIANNE WOKE UP in the early morning hours of May 15, 1939, with a sharp pain that took her breath away. She knew their child was sending out a calling card that required an immediate RSVP.

Marianne woke up Louis and said simply, "It's time, Louis."

"Hmm? You want to know what time it is? Why, it's only three thirty, honey. Go back to sleep."

Less than a minute later, mid-snore, Louis was again awakened.

"No, Louis, I mean it's *time*."

Louis smiled. "Now it's three thirty-one, darling." But somewhere in the recesses of his sleep-addled brain, the implication of his wife's statement hit home. He bolted out of bed so fast he ran right into a wall. Dazed and rubbing his forehead, Louis fumbled with his pajama buttons. Mumbling to himself, "How strange. I don't remember this task being so difficult." But when he looked down and saw his hands shaking, he gave himself a little pep talk. "Okay, Louis, calm down." Once he finished getting dressed in the dark, he rushed over to help Marianne.

When he turned her bedside lamp on, Marianne laughed out loud in between contractions. She tried not to but couldn't help herself. "Louis, take a look in the mirror."

Louis, agitated at the loss of precious time, obliged his wife and couldn't help but smile at his unusual appearance. His hair stuck up so straight it resembled a soldier standing at attention. With his shirt haphazardly buttoned and tucked into his pajama bottoms, mismatched shoes, and no socks, he could have easily been mistaken for a drunken bum. It was quite a sight for a man who normally prided himself on his impeccable attire.

With Marianne's delivery imminent, Louis had prearranged to have both Ellen and Clifford remain overnight at the estate until the baby arrived. Louis rang for the butler to bring their car around. He then called out to Ellen, asleep in the next bedroom.

After Louis changed his clothes, he tried to help Ellen as she dressed Marianne; but he only got in the way and stood in the doorway feeling useless. In less than five minutes, while contractions continued to build, Louis carried her to the car. Ellen ran behind them carrying Marianne's suitcase that she handed to the butler before the car sped away into the night.

Ellen silently prayed the delivery would be quick and the drive without incident. Although given the sight of the auto careening into the street, the outcome of the latter remained uncertain.

"Clifford, perhaps you could slow down a bit? We don't want to shake the baby out. I'd prefer to have this child at the hospital."

However, her request was ignored. Marianne kept her eyes closed while he drove the car at breakneck speed to the hospital. With his wife safely in the care of hospital staff, Louis ended up in the fathers' waiting room. He wished he smoked to pass the time. Instead, he paced and tried to read yesterday's newspaper. As he began to doze, a nurse shook him awake and brought him to see his wife.

At 9:00 a.m. Marianne gave birth to their daughter, Bridget. The nurse brought Louis into Marianne's room as she held their beautiful baby. Marianne was enthralled at her daughter's blond waves, large blue eyes, and long, dark eyelashes.

"Oh." Momentarily speechless, Louis gazed at the bundle of happiness and sunshine wrapped in his wife's arms. "She's so beautiful. I'm so proud of you, Marianne." Kissing her tenderly, tears dropped onto Bridget who let it be known she did *not* like being wet. Louis and Marianne laughed, knowing she would be the center of the Sheridan universe.

When the family returned home a week later, Ellen held Bridget for the first time. As the baby settled contentedly into Ellen's arms, she felt her eyes filling up at the sight of the tiny infant completely dependent on others for care and love. She remembered her own mother's words, "There's nothing more helpless in the world than a newborn infant." But Ellen's happiness was temporarily marred when an image of Patrick surfaced. How she missed her sweet brother! Shaking off her momentary melancholy, Ellen returned to the joyous occasion at hand.

Ellen couldn't believe she received wages for a job that gave her so much pleasure. She came to think of both Louis and Marianne as friends, not just employers. Ellen knew how fortunate she was to procure her first job with a loving and wonderful family. They believed in her capabilities and trusted her to care for their precious newborn daughter.

Time passed quickly as Ellen reveled in her good fortune

and newfound confidence.

TWENTY-EIGHT

"I SHOULD HAVE *known it couldn't last forever,"* he lamented.

While attending the funeral parlor, families now hired police to guard the home and ensure the grieving family returned to a home free of unwanted intruders.

He now reverted to the time-honored profession of robbing people at gunpoint. He couldn't believe his new vocation could be so easy, especially when he targeted well-dressed businessmen leaving the bank. His operation was a huge success until he accosted a man who refused to part with his wallet despite a gun pointed directly at his heart. Blinded by fury, he pistol-whipped the man into a bloody mess on the sidewalk. Furious at his new venture being thwarted, he probably would have killed the man but stopped abruptly when someone across the street shouted for the police. Although a crowd had formed, he never forgot the person's face who interrupted his latest caper and smiled at the thought of paying the stranger a well-deserved visit.

After he ran two blocks to his car and finally catching his breath, he shook his head to clear the lingering effects of his almost-murderous rampage. He didn't understand how a simple job could have gone so wrong. With his moods fluctuating from easygoing to fits of rage at the slightest provocation, he sometimes felt like two different people. In a rare moment of clarity, he assumed it had something to do with his upbringing but lacked the patience and ability to further dissect his problem.

Later that afternoon, keeping his hat pulled down over his eyes, he returned to the scene of the crime in search of his pocket watch that slipped off its loose chain. He saw an unlikely object across the street, lying on the ground for all to see. He picked it up with shaking fingers and knew he found something of great value.

By the next day, and several beers later, the anger went away and he devised an alternate plan to augment his dwindling finances. He checked the society pages for clearly defined events leaving mansions with skeletal forces.

The next week, armed with the tools of his trade, he arrived at the Prescott mansion. He wrapped his hand in a thick woolen scarf and broke a windowpane in the back door and turned the lock. He knew the owners attended a banquet hosted by the Cleveland Museum of Art and smiled at the irony. "They're not the only ones who appreciate works of art," he chuckled to himself as he cut expensive paintings from their frames. He leisurely looked in closets and dressers while selecting treasures that would increase his diminishing bank account.

The following day, he took the newest possessions to his fence, Blackie. Astounded at the large sum from his latest project, he smugly thought how profitable and smart he was to change his career path.

TWENTY-NINE

"**H**ELP, POLICE. PLEASE, someone help this poor man!" Ellen's frantic cries at witnessing the brutal assault were promptly answered by the beat cop a few blocks away.

Oblivious to anything other than the beautiful but distraught woman in need, he inquired, "What's wrong, Miss?"

Ellen pointed across the street at the man lying on the ground in a pool of blood. "That man was assaulted. His attacker ran when I called for help." The police officer ran across the street and whistled for a patrol car who escorted the man to the hospital.

Returning to Ellen, shaking from the ordeal, the officer kindly asked, "Did you get a good look at him?"

"Yes," she whispered.

"My name is Officer O'Donnell. Do you think you could come to the station and make a statement?"

"I think so."

The officer assisted her into the police car. When she entered the station, Ellen was led to Office O'Donnell's desk. "Can you please write down everything you remember?"

"I'll try." Ellen wrote a brief narrative, which included a general description of the assailant. Handing the statement to the officer, Ellen said in a weary voice, "I'd like to return home now."

"Of course. We'll have a car drive you home. Could you return tomorrow and sit with a sketch artist?"

"I'll do whatever I can to help."

When Ellen returned home, she described the awful events to her mother. After sipping a cup of tea, Ellen called the Sheridans and explained why she was unable to work.

It wasn't until the next morning Ellen realized one of her clip-on earrings had fallen off during the excitement. She thought nothing of it and grabbed another pair of earrings from her drawer. When Ellen left her home, she was feeling somewhat better. The shaking had disappeared, and she no longer jumped at every sound. Exiting her home with a set destination—the Cleveland Police Station—she had every intention of assisting with a sketch of the thief that would result in his capture. His murderous look would be forever etched in her brain. She was confident in the clarity of his image, which returned now that her fright had subsided. Carefully adjusting her hat and putting on white gloves, Ellen descended the front steps when she saw someone across the street. A man dressed in a tailored suit leaned casually against the lamppost. At a distance there was something familiar about the man, but she couldn't see his face clearly.

When the stranger lifted his jacket and pointed to a pistol in his holster, Ellen recognized him and her entire body trembled. How did he find me? she thought.

The man placed his finger in front of pursed his lips and said, "Shhh," He then pointed to her home and waved. What was he up to? Ellen looked back and noticed her brother was still looking out the front window—and waving back! Ellen got the message and the murderous intent, loud and clear. Ellen knew she was in danger but surely the assailant wouldn't go after her family—or would he? Ellen wasn't about to take that chance. She already lost her baby brother to a kidnapper. Ellen wasn't about to let another family member be harmed at the hands of another.

Ellen would have to break her promise to help the kind police officer because her family's safety came first. Struggling to maintain her balance as dizziness and nausea overwhelmed her, Ellen held onto the railing and dragged herself back through the front door.

"Are ye all right, me darlin'?" her mother asked with concern as she helped her daughter in the front door. It seemed as though her mother's voice was a million miles away as she staggered into the chair.

"I don't feel well, Ma. Perhaps I should return to bed."

"Yes, me dear. Just lie down. If'n ye like, I'll call the Sheridans ta say yer still not feelin up ta work. I'm sure they'll understand yer bein' ill fer two days since ye nev'r missed a day b'fore."

"Thank you." She turned away from her mother to hide the rage and frustration at being threatened by someone whose identity she would be forced to protect. With her head held high, despite legs that threatened to give way, Ellen slowly climbed the stairs and barely made it into the bathroom where she vomited her breakfast.

Ellen got into bed and tried to sleep but kept tossing and turning. When she finally did fall asleep, her dreams were filled with nightmarish screams and blood-filled images as she watched her family suffer at the hands of a monster. Waking up in a cold sweat, Ellen paced her room and wrestled with her conscience. Exhausted by recent events, Ellen went downstairs to eat a light supper, hoping some degree of normalcy would return if she were surrounded by her family. But, once again, Ellen was unable to keep her food down and ran into the bathroom.

When she returned to her bedroom, Ellen noticed a chill in the air. Her window was fully opened yet she distinctly remembered closing it against the cold night air before going down to the kitchen. Approaching her bed, Ellen noticed something shiny. She cautiously reached for the object but recoiled when the realization hit home. It was her earring missing since yesterday's incident. Ellen knew it was left by the attacker. She surmised from his bold actions that her family might be accosted if she ever went to the police. Indecision was no longer a problem, and mustering what little strength she had left, Ellen carefully walked downstairs and made sure no one was around as she picked up the telephone.

"Operator, please connect me to the Cleveland Police Station. The number is CLearwater 1-3787," she spoke firmly while clutching the card in her fisted hand. When the call was placed, she asked for Officer O'Donnell and Ellen informed him she was unable to meet with a sketch artist. Despite his best attempts to change her mind, Ellen remained firm and apologized to the officer before hanging up. Ellen felt helpless and ashamed of her inaction, the same feelings she experienced when Patrick was abducted.

Although she was now an adult facing a similar dilemma, Ellen knew her main job was to protect her family at all cost. If it meant withholding information from the police and those she loved to accomplish this, Ellen would do what was required. But inside, her culpability festered like a cancer and went against everything she believed in. Ellen had been raised to be truthful in all things and reach out to others in need.

If only life were that simple, Ellen thought. She found herself caught up in the complexities of everyday life and realized the consequences of going against her beliefs were sometimes necessary to keep her family safe. There were days when the pressure inside Ellen's head threatened to explode because she couldn't unburden her soul. But Ellen was strong in spirit and love guided her way through life's difficult decisions. She prayed God would understand her actions and absolve her guilt.

THIRTY

O N THE FIRST day of October, nature's dizzying array of colors brightened Ellen's soul. She was grateful for the resplendent feast surrounding her as she entered the Sheridan household.

Shaking with excitement, Alice burst through the Sheridans' back door.

"Ellen! Where are you?" Alice's voice was unusually loud.

Ellen ran to the kitchen, breathless. "You sound upset. Is everything okay?"

"More than okay. I've met someone. And he's so dreamy, I can't believe we'll be dating."

Ellen had never seen Alice like this. Her effervescence reminded Ellen of the spray from a soda bottle when opened after being thoroughly shaken.

Curious, but not wishing to pry, Ellen asked what he looked like.

"I feel like I'm in the middle of a grand adventure. Pinch me so I know this isn't a dream."

When Alice loudly responded to the pain stimulus, she grinned. "We met at the West Side Market, and I literally ran into him with my arms filled with fruits and vegetables. He helped me pick up the food scattered across the sidewalk and we actually talked, once I could control my tongue and get over the shock."

Ellen noticed Alice avoided her question. Suspicious about the clandestine affair, but not wanting to voice her misgivings and spoil Alice's happiness, Ellen asked, "When is your date?"

"We'll meet next Saturday in front of the market. From there, we'll go to The Hippodrome for the latest movie followed by dinner. Who knows? It's all so exciting. Oh, Ellen, will you help me select an outfit?"

"Of course! And, if we can't find something suitable, we can go shopping."

"You would do that for me?"

"Sure, it's what friends are for."

After searching through Alice's dowdy wardrobe, Ellen recommended a nearby clothing store. Seeing the look on Alice's face as she tried on a beautiful outfit, Ellen was happy to see her friend excited at the prospect of a new adventure. Everyone deserved a little fun, and Alice was overdue. Ellen secretly wished Alice's dream date would be everything she hoped and more.

THIRTY-ONE

T HE FOLLOWING SATURDAY, Alice compared her prior drab and lonely existence to the wonderful relationship she currently found herself immersed. She gazed at her new boyfriend in absolute wonder. Brett Roth had a muscular build, stood tall and proud, and with his ruddy complexion, perfectly-styled red hair, brown eyes with flashes of green, and a full beard, he could easily be mistaken for a movie star. Alice's new friend drew the stares of many beautiful women, an experience foreign to her, but one she secretly delighted in because he was with *her*.

As they stood in line for tickets to *Gone with the Wind*, Alice and Brett's conversation flowed smoothly and easily.

"Where do you work, Alice?"

"I'm in charge of running a very large estate on the east side of Cleveland," she proclaimed with an air of self-importance to overcome her feelings of inadequacy.

"I used to work in construction on the east side. Which home?"

"The Sheridan home on Millionaire's Row."

"No kidding? I worked on that home. Do they still have a lake in the backyard large enough for a rowboat?"

"Oh, yes. That's my favorite part."

"I always thought it strange a home so fancy had a back door with such a flimsy lock."

"Oh, they've had the lock replaced. All shiny and new, it's quite lovely."

Her new friend smiled tentatively as they approached the ticket window. Alice's dream date was everything she hoped it would be. They made plans to meet the following Saturday; same time and place. She couldn't wait.

Alice continued their fling over the next four weeks and even thought about walking down the aisle with Brett. They got along so well, never argued, and always had something to talk about.

However, the last time they met, he seemed different and aloof. Alice had a feeling her trip down the aisle was nothing more than fantasy as they struggled through the meal barely speaking to one another. Alice tried talking to him, but he kept his answers curt and short.

Alice couldn't stand it any longer. "Will I see you next week? We could see a great new movie, *The Wizard of Oz.* They say it's in Technicolor and it's sure to become all the rage."

"No, Alice. I've met someone else who's much prettier, and I'd rather spend time with her." Seeing her distress made Brett smile as he ravenously ate his food.

Alice remained quiet and stopped eating, unsure how to respond and afraid to move. She sat still and waited for him to say his cruel remark was a joke. "Then why did you ask me out to dinner?"

Leaning in close with a sneer on his face, Brett grabbed Alice's arm forcefully and said in a threatening manner, "To tell you something really important and make sure you understand with that small brain of yours."

Alice flinched as Brett laughed. "You'll do well to forget about me. I'm warning you not to speak to anyone about me. I know where you live and if I had to pay you a visit, I guarantee you wouldn't like it."

Alice tried to hide her terror and walked away with her head held high. She heard his callous laugh in the distance, and after she rounded the corner, ran all the way home. Luckily, her only discussion with Ellen about the new man in her life didn't include his name or any description. Sick with rage and feeling manipulated, Alice knew she was a pawn in whatever sick game Brett was playing.

THIRTY-TWO

O N DECEMBER 23, 1939, Ellen prepared for a routine workday, excited at the prospect of two paid holidays, thanks to the generosity of her employers. However, Sadie's absence cast a slight pall on her anticipation when she left the Sheridan employ two weeks earlier to care for her ailing aunt. Poor Sadie lamented the missed opportunity to meet Edward and Timothy Sheridan during their holiday break from school.

Feeling distracted, Ellen's annoyance grew as she traipsed through the house looking for her shoes under cushions and beneath chairs. "Ennis, I don't suppose you know where my shoes are?" When their Irish setter didn't respond, other than snoring, Ellen added, "What's the matter? Cat got your tongue?"

Laughing at her own joke, she continued her search and noticed Ennis's makeshift bed seemed lumpier than usual. Sure enough, snuggled under her front paws, Ellen found her slightly slobbery shoes. She patted Ennis on the head and received a loud snort in return as her protector turned onto her back, paws in the air. The sight made Ellen smile every time. After wiping her shoes off and applying a fresh coat of Vaseline for a beautiful shine, Ellen was ready to leave.

Although running late again, Ellen prided herself in the fact she only missed two days of work. While putting on her winter coat, Ellen stopped briefly when she saw her youngest brother, Thomas, kneeling on the couch looking intently out the living room window. He held his face in pudgy hands and sighed with contentment. Curious, Ellen knelt next to him and asked, "So, what are we looking at?"

"Beautiful snowflakes. Aren't they neat?"

"They sure are. Do you know each one has a unique shape?"

"Really? But where do they come from?"

"They're raindrops dressed up in little white coats to celebrate the birth of Baby Jesus."

"Keen. Ellen, you know *everything*."

Ellen lovingly hugged her brother and kissed the top of his head before leaving to catch the next streetcar.

PART TWO

The Murder Investigation

(1939-1941)

THIRTY-THREE

ELLEN WAITED OUTSIDE Bridget's bedroom while Marianne read to her daughter. Peering over the balcony, Ellen recalled Louis Sheridan had looked dashing in his form-fitting tuxedo, bouncing his top hat on his knees and tapping his foot on the floor.

"Marianne, are you ready *yet*? As the guests of honor, we don't want to be late."

As Marianne exited her daughter's room, she descended down the winding staircase.

"Hush, Louis," Marianne admonished her husband. "You know the least little sound could wake up Bridget. Why, I believe she could hear a bird's wing flapping in the next county. The little darling just closed her eyes, and hopefully will soon be fast asleep."

Louis turned and watched in undisguised appreciation as Marianne approached with a smile that could melt hearts from across the room. Her petite figure, expressive hazel eyes, and soft brown curls were gathered together in an updo and held with a decorative clasp making her look demure and sensual at the same time. She wore her newest purchase—a long mint-green, silk gown enhancing her eyes and a plunging neckline that accentuated her figure.

"Why, Louis Sheridan! The way you look at me, you'd think we were newlyweds, not an old married couple of twenty-one years with three children!" With a sparkle in her eye and a bloom of color in her cheeks, Marianne entered her husband's arms for a warm and loving embrace.

"My dear, seeing you like this makes me feel like a newlywed," Louis said as he scooped her up in his arms and headed toward the front door.

"Louis, put me down this instant!" Marianne laughed, failing miserably at her attempt to sound stern. "You know it's freezing outside and I need a warm coat."

"I could keep you warm, my love."

"Oh, I know that look. My coat will have to do or we'll never make it to the fundraiser. We're the guests of honor, remember?"

With a shake of his head, Louis relented and gathered their coats before exiting.

"Ellen, we won't be too late. Hopefully Bridget will stay asleep for you." On cue, they could hear the tiny infant's loud objections. "Or maybe not."

Ellen laughed as she ushered them out the door before dashing upstairs to care for Bridget.

THIRTY-FOUR

AT 9:15 P.M., the radio-dispatched unmarked detective car received an urgent call in response to screams and possible gunfire at 7525 Euclid Avenue. With senior members of the Cleveland force on holiday leave, newly-appointed detectives Frank Szabo and his partner, Kevin Collins, were working a double shift the night before Christmas Eve. Although their second shift involved a transfer to the short-staffed East Side District, they welcomed the transition. As the sole breadwinner for his elderly parents, Frank was grateful many officers were on vacation which provided much-needed overtime pay.

They were advised to proceed with caution to the residence belonging to Cleveland socialites Louis and Marianne Sheridan. Frank and Kevin had never met the Sheridans but knew of them from articles and photos in the society pages. Cruising a few blocks away, they radioed their location and within a few minutes arrived at a home where bedlam reigned.

"Turn in here," nervous neighbors said as they directed them into the Sheridan driveway.

"Do you know what happened? Was anyone hurt?" Questions were hurled at Frank and Kevin from all directions in the ever-growing crowd.

Frank took control. "Folks, please stay outside and let us do our job. Once we begin the investigation, we'll be out to take your statements later. But first, we need to go inside and determine what happened."

Approaching the home, weapons drawn, they cautiously entered the partially open front door. They discovered a young woman, covered in blood, attempting to revive Mrs. Sheridan. Lying next to her in a large pool of blood, with a death stare fixed on his face, lay the lifeless body of her husband. Another female, pale and anxious, stood in the background.

This would be Frank and Kevin's first murder scene, although they, along with other detectives in the academy, received training in homicide procedures as part of their indoctrination. Frank enjoyed working with Kevin and found him very competent. They got along well together, aggressively approached any police emergency, and in general, made a great team.

Frank said to the women, "We need you to step away from the body." Over his shoulder, Frank could see an abundance of curious neighbors attempting to enter the home. Frank announced, "You need to stay outside. We don't want to trample the crime scene with excess foot traffic."

Everyone responded to the authority in Frank's voice, which surprised him. He thought his naiveté would be obvious to everyone since the academy only taught him the basics of how to proceed. The remainder of his investigative techniques were self-taught through library books.

Given the disarray of the downstairs and several prominent paintings missing from their allotted frames, Frank and Kevin assumed a robbery had gone awry. After cordoning off the crime scene, they made a thorough search of the house and surrounding grounds to confirm the burglar had fled the premises. With this accomplished, they isolated the witnesses for interrogation.

Seeing Mrs. Sheridan had struggled to her feet, Kevin led her to a chair before she collapsed.

"I'll give you a few minutes to collect your thoughts, Mrs. Sheridan. Please try to relax if you can."

Ignorant of Kevin's inane directive, she nodded her head. She remained catatonic as her gaze transfixed on the bloody mess surrounding her beloved Louis. Kevin then brought a chair over to a woman standing in the corner as she shook uncontrollably while staring at the grisly scene.

"Can I get anything for you?"

"N-n-no th-thank you, officer," she said through chattering teeth.

"I need to ask you a few preliminary questions. Please try and provide as much detail as possible. First, what is your name and relationship to the Sheridans?"

She turned the chair away from the ghastly scene and waited until the shaking subsided before responding. "I'm the housekeeper, Alice Webber. I work five days a week. But I came down with a stomach flu yesterday and was too weak to leave the house. The Sheridans kindly offered one of their spare bedrooms until I was stronger."

"Did you hear any suspicious noises or witness the attack?"

Alice slowly dried her eyes as she wrestled with her conscience. But recent events in her own life and overwhelming fear clearly dictated the only response she could provide. "No, sir. I was asleep until I heard Mrs. Sheridan scream. By the time I came out of my room, the front door was open, the Sheridans were on the floor, and Ellen was reviving Mrs. Sheridan. I didn't see any intruder."

"Besides yourself, how many people were in the home before the Sheridans returned?"

"Just the nanny, Ellen O'Malley, and the Sheridan's seven-month-old daughter, Bridget."

"Did the Sheridans regularly employ anyone else?"

"Well, Sadie, the temporary cook, was employed from January until two weeks ago, and the butler had the evening off."

"I'll need information on both of them for interviews in addition to the name of the regular chef. Let's begin with the cook most recently employed. What was her full name and circumstances regarding her departure?"

"Sadie Leibowitz just turned fifteen and started working this year following a recommendation by Miss O'Malley. But Sadie's last day was December ninth when her aunt took ill, and she was forced to quit. The Sheridans asked the butler, Clifford, if his wife, she prefers to be called Sara B., would consider returning after she had her baby. She's expected to start after the first of the year."

"Can you provide more information on the butler?"

"Clifford Smith has worked for the family forever—long before I came along. He usually works Monday through Saturday but was given tonight off as a holiday surprise."

Kevin noticed Miss Webber's color was turning a slight shade of green and guided her toward the open doorway of a guest bedroom. He then turned his attention to Mrs. Sheridan, sitting in a corner, sobbing.

THIRTY-FIVE

ONCE MARIANNE REGAINED some semblance of composure, Kevin brought her a snifter of brandy to steady her nerves. Although she initially refused, he insisted. Despite her resistance, the drink had a calming effect.

"I want you to know we've already called the doctor. Is there anyone else you'd like us to contact?"

Speaking through a haze, Marianne said, "Yes, both my sons. They're attending a party at their friend's home." Reaching for her address book on the table, she provided the phone number.

Kevin asked Frank to call the sons and continued his interrogation. "I'm so very sorry for your loss and apologize for asking questions at a time like this. I'll try to be brief. Can you think of anyone who would want to harm your husband?"

"No one. Both his colleagues and employees highly respected and admired him."

"Did you see or hear anything during the scuffle? Perhaps any noticeable marks on the murderer's body like an unusual accent or physical deformity?"

"I was too distraught to notice any details but I believe my husband pulled off the thief's mask. I remember seeing red hair but only caught a brief glimpse before I passed out."

"Did you get a sense of his height? For example, was he taller or shorter than your husband?"

"They were the same height—about six feet tall."

"Were there any recent repairmen or construction workers in your home?"

"We added a new bathroom downstairs and a spare upstairs bedroom was renovated into a nursery before Bridget was born."

"Was the same company employed for both renovations?"

"No." Her hands shook as she dabbed her eyes with a handkerchief, her memory clouded by grief and sorrow. "I'm certain our accountant, Ken Knabe, could provide the information you need."

"Thank you, we'll contact him tomorrow. Do you recall if any construction workers had red hair?"

"Not that I recall, but, again, I only saw part of the workforce."

"Were you aware of other break-ins in the area?"

"My husband told me not to worry because those involved empty homes. Ours is always occupied."

"How did workers access the home?"

"Either the butler or housekeeper let them into the home. We never thought anything like this could happen to us . . ." Mrs. Sheridan's nervous discourse stopped and her eyes glazed over as copious tears cascaded down her cheeks.

Kevin glanced at Frank, tilting his head toward the woman covered in blood and sitting by herself. Both assumed this was the nanny, Miss O'Malley, and after Frank completed his phone calls, Frank would conduct her interview.

Kevin continued. "We appreciate everything you told us. Any further recollections will assist in apprehending the man who murdered your husband."

At the mention of her dear Louis, Marianne continued to cry. The physician arrived to verify Louis's death and sign the death certificate. He also prescribed a sleeping draught for Marianne with strict instructions that she return to her bedroom. As she left, Kevin thanked her for her cooperation and felt sorry for the bereft lady as she faced what would undoubtedly be the worst Christmas of her life.

THIRTY-SIX

FRANK GAZED UNABASHEDLY at the beautiful woman standing in front of him. He saw past the smear of blood on her face, clothes soaked in blood from helping Mrs. Sheridan, and hair in disarray with bits of red curls softly framing her face. Captivated by the striking woman whose hard-fought composure in the grueling backdrop revealed an inner strength which enhanced her natural beauty, Frank forced himself back to the matters at hand. Luckily for him, Ellen's current state prevented her from noticing his intense stare.

Taking out his pen and notebook, Frank cleared his throat before he began his interrogation. "What is your name, Miss?"

Frank saw the woman's shaking hands and tear-streaked face. What he mistook moments ago for composure was clearly shock.

"Ellen O'Malley," she said in a monotone voice.

Frank noticed the blank stare on Ellen's face. "Miss O'Malley? Miss O'Malley, can I get you a drink?"

Ellen dabbed her eyes. "No, thank you."

"I understand you work for the Sheridan family."

"Yes, I'm the Sheridan's nanny for their seven-month-old

baby, Bridget."

"How long have you worked for the Sheridans?"

"Approximately eleven months—I helped care for Mrs. Sheridan during her difficult pregnancy."

Looking back at his notes, Frank continued. "Was there anyone else in the house other than yourself, the baby, and the housekeeper before the Sheridans arrived home?"

"No, only the three of us. Thankfully the Sheridan's two sons were at a party, the temporary cook left two weeks ago when her aunt became ill, and the butler had the night off."

"Was anyone else aware of the Sheridans' schedule this evening?"

"Their attendance at the charity event was well publicized in the society pages. Anyone who read the newspaper probably knew their plans for this evening."

"We couldn't find evidence of a forced entry. Any idea how the burglar got in?"

"No sir, I don't. As usual, I saw them lock the front door as they left before I went upstairs to take care of Bridget."

"Did you hear or see anything before Mrs. Sheridan's scream?"

"Yes—I heard a noise." Ellen stopped as the gravity of events witnessed was etched into her memory. She rubbed her face to try and erase the image of death. "I'm sorry—I still can't believe he's dead."

"I know this is difficult, but you mentioned a noise."

"About an hour after the Sheridans left, I heard a noise downstairs while taking care of Bridget in the nursery. After a brief search, I couldn't find anything unusual, and the baby was crying for attention, so I returned to the nursery." Ellen's face softened when she added, "I completed the lengthy process of getting Bridget to sleep. No small task with that one, but I love her dearly." Ellen stopped mid-thought and her face became flushed.

"What happened after you put the baby to sleep?"

Realizing the void facing the Sheridan family—especially the cherished infant sleeping in her crib, oblivious her beloved father was forever gone—Ellen's tears flowed again and her expression reflected a profound sadness. She knew the suffering ahead for Mrs. Sheridan—she'd seen it firsthand when her brother was kidnapped. "I'm sorry, wh-what . . . ?"

"Once the baby was asleep . . ."

"Oh, yes. Let's see. After Bridget began to snore softly—a sure sign she was out for the night—I tucked her into bed with her favorite stuffed animal and kissed her forehead. When I slowly tiptoed out of the nursery room, I heard the front door open."

"What time were the Sheridans expected home?"

"Around eleven but lately, Marianne experienced migraine headaches often triggered by stress or excitement. When they arrived home at nine o'clock and unlocked the front door, I assume they came face-to-face with the burglar."

"We try not to base our investigations on assumptions, just facts as you know them. You mentioned the front door opened. Where were you and what exactly did you see?"

Once again, overcome by her emotions, Ellen knew she had to concentrate and continue her narrative. "I had exited the nursery upstairs—it's the third door on the right—and was at the top of the staircase. When Louis turned away from the stranger to check on Marianne, the burglar took advantage of the momentary confusion and pulled out a gun. Louis attempted to wrestle it away from the intruder and during the struggle, pulled off the thief's mask. The next few moments passed in slow motion as the room filled with a loud explosion and gunpowder. The gun, slick with blood, fell to the floor with a resounding thud. For a brief moment I prayed the thief, not Mr. Sheridan, had been shot. God forgive me . . ." Ellen made the sign of the cross. "My prayer was not answered. As Mr. Sheridan pitched backward, his wife fainted, and they both fell to the floor."

"What happened next?"

With her head bowed in shame, Ellen continued her narrative. "At the time, it seemed like I was in a fog and my movements were in slow motion, as if my brain was disconnected from the rest of my body. It wasn't until I heard Mrs. Sheridan moan that I felt my reflexes return. I ran to the bottom of the stairs to help her and, out of the corner of my eye, I saw someone dressed in black run out the front door with what appeared to be a pillowcase slung over his shoulder."

"How much time elapsed from the time the Sheridans entered the front door until Mrs. Sheridan began to come around?"

"Probably a minute or two, but it seemed like so much longer. Mrs. Sheridan wasn't fully conscious for several minutes later."

"Did you get a good look at the murderer?"

Ellen, uncertain what to reveal, decided to provide clues anyone would have noticed. "He was white, about the same height as Mr. Sheridan, and although I only saw the back of his head, I noticed he had red hair."

"Did you recognize him? Perhaps a former employee or construction worker in the home?"

Ellen hesitated slightly as she relived ugly flashbacks that laid the groundwork for her culpability. She realized the irony of history repeating itself. Recently, she witnessed a thief, now a murderer, who forced her to choose the protection of her loved ones while she maintained the lie about his identity

Ellen could not forget the earring he left on her bed as a warning. If he got out on parole, he knew where Ellen and her family lived. Would he come back and hurt them, maybe even kill her family? Ellen couldn't take the chance. Although cognizant of the price she paid with her silence, Ellen felt any other recourse would have left utter desolation in its wake. Ellen was fearful of saying too much—especially in her heightened state of anxiety. She thought it best to wait until her head was clear before she inadvertently opened the door that housed her secret and exposed her family to mortal danger.

Making a decision, she said with a sense of calm foreign to the battle waging within, "No, detective, I did not."

"Did Mr. Sheridan have any enemies you're aware of?"

"Goodness, no. He was beloved for his generosity, and his compassionate treatment of employees earned him the respect of all. I can't think of anyone who wished him any harm."

Ellen responded to Frank's basic questions and stifled anguished cries as he took detailed notes. Frank noted her sparse description of the assailant despite extensive prodding. He instinctively knew Ellen's brief responses were an act of self-preservation while she battled shock and mentally confronted the cruelty of violence. He knew, for the time being, any further details about the assailant would not be forthcoming.

"Thank you, Miss O'Malley. Here's my card and badge

number. If you can think of anything else, please call the station house and they will make certain I get the message."

Taking the card while glancing down so the detective wouldn't see the shame in her eyes, Ellen was filled with desperation and helplessness. She didn't mention the scream she stifled as she gazed at the man who had murdered her employer and friend. With the abrupt removal of his mask, Ellen had recognized him. With police sirens growing louder, the burglar had run toward the front door in a hasty retreat, but stopped momentarily as Mrs. Sheridan moaned. Hearing Ellen's muffled gasp as she made her way down the stairs, their eyes locked for what felt like an eternity. When the murderer put his finger to pursed lips, he mouthed a threatening message that struck her heart with its chilling intention. "Shhh. I know where you live."

"Thank you for the card, Detective. I really can't think of anything else at this time."

"Oh, before I forget, would you be willing to come into the station to review mug shots and perhaps sit with a sketch artist?"

"I'll be happy to, but I didn't see much."

"You'd be surprised how much you remember once the initial shock has passed. All we can ask is that you try."

"I'll stop in sometime within the next few days."

"Thank you for your time, Miss O'Malley," Frank said as he left the home to assist his partner with interviewing neighbors.

THIRTY-SEVEN

Frank and Kevin canvassed the area—a relatively easy chore with the entire neighborhood milling around the Sheridan property. Frank smiled to himself and watched Kevin work his magic. Women in the neighborhood vied for the attention of a detective with thick blond hair, ruddy complexion, and blue eyes. Despite reassuring those lingering out in the cold, Frank and Kevin didn't obtain much useful information until they spoke to one very anxious neighbor, bursting with apprehension.

"I'm Paul Carns and I live next door to the Sheridans. I sure hope they're all right. They are the nicest people on the block."

Ignoring the tacit question, Frank asked one of his own. "Did you hear or witness anything regarding tonight's burglary?"

"I saw a young fella hightail it down the street and jump into a late model Ford V-8. I bought a similar car for my son's birthday."

"Did you notice in which direction he was headed?"

"West on Euclid Avenue."

"I don't suppose you saw the license plate number?"

"No, sorry. The car was near the end of the block. But it had a 1939 Ohio license plate. I remember the year because 1939 plates had blue letters on a white background. I could see that much because it was parked under a street light."

Frank decided to walk the escape route described by Mr. Carns and noticed a set of large footprints leading to the empty space previously occupied by the Ford. The depth of prints in the snow captured his attention although their significance eluded him, like a feeling of déjà-vu. In his thorough and methodical manner, Frank recorded this obscure finding with other potential clues in his notebook. He could not shake the feeling he overlooked something of importance. But given the early stage of their investigation, he assumed the omission would become apparent once they sifted through the evidence.

Eager to use his new Kodak camera with a flash attachment, Frank had taken pictures of the crime scene. On a whim, he also photographed several images of the strange footprints leading to the vacant parking space.

With sufficient information, they radioed dispatch with the following bulletin:

"All cars be on the lookout for a white male, average build, approximately six feet tall, red hair and possibly a full beard, driving a late model Ford V-8 with current Ohio license plates, number unknown. Suspect was last seen heading toward the west side of Cleveland from 7525 Euclid Avenue. Any cars with occupants matching this description should be searched for a large pillowcase filled with stolen property. Approach with caution—this man is armed and has already committed one murder. We believe he's responsible for other robberies on Millionaire's

Row and adjacent cities."

When they returned to the house, they separated to cover the massive estate.

"Kevin, did you finish checking the upstairs?"

"Sure did, Frank. Couldn't find a murder weapon or the discarded mask."

"Neither did I. But come down here. I want to show you something."

Together they examined the back door. It stood slightly ajar and had clearly been tampered with. Broken pieces of wood surrounded scrape marks along the lock. After securing the door as much as possible, Kevin said, "Someone picked the lock like the other homes robbed in this area."

"I agree. It's probably the same person but this time, he was unlucky enough to pick a home that was occupied."

Frank and Kevin compared notes to confirm the accuracy of contact information for Mrs. Sheridan, Ellen, and Alice. They looked around at the large Christmas tree, ornately decorated, with presents beneath it and holiday lights strung across the fireplace mantel—stark reminders the holidays would be abysmal for the Sheridan family.

THIRTY-EIGHT

WHEN FRANK AND Kevin were preparing to leave, they found Ellen sitting alone in the parlor looking lost and forlorn.

"Miss O'Malley, are you going home or staying? If you need a ride home, we'd be more than happy to give you a lift," said Frank.

"I asked Marianne if she would like me to stay. She told me to return home. Her sons are on their way here and she prefers to be alone with her family. But, no, thank you for the offer. I can take the streetcar."

Despite her resistance, the detectives insisted. "Ma'am, we wouldn't be doing our jobs if we didn't look out for you."

After the traumatic night and withholding information from the police—something that went against everything she believed in—Ellen, devoid of energy, gladly accepted their kind offer.

"Where do you live?" asked Frank.

"At 3104 Carroll Avenue, across from the building that houses St. Ignatius College and the high school."

"I grew up not far from there. Isn't Carroll Avenue near St. Patrick's Church?"

"Yes, Detective," Ellen said in a tired voice.

"Please, call me Frank."

"Okay, Frank. Please call me Ellen." Although she didn't feel like talking, Ellen wanted to continue any conversation to remove the deafening sounds of silence. She asked out of courtesy, "Where did you go to high school?"

"West High." Ellen became more attentive and informed Frank she had attended the same school.

Frank tried to keep the excitement out of his voice. "I live on West Thirty-first Street."

"That's just around the corner from my home," Ellen said with more energy than she thought possible.

For the duration of the ride, Frank and Ellen conversed about similar neighborhoods and shared experiences at West High and St. Patrick's School. But Ellen, distressed at having to keep her secret, was overwhelmed and remained ignorant to Frank's attentiveness.

"If it would be all right with you, I'd like to follow up and make sure you're doing okay."

"All right, Detective—I mean, Frank." When the police car arrived at the O'Malley residence, Frank and Kevin accompanied Ellen to her front door.

Mary flung open the door, wide-eyed with fear at the distraught look on her daughter's face and blood-stained clothing. "Sweet Mother Mary, are ye all right, me darlin'?"

Ellen collapsed into her mother's arms, sobbing. She explained the ghastly details and introduced the detectives.

"What dear men. Would ye care for a cuppa' tea?"

"No, but thank you, Mrs. O'Malley. My partner and I are still on patrol, but we wanted to see your daughter home safely."

"We'd be thankin' ye kindly for your concern and bringin'

our lovely Ellen home after such a tryin' day."

With the help of her mother, Ellen made it to her bedroom before she fell onto the bed, worn out from apprehension and sorrow. She couldn't believe the ominous day had started with something as pure and simple as a snowflake. She wondered how life, in the blink of an eye, could morph from happiness to circumstances mired in tragedy and despair.

To assuage her guilty conscience, Ellen made a solemn oath. She didn't know how or when but one day, when it was safe to do so, Ellen would make certain the Sheridan family knew the entire truth. Ellen fervently hoped they would understand and forgive her.

Secure in the home of her parents and with Ennis, ever the protector, at her side, Ellen replayed the evening's events over and over like a repeating melody from a needle stuck in the groove of her favorite record. She cried herself to sleep as Ennis kept guard at the foot of her bed.

THIRTY-NINE

H E ESCAPED THE *manhunt and silently thanked John Dillinger, the greatest American gangster and his hero. Since Dillinger bought a Ford V-8, faster than the six-cylinder engines used by G-men, he had to have one, too. But when he heard Dillinger had the balls to write a thank-you note directly to Henry Ford for the powerful V-8 engine in his 1932 Ford, he couldn't stop laughing. His mind worked like Dillinger's—a quick getaway was essential to any successful operation.*

"Too bad Dillinger's not still around. We would have made a great team," he mused.

After pulling into a dark alley, he was surprised to see blood on his hands and guessed it was from picking up the pillowcase from the floor after the shooting. He wiped the blood away and removed his dark clothing, throwing it into the backseat before changing into his classier duds—a double-breasted navy blue suit with wide lapels, pinstripe shirt with matching pocket handkerchief, brand new red silk tie, suspenders, and black fedora with the brim snapped down over one eye. He drove to Gleason's, a well-known jazz club on Cleveland's East Side, where B. B. King sometimes played as a featured performer.

The moment he walked into the bar, all the ladies turned an appreciative eye on his well-groomed appearance. He lit a cigarette, laid a C-note on the table, sat back and waited. It didn't take long before a bevy of beauties surrounded him.

"Thanks to that last caper, I'm on top of the world. These lovely ladies have no idea they're sitting with a celebrity. Why, I bet the Cleveland Irish Mob down at the docks would be happy to work with me. I've certainly got the looks," he laughed to himself.

Although he had shot a man earlier, he wasn't worried—it probably wasn't a life-threatening wound, given the man's physical stature and heavy winter coat.

"Guy should've known better. Those new shiny locks look pretty but they're the easiest to pick. Why, it's an open invitation to any thief with a penchant for gold. Or, silver in my case," he thought.

When he arrived home, he threw the bloody clothes from his backseat in the trash without giving it a second thought.

"After a good night's sleep, I'll contact Blackie to cash in the goods. Wonder how the papers will report the story. They may even give me a special nickname, like The Thief Extraordinaire. Yeah, that has a classy ring to it."

FORTY

ℓℓ S SHE CLEARED away the breakfast dishes on Christmas
Eve in 1939, Sadie turned on the radio in her aunt and
uncle's home. While humming to her favorite tune, she
stopped working and sat down when the news commentator
broke the lead story. Events at the Sheridan mansion left Sadie
at a loss. She couldn't believe Louis Sheridan was dead.

When Sadie heard a description of the murderer, she
panicked. She had seen Alice with a man who fit the description
at the West Side Market two months earlier. At the time, Sadie
was pleased Alice had finally found a man—and a handsome
one at that. His full head of red hair, neatly coiffed,
complemented his well-groomed beard.

Now, she didn't know what to think. Sadie's first thought was
to ask Ellen for advice, but decided against it when she saw the
barrage of reporters outside the O'Malley home. Going to the
police never even entered her mind after her traumatic
experiences in Germany and their Gestapo tactics. She stifled
the panic rapidly building within her. Shivering from rivulets of
sweat pouring down her back, the nightmare returned.
Thoughts of Nazis strutting around threatening all who dared to
cross their path—especially Jews—filled Sadie Leibowitz with

abject fear and made her reticent to approach the authorities.

Without a clue where to turn, Sadie decided to speak with Alice directly. When Alice answered the door at the Sheridan estate, Sadie was astonished at the change in her friend's appearance. Alice gazed at her with puffy eyes set in a desolate face while shaking hands unconsciously fussed with her hair.

"Goodness, dearie. Why are you here?" asked Alice with concern etched in her voice.

As she got closer, Sadie noticed her friend looked haggard and older in the two short weeks since they had worked together.

"We need to talk, Alice. Alone."

Alice donned a shawl to join Sadie outside.

"I saw you with a red-haired man a few months ago at the market. His description is remarkably similar to the police suspect from today's radio broadcast."

Alice's pallor turned a ghostly white as she said in an uneven voice, "Oh, that's just a coincidence. I was meeting my . . . my cousin for an early dinner. No need to worry yourself. And poor Mrs. Sheridan, she's at a breaking point so I wouldn't bother her either."

"But don't you think the police—"

"No!" Alice said before composing herself. "I meant to say, my cousin went back home to Chicago, so he couldn't have anything to do with this."

"Well, if you're sure—"

"I am, dearie. Now hurry along home before your aunt needs you."

Alice practically ran into the home and left Sadie standing alone.

Although she didn't believe Alice's story, Sadie had nowhere else to turn and went home.

THE FOLLOWING DAY, Sadie answered a knock at her door. Confronted with a handsome man, Sadie's eyes widened in surprise when he displayed his detective's badge.

"Hi, my name is Detective Kevin Collins and I'm investigating the Sheridan murder. Is Sadie Leibowitz home?"

"Th-th-that's me. Come in, p-p-please." She opened the door wider as her face became hot, frightened at the prospect of a police interrogation.

"Thank you, Sadie. Is it all right if I call you Sadie?"

"Yes."

Kevin's friendly and kind demeanor slowly put Sadie at ease.

"I understand you worked at the Sheridan home but left two weeks before the murder. Why did you leave?"

"My aunt was ill, and I came home to care for her."

"While you worked there, did you ever see anything out of the ordinary or witness any red-haired men near the house?"

Sadie thought of Alice's "cousin." Although she didn't believe Alice's story, she knew Alice was frightened. In a spontaneous decision to protect her friend, Sadie responded, "No, sir. I didn't." Despite her mere fifteen years, Sadie could easily relate to being intimidated by powerful men and didn't want to increase Alice's obvious terror—no matter what the cause.

The detective gave her a curious stare as though waging an internal debate.

Sadie was filled with desperation, afraid to say the wrong thing. She remained silent and looked down at the floor.

However, before her anxiety skyrocketed, he said, "Well, we knew it was a long shot but we have to pursue all leads. Here's my card if you should think of anything else."

"Of course, Detective." After escorting him out the front, Sadie leaned against the closed door and breathed a deep sigh of relief.

On the front stoop of Sadie's home, Kevin Collins glanced backward with an uneasy feeling. His gut told him she was withholding something. But given the extent of her fright, she may have been reacting to involvement in a murder investigation or perhaps rumors she heard about mistreatment of the Jews in Nazi Germany, especially by the police.

FORTY-ONE

THE NEXT DAY, Kevin returned to the Sheridan home to interview the butler, Clifford Smith. However, Mrs. Sheridan answered the door instead.

"Good morning, Mrs. Sheridan. I'm here to question Mr. Smith. I expected him to answer the door."

"Usually he does. But I can't seem to sit still and told Clifford I would get the door. I feel powerless." Marianne's nervous energy seemed to vibrate throughout her body as she anxiously twisted her hands.

"There were a few questions we didn't ask last night. Would this be a better opportunity before I meet with your butler?"

"Of course. Anything I can do to help." She led Kevin into the living room and two handsome but severely distraught young men jumped up and kindly waited for the detective to remove his coat before speaking.

"Detective, my name is Edward and this is my brother, Timothy. We are . . ." his voice faltered ". . . *were* Louis Sheridan's sons."

As Kevin shook their hands, he attempted to put them at ease. "Please call me Kevin and accept my condolences on your loss."

"Thank you. May we remain with our mom while you question her?" Timothy asked.

"That's a good idea. Actually, I have a couple of questions for both of you."

Edward and Timothy were eager at the prospect of assisting the investigation—anything to avenge their father's murder and ease their mother's pain.

"Certainly. Anything we can do." The brothers shared a look of support and strength.

"Where were you both on the night of your father's murder?"

"We attended a Christmas party at a friend's home with plans to spend the night, but then we got a call . . ." Timothy's voice quivered and Edward put his arm around his brother's shoulders for support.

"Were either of you aware of any enemies your father may have had?"

"None. Everyone who knew our father admired and loved him," said Edward as Timothy nodded his head.

"Were either of you home during construction of the bathroom and nursery?"

This time Timothy responded for both. "No. Renovations were done while we were away at school. Our parents are, I mean were . . ."

Timothy became flustered and his brother finished his thought. ". . . considerate and always went out of their way to make sure we were not inconvenienced."

"I have one more question for you boys. Have you ever seen anyone with red hair, about six feet tall, near your home? Perhaps someone out of place or lingering too long in front?"

Both Edward and Timothy shook their heads, disappointed they were unable to assist in the investigation.

"Thank you for your honesty." He turned to Mrs. Sheridan. "Can you provide us with a list of missing items and their approximate worth?"

"Anything of value was insured by The Dunbar Mutual Insurance Company. I will ask them to prepare a list of items and their monetary worth. However, from a brief glance, I can see many uninsured items are missing, and they carried a far greater sentimental value."

"Can you please have Dunbar Mutual contact me directly at this number?" Kevin handed over his card and printed his badge number on the back.

"Of course."

"We will also need a list of missing uninsured items."

"I can pull the information together over the next week and will send it to your attention."

"Thank you, Mrs. Sheridan." Turning to Edward and Timothy, Kevin added, "It was a pleasure to meet you both, and again, I'm sorry for your loss. I'm glad you can be here for your mother."

Marianne said with a radiant smile, her loss temporarily forgotten. "They follow me around like a couple of lost puppies, attentive to my every need." But the moment passed quickly and despair surrounded Marianne like a heavy fog threatening to encompass her universe.

"Could you please tell Mr. Smith that I'm ready to see him?"

Edward rushed into the kitchen to fetch the butler.

Kevin got up to stretch his legs and, when he turned around, suppressed his astonished reaction as Clifford Smith entered the room resembling a typical English butler seen in the movies—similar to *My Man Godfrey* starring William Powell. Standing six and a half feet tall with thick black hair and a ruddy complexion, Mr. Smith exuded a confidence and aristocratic air as he seamlessly managed to put others at ease.

"Mr. Smith, I'm Detective Kevin Collins and I need a few moments of your time to discuss Mr. Sheridan's murder."

"Anything I can do to help, Detective. What would you like to know?"

"Where were you the night of December 23?"

"I had the evening off and was home taking care of my wife and our baby."

"How long have you worked for the Sheridans?"

"My goodness, Sara B. and I have been with the Sheridans for fifteen years." At the mention of his wife, Clifford unconsciously smiled as his eyes twinkled in delight until he remembered the gravity of the situation.

"Have you encountered problems with anyone working at the mansion or witnessed any disagreements with anyone?"

"No, I haven't. If anything, I'd have to say everyone has been treated with respect and they respond in kind."

"Have you ever seen a construction worker about six feet tall with red hair?"

"No, I'm sorry, I can't help you there. Mr. Sheridan trusts my judgment and requested I oversee all workers who entered the home, but I never saw anyone matching that description. I do know there were two separate companies hired for renovations and did my best to monitor their activities, but I had numerous other duties to attend to. I'm certain the foremen would have more information."

"Well, thank you for your time, Mr. Smith. Here's my card with the station house phone number if you think of anything else. Would it be all right if I pay a call on your wife to ask a few questions?"

"Yes, you can contact my wife. Let me call Sara B. to make sure she's available."

Kevin patiently waited for Mr. Smith to provide his home address and, after placing a call to his wife, informed Kevin that she would expect him shortly.

"Thank you, sir. You've been most helpful."

"Not at all, young man," Mr. Smith said as he walked Kevin to the front door.

When Kevin arrived at the Smith residence, Sara B. met him at the door. Bursting with energy, she couldn't have been more than five feet tall and 100 pounds with dark, curly hair clipped on top of her head. But looks were deceiving as Sara B. bustled about her home concentrating at making Kevin feel at home.

"Have you eaten yet, Detective?"

"Yes, ma'am, but thank you. Out of curiosity, where did your name Sara B. come from?"

"The neighborhood where I grew up had several girls with the name of Sara. We each chose to use the initial of our middle names to differentiate between us."

"Makes sense."

"So, Detective Collins, how can I help you?"

Kevin, astute at judging others, accurately surmised the petite woman sitting across from him as a no-nonsense type of person who got down to business quickly. "I understand you've been on pregnancy leave from the Sheridan's household."

"Yes sir—it's my third and won't be my last if Clifford has anything to say about it," Sara B. blurted out before she remembered Kevin's proximity and her gaze shifted downward.

Kevin asked the same questions posed to her husband and appreciated Sara B.'s keen eye for detail delivered without aplomb as her calm demeanor remained unfazed throughout the interview. Both Clifford and Sara B.'s responses were similar; however, Sara B. broadened her replies to include Clifford's work ethic, impeccable attendance record, and chivalrous nature to everyone.

In the distance, Kevin heard a baby squealing. After a few minutes, and with thoroughly frayed nerves, he concluded the Sheridans were fortunate to employ such an honest and forthright worker. Kevin handed his business card to Sara B. before dashing out in a hasty retreat. Kevin reveled in the tranquility of his car, although his ears were still ringing. He decided to head for home with the beginning of a headache.

FORTY-TWO

GLANCING AT THE *next day's shocking headlines, he couldn't believe it.*

"I'm sure the bullet only grazed him. But it's Sheridan's own fault—fighting over a loaded gun. No way am I going down for a murder rap. I need to get out of town—the sooner the better," he thought sagely.

He packed a bag and traveled to his favorite pawn shop on Ontario Street sandwiched between a hotel and a saloon.

"Hey Blackie, guess who?" He tried to be casual but didn't quite pull it off.

The shop's owner gave him a strange look before asking, "Well, what do you have for me today?" Blackie gave a sharp whistle when he saw the fine quality of goods his long-time customer presented. "Who'd you have to kill for this stash?"

The murderer swiftly glanced around and shifted from one foot to another. Did Blackie suspect something? When he realized it was Blackie's attempt at humor, his laugh sounded forced.

"I'll give you five hundred for the lot."

"Are you kidding? It's worth ten times that."

"Here, then, take the goods back and see if anyone else will

give you more. Besides, I don't need the trouble."

Out of options, he reluctantly accepted the money while grumbling about honesty among thieves. After he left the shop, he cursed the day he bought a gun as he hightailed it out of town in his coveted Ford V-8.

FORTY-THREE

FRANK INTERVIEWED THE Sheridan's accountant, Kenneth Knabe, who provided names of two construction companies involved in renovating the Sheridan estate. Frank contacted the owner of the most recent company—Pappas Construction—and learned they were a small company with no employee, then or now, matching the suspect's description. Frank's second call to the owner of Schmidt Construction yielded the same response.

Despite the high profile nature of the Sheridan case, the CPD was understaffed and Kevin was transferred to the Third District. Before his scheduled departure, Kevin gave Frank summaries of his interviews with Mrs. Sheridan and her two sons, both cooks, and the butler. Frank would continue the investigation alone, pleased his superiors afforded him confidence to handle the responsibility solo.

The crash course in homicide investigation provided by the CPD did little to assist Frank with investigative methods. Luckily, the books he read before entering the Academy, and subsequent night courses, proved to be a wealth of information mostly based on common sense and analysis of available clues.

His next course of action involved exploring their only solid lead—a late model Ford V-8. Given the suspect's description and direction he was last seen heading, Frank assumed the murderer resided in Ohio City, near West 30th Street with other Irish immigrants; however, he did not limit the scope of his investigation at this early stage. He contacted the Cuyahoga County Deputy Registrar's office to review the Certificate of Title records for all Ford V-8 autos registered to Cleveland residents in 1939.

Initially, Frank found ten names of 1936–1939 Ford V-8 owners with current license plates. Of these, five relocated outside the state several years prior and one currently resided as a guest of the state penitentiary.

He then compared the remaining four names against potential title transfers and available banking data listed on auto loan documents. His painstaking search took a few days but yielded a viable list which fit his parameters:

Jonathan Hershberger—deceased 11/01/39.
Title transferred to nephew, Todd Hershberger.
Former residence: 3890 Fulton Road.
Paid cash: no bank listed.

Robert O'Riley—deceased 1936.
Title transferred to son, Joseph O'Riley.
Former residence: 3494 Carroll Ave. No current address.
Central National Bank: borrowed funds using the car as collateral.

Kurt Mueller—3165 Bridge Avenue.
Current titled owner.
Paid cash.

Katie Gallagher—2836 Jay Avenue.
Current titled owner.

Feighan Bank: financed loan, PIF one month later.
New bank deposit in the amount of $10,000 on 12/26/39.

FORTY-FOUR

WORKING HIS WAY down the list, Frank verified Jonathan Hershberger transferred his 1937 Ford to his twenty-year-old nephew, Todd Hershberger—a man with no criminal history. After calling major banks in the Cleveland area, Frank discovered Todd's balance was $100. Based on this, Frank ruled him out as a suspect for the highly lucrative robbery, given his paltry balance, but needed to be thorough in his investigation.

Armed with his research, Frank drove to the Hershberger home the day after Christmas for an interview with Todd. The young man appeared forthright and eager to please. Frank knew instantly this was not his suspect. Towering over Frank with a dark complexion and well-groomed features, Frank launched into his inquiry.

"We are conducting an investigation into the Sheridan murder on December twenty-third. Based on eyewitness testimony, a model Ford V-8 was identified as the escape vehicle."

"I'll help any way I can, but I drove my car out to a family reunion in Pittsburgh the weekend Mr. Sheridan was murdered."

Frank handed Todd a notepad and asked him to provide the names of at least five witnesses, with their respective phone numbers, to confirm his story.

"Thank you for your time. If we receive witness corroboration, there should be no further need to bother you." Frank headed out to his patrol car, list in hand.

Strike one.

The O'Rileys would be next on his list. Frank questioned their former neighbors and confirmed Bob O'Riley's death in 1936 resulted from a drunken fall shortly after winning his car in a poker game. The Ford was transferred to his son, Joseph, well known in his neighborhood by his flaming red hair. Frank also discovered Joseph ran with a rough crowd, known for petty larceny, prior to the O'Rileys departure in 1937. Given the suspicious circumstances surrounding their disappearance and Joseph's description similar to the murderer, he became number one on Frank's suspect list. However, no one knew his current whereabouts.

Frank researched and found documentation in the County Recorder's Office that the O'Riley home went into foreclosure after Mrs. O'Riley and her son left their Carroll Avenue residence in March 1937. Frank's next stop at Central National Bank, where the O'Rileys obtained a loan using the car as collateral, revealed the account was paid in full, with remaining finances cleaned out in 1937 shortly before their departure.

With one last phone call to the East Ohio American Gas Company, Frank discovered the final O'Riley bill, forwarded to an address in Columbus, Ohio, belonged to Michael and Lynn Bycko. He contacted the Columbus telephone operator who placed a long-distance call to the Bycko residence. Once connected, Frank again introduced himself and provided a brief recap of events as the reason for his call.

"Mrs. Bycko, what is your relationship to Joseph O'Riley?"

"He's my nephew."

"Since the 1936 Ford title was transferred to Joseph, we need to verify if the car is still in his possession. If not, we need to locate the current owner."

"Joseph drove the car to our home in 1937 with his mother. He obtained a job in the city and over the next two years, used the car for work and weekend trips to visit friends in Cleveland."

"Do you know if Joseph was in Cleveland last weekend?"

"Well, I'm not sure. He drove to an out-of-town wedding, but I can't recall where it was."

"If Joseph is home, I'd like to speak with him."

"He's out back. Hold on and I'll get him."

Five minutes passed before Joseph, out of breath, picked up the call.

"Detective Szabo? Sorry for the delay; I was chopping wood for kindling. My aunt explained the reason for your call and said you'd like to talk to me. How can I help?"

"Your aunt mentioned you drove your father's—now yours—1936 Ford to a wedding last weekend. Can you tell me the location of the wedding?"

"It was held in Dayton, Ohio. I arrived the evening of December twenty-second and returned home in time to spend Christmas Eve with my mother."

"At any point during the weekend, did you return to East Cleveland?"

"No, sir, I did not. It would have involved a detour of several hours each way and there wasn't enough time. Besides, I usually get together with my friends several times a year, so there was no need for me to go out of my way to see them."

"Will you provide the names and contact information of at least five people to confirm you remained in Dayton the entire weekend?"

"I'll be happy to."

After Frank provided his mailing address, he thanked Joseph for his cooperation before hanging up. But, despite Joseph's prompt answers, Frank remained unsure if his responses were forthcoming, especially given his prior gang affiliation in Cleveland and frequent weekend trips to consort with Cleveland friends. Discouraged, Frank glanced at the clock and decided to conduct the last two interviews on the following day since his shift was nearing an end.

FORTY-FIVE

A FTER CHECKING HIS messages at the station house the next morning, Frank reviewed his prior notes and planned to interview the next person on his list—Kurt Mueller. Frank assumed Mr. Mueller would be at work and went down to the main Social Security Office to check employment records and obtain work and home addresses. When he discovered Kurt was employed by Pappas Construction, his pulse quickened. Address in hand, Frank traveled to the site where he asked the foreman if he could speak with Mr. Mueller.

The foreman looked Frank up and down. He responded, "What's this about? I don't like to give out information on my guys."

Frank showed his badge and said, "This is an official police investigation."

"Okay. Sorry. He went home early. Said he wasn't feeling well."

Frank compared the SSO address against the foreman's records to confirm the information's accuracy; within fifteen minutes, he arrived at the Mueller home.

Kurt opened the front door, his shoulders draped in a blanket, and sneezed at the blast of cold air. His nose was bright red and conversation was impossible until his hacking cough subsided. Once they made eye contact, Frank could see Kurt would not be a cooperative witness. He exuded a belligerence borne of misfortune, and his deeply lined face was a road map of heartache. Mr. Mueller was a husky man, about thirty years old, and missing most of his teeth. Over the years, Frank's exposure to riffraff included many men like Kurt—a street brawler who carried life's troubles around like a badge of honor, taking pleasure at disrespecting those in authority while feigning ignorance by talking like a common street thug.

"Whaddya want?" he asked, while blowing his nose.

Frank flashed his badge and said, "I need to ask you a few questions."

"Hey, how'd ya know I was home?"

"Your foreman said you left early because you were ill."

"I don't appreciate you talkin' to my boss. Looks bad when a cop comes around." With a fresh round of coughing from the blast of cold air, he grudgingly allowed Frank to enter his home.

"Sorry to inconvenience you, Mr. Mueller, but this shouldn't take long. How long have you worked for Pappas Construction?"

"A little more than a year."

"Did you ever work on the Sheridan home at 7525 Euclid Avenue?"

Kurt hesitated. Suddenly he looked *very* nervous. "Yeah, we worked there on a nursery, I think." Kurt failed to mention his involvement in additional renovations the year before while employed by Schmidt Construction.

"Who is 'we'?"

"Me and my brother, Stephen."

"Did anyone in your crew have red hair?"

"What is this, twenty dumb questions?"

"Please, just answer the question."

"No."

"Thank you. Now, I need to confirm if you still own a 1937 Ford V-8."

"Yeah, so what?"

"Can you verify your whereabouts the evening of December twenty-third?"

"Hey, wait a minute. I read 'bout that—it's the same night as the Sheridan killin'. I ain't got nothin' to do with that. I was home in bed with a wicked hangover and the start of this here cold."

"Could anyone else have borrowed your car?"

"Well, my brother, Stephen, stayed with me for the holidays. He wanted to take the car for a spin to see some friends. I told him no 'cuz he drives too fast, but he went ahead and took the car anyways. I was too sick to stop him." As he mentioned his brother's name, Kurt glanced over at a photo above the mantel. The man, standing next to his brother, bore a strong resemblance to Kurt, but he took much better care of himself. Stephen's build, similar to his brother's muscled physique, was contrasted by his short stature. Also unlike his brother, Stephen's smile reflected straight, white teeth with full lips curled in a smile, dark eyes, thick mustache, and short brown hair.

"I assume that's your brother in this picture?" Kurt nodded. "Could you provide a list of Stephen's friends and their addresses?"

"I got no idea. Why not ask him?"

"I'd be happy to. Is he still at your home? If so, I can talk to him now."

"Nah, he left after Christmas."

"Any idea where he went?"

"What am I s'pose to be, his keeper? He didn't say nuthin' and I didn't ask."

"Well, if he does show up, please have him contact me at this number." Frank handed his business card to Kurt, which was promptly stuffed into a pocket before he showed Frank the door. After the door slammed shut behind his hasty departure, Frank instinctively knew Kurt had withheld information and held out little hope he'd ever hear from Stephen.

When Frank returned to the station, he checked outstanding warrants involving Stephen Mueller and discovered a long list of petty larceny and drunk-driving charges. Although the picture in Kurt's home didn't fit the witness description, Stephen rose to the top of Frank's suspect list as a possible accomplice to Joseph O'Riley.

FORTY-SIX

FEELING ENCOURAGED WITH his increasing list of viable suspects, Frank conducted his last interview at the residence of Katie Gallagher. A diminutive young woman with wavy, short brown hair, emerald-green eyes, and a warm, accommodating manner, she graciously welcomed the detective into her home.

Following a crime recap and reason for the visit, he asked Miss Gallagher, "Are you still in possession of the 1938 Ford V-8?"

"Yes, I am. It's parked behind my home."

"Did you use your vehicle on the evening of December twenty-third?"

"I was home with a bad headache and even if I felt better, I couldn't have driven my car because it was in the shop. Although, come to think of it, my fiancé asked if he could borrow the car to attend a Christmas party on the twenty-third, but I had to tell him no. Sometimes I get the feeling he was more interested in my car than me." Katie became embarrassed at voicing her private thoughts aloud and countered with, "Of course, I'm kidding."

Frank smiled before he continued the interrogation.

"What's your fiancé's name?"

"Brett Roth."

"Can you provide a brief description of Mr. Roth?"

"Oh, sure. He's very handsome with large green eyes, wavy ginger hair, a thick beard, and fairly tall."

Frank's heart pounded when Miss Gallagher unwittingly described the killer. Working hard to keep his voice neutral, Frank's questions took a new turn. "When, and under what circumstances, did you meet Mr. Roth?"

Katie, glowing at the happy memory, recounted the joyous occasion. "While I was taking care of early Christmas shopping in November at Higbee's Department Store, he bumped into me and my packages spewed across the floor. He graciously helped pick up the numerous boxes and bowed with a quaint apology about his clumsiness. After introductions, he said he was there to purchase a gift for his mother and asked my opinion. When he said price was no object for the number one lady in his life, how could I not be impressed? Brett certainly displayed the manners of a true gentlemen, and I accepted a lunch invitation the same day. From his confidence and aristocrat bearing, I believed there was nothing to fear." Blushing, and a bit defensive, she added, "I mean, the restaurant would be crowded in the middle of the day. I don't want you to think I make a habit of dating complete strangers."

"The thought never crossed my mind. Where did you go from there?"

"We exited Higbee's lower level into the underground Terminal Tower Complex and walked over to the Old English Oak Room. We had so much in common and talked for hours. Before I knew it, we saw one another about every day and spoke on the telephone frequently. When Brett asked me to marry him shortly before Christmas, I eagerly accepted." Her eyes glazed over at the thought of walking down the aisle with the man of her dreams.

"Now, Miss Gallagher, where was the party he attended on the twenty-third?"

"At a friend's home in a western suburb of Cleveland. Lakewood, I believe."

"Are you certain it wasn't *East* Cleveland?"

"I'm positive."

"Was Mr. Roth at the party around nine p.m.?"

"Oh, yes. It began at eight and didn't end until eleven-thirty. Brett arrived back at his home around midnight."

"How do you know what time he arrived home?"

"He told me."

"Can anyone confirm your fiancé remained at the party until after nine?"

"Yes, I can provide a list of at least a dozen people at the party. I'm certain they will confirm he never left before eleven-thirty."

"A list of five witnesses, including their phone numbers, should be sufficient." Frank handed his card to Miss Gallagher for the address, and hoping to keep her off-balance, asked, "Can you explain the source of the ten-thousand-dollar deposit into your account at Feighan Bank on December 26?"

"It was a Christmas gift from my fiancé. I resent the implication, Detective."

"Sorry ma'am, but the murder of Mr. Sheridan also involved a theft of highly valuable property. We need to cover all the bases."

"In that case, you may contact Brett, although he must be out of town. He hasn't called for several days, and we usually speak daily."

"Does he have a phone?"

"Well, no, he calls me from a neighbor's phone."

"Do you know his current address?"

"No. He always picked me up at my home. I've never seen where he lives." She sounded defensive as she added, "We've only been dating a little over two months and it's been a whirlwind romance."

Frank's disarming smile helped ameliorate Katie's defensiveness. "Did anything unusual happen the last time you saw Mr. Roth?"

"Well, he did seem a bit distant after he met my father. When I saw Brett next, I asked him about it, but he told me not to worry, it was nothing. He was nervous about meeting my father." But Katie's demeanor temporarily changed.

"And what happened during the meeting with your father?" Frank prodded.

"I was so excited, I called my father to join us for a light supper at my home so I could tell him the wonderful news about our engagement. I hinted about an extraordinary surprise I'd share with him. My father and Brett hit it off. In honor of our news, my father asked me to fetch some glasses for the champagne he brought. When I came back with the crystal goblets, Brett complained of a stomachache before leaving ten minutes later."

"Have you seen him since that night?"

Disturbed from her reverie, Katie asked the detective to repeat the question.

"No, I haven't. But I'm sure he'll call again soon. He has many out-of-town clients."

"What type of business does he manage?"

"Mainly exports. I don't have a head for business, but his venture must be very successful to afford my expensive Christmas gift. I believe he wanted to impress my father. Oh, and me, too."

"I understand. When he does contact you, please ask him to give me a call." Frank handed Katie a business card for her to mail the list of friends confirming her fiancé's alibi. "Would you mind if I contacted your father?"

"My father? Whatever for?"

"He may be able to provide some insights into your fiancé's status."

"I doubt if he would know anything, since he is *my* fiancé. But if you need to contact my father, his name is Robert Gallagher. Let me give you his address and phone number."

"Would you mind writing down your phone number in case we have any updates?"

"Of course." In careful penmanship, Katie handed Frank a decorative piece of paper with her contact information.

Frank thanked Katie for her cooperation. He knew Mr. Roth would not be returning to her. His gut also told Frank he'd found his number one suspect. Despite this setback, Frank marveled at the strides his investigation advanced in one day as he glanced at the list of three potential suspects: Joseph O'Riley, Stephen Mueller, and Brett Roth.

FRANK'S MEETING WITH Mr. Gallagher the next day proved to be informative. Frank performed background research and discovered Mr. Gallagher was president of First National Bank and Loan. When Frank arrived at the Gallagher estate, it confirmed Katie's father had a lucrative and successful career.

After being shown into the parlor by a butler, Frank waited five minutes until Mr. Gallagher confidently strode into the room and shook Frank's hand once introductions were made. "Thank you for seeing me on such short notice, Mr. Gallagher. As I explained on the phone, I'm the lead detective for the Sheridan murder and hope you can fill in a few details that at this point don't seem to add up."

"Be happy to, but I'm not sure how I can be of any help."

"As you know, I met with your daughter, Katie, and she's concerned her fiancé is missing. She believes it could be the result of your meeting."

"And what bearing does this have on a murder investigation?"

"We need to question Mr. Roth about his whereabouts the evening of the murder based on matching witness descriptions."

To Frank's surprise, Mr. Gallagher chortled, but it contained a note of derision. "I can explain what happened and the reason he's missing, but I need a promise from you this information will not get back to my daughter."

Frank nodded before Mr. Gallagher continued. "I consider myself an excellent judge of character, and the evening I met Katie's fiancé with his polished veneer and phony attitude, I knew he was an imposter. I asked my daughter to find her crystal glasses so I could have a little chat alone with Brett. When she left the room, he relaxed, fully confident of my acceptance."

This time, Mr. Gallagher did laugh out loud at the confused

and angry response from his daughter's intended. "I told him in no uncertain terms that my daughter's fortune was in a trust controlled by me and in the event of my death, a law firm has been placed on retainer to resume these duties. When I mentioned he would never see a dime, he looked distinctly ill. My poor daughter bought the whole 'stomachache' routine, but I knew it would be the last time Brett would impose on my daughter's time. Turns out, I was right, although it gives me no pleasure since his disappearance has brought Katie nothing but grief. Before he left, I pretty much knew what he was thinking since unfortunately, I've been down this road before—his vision of an easy mark with quick access to my fortune disappeared after our little talk."

"Thank you for your candor, Mr. Gallagher. Although I will do my best, I can't guarantee your statements will remain confidential but I won't mention our discussion to your daughter. I'm sorry to say we have exactly the same assessment of Mr. Roth."

Both men shook hands and Frank returned to the station and wrote up a summary of the latest interviews.

After reviewing all witness statements to confirm there were no additional clues, Frank's next step would involve alibi confirmation of the Ford owners. He looked forward to receipt of the list of contacts from Todd Hershberger, Joseph O'Riley, and Miss Gallagher; he did *not* expect any response from either Kurt or Stephen Mueller. Frank intuitively knew the case would be resolved once he defined the missing puzzle piece that continued to elude him. In the interim, Frank hoped the clues would gel into a workable theory and help identify missing facts to capture and prosecute the man who callously took the life of a husband, father, and esteemed member of the community.

FORTY-SEVEN

WITHIN A WEEK, Katie Gallagher drove to the station house asking to see Detective Szabo. When Frank walked to the lobby, he noticed Katie seemed close to hysteria, constantly wringing her hands as she dabbed her eyes.

The words gushed out in a rambling speech. "I haven't heard from my fiancé, Brett Roth, and believe something may have happened to him. He had many friends in East Cleveland near the Sheridan robbery. Perhaps he was in the wrong place at the wrong time?"

Although Frank found it difficult to see her so distraught, he kept his promise to Mr. Gallagher and did not divulge any information about their meeting. Now more than ever, he believed the events of December 23rd to be the handiwork of Brett.

He said, "We're following up on all leads but will keep a special lookout for Mr. Roth. If we find anything you need to be aware of, we'll keep you posted. You already have the precinct phone number on the card I gave you. Feel free to call me with any questions. I'm sure everything will be fine," Frank said.

After she left, Frank shook his head, knowing the heartache

she faced. He sagely decided not to inform her that, during the past week, he had contacted the list of five witnesses she provided. None could corroborate her fiancé's attendance at the Lakewood party between 8:00 p.m. and 11:30 p.m. The majority couldn't recall even catching a glimpse of him the entire night. With enough on her plate, she seemed too fragile to handle the truth.

FORTY-EIGHT

REPORTERS CONTINUED TO hound the O'Malley home to interview Ellen, but she refused to leave the house for several days after the murder.

A week after the murder, Ellen sneaked out the back door and took a streetcar to the Second District and requested Detective Szabo.

"Thank you for coming in, Ellen. Please follow me into an interview room and I'll bring you some mug shots to review. Can I get you a cup of coffee or tea?"

"No, thank you. I'll be happy to look at the mug shots, but I can't help a sketch artist. I was at the top of the staircase in the dark hallway when I heard the commotion and only saw the back of the intruder."

"No problem, then. I'll be right back." Frank left and returned to the interview room with two books containing composites of known criminals in the area. When he left, Frank kept the door slightly ajar to gauge her reactions. Despite her outward tranquility, Frank observed Ellen's angst. She seemed oblivious to a nervous twitch in her right eye as she unconsciously fussed with a handkerchief. Frank noticed halfway through the first book, her gaze lingered on one photo just a moment too long. But the longer she gazed at the picture, her features relaxed and she unconsciously shook her head in what appeared to be relief. Ellen spent the remaining two hours carefully reviewing both books.

"I'm sorry, but I don't see anyone that resembles the murderer." She added, "But then, I didn't have a clear view of his face."

Frank had a feeling Ellen was withholding information. Despite being a professional who pursued all possible leads, Frank was drawn to this lovely woman and couldn't understand his need to protect her. Even though they had only met recently, Frank couldn't ignore the closeness with Ellen that defied all logic. Perhaps it was the result of growing up near one another and attending the same schools. Frank found it hard to believe a woman as refined and forthright as Ellen had been during questioning could withhold information pertaining to the gruesome murder she had witnessed. He suspected she would reveal whatever information appeared to weigh upon her when she was ready. Perhaps allowing time to overcome the shocking events would give her confidence to reveal her secret. Despite his confusion, there was one thing Frank was sure of—he didn't want to lose touch with such a lovely lady and was willing to wait until she felt comfortable enough to confide in him.

"Thank you again for coming in. If it would be all right with you, I'd like to check up on you from time to time and make sure you're doing okay."

Ellen was grateful for his concern and responded in a neutral tone. "That would be fine. Thank you." She walked out of the station with a poise she didn't feel.

Ellen worked hard to dismiss feelings she couldn't quite

define. When she did examine her reaction, Ellen realized one positive thing occurred from that unfortunate night—meeting Detective Szabo. He stopped in to see her every day on his way into work. He offered to accompany her to the train station, escorted her through the door, and held her hand as she descended the steps. Ellen asked the detective to keep her in the loop as his investigation continued. When he promised he would, she smiled but forced herself to maintain an even demeanor although her heartbeat accelerated.

FORTY-NINE

HEEDING THEIR MOTHER'S advice, Edward and Timothy Sheridan returned to their respective schools two weeks after their father's death.

"There's no sense staying around here and following me around like lost sheep. You boys need to return to school and a normal social environment. And I need some time alone to grieve your father's passing."

"But Mother . . ." Neither son got any further before their mom put her hand up in resignation and walked out of the room.

Despite much persuading and cajoling, they realized their mother would never unleash her grief in their presence. They understood her need for space to deal with the sorrow she kept deeply buried after losing the love of her life.

Once her sons departed for school, Marianne relied on the comfort she received from her daughter, Bridget, and the encouraging support from Ellen who returned to work a week after the murder.

Marianne preferred to sleep in a guest room and entered their former shared bedroom sparingly, afraid she would lose the wonderful scent of her beloved Louis before it dissipated into thin air.

"Oh, Louis," she'd cry when alone. "Why did it have to be you? Didn't that horrible man know we would have given him anything he wanted? I miss you every second and don't know how to go on without you." Marianne rested her head on Louis's pillow as she cried herself to sleep. When Ellen passed by, she quietly closed the door to ensure Marianne's grief remained private.

Marianne couldn't part with Louis's personal items. She kept his dresser the same, and the familiarity comforted her soul. Whenever a pang of loneliness struck, Marianne would enter his den and glance at his important papers or open a spare bottle of his cologne. With these simple acts, his presence surrounded her as soft as a reassuring hug and it momentarily eased the pain.

However, as time passed, the need to evoke her husband's memory occurred less and less. He still lived in her heart and remained the only man she had truly loved. Marianne also took pride in the accomplishments of their children, who unwittingly emulated their father's fortitude and generosity.

FIFTY

ONCE ELLEN WAS somewhat back to normal after the murder, she analyzed her feelings toward the handsome detective. She instinctively knew his attention remained separate from her status as a witness. But Ellen couldn't understand what he saw in her. Although friends commented frequently on her beauty, she didn't see it. She wore minimal makeup (pancake face powder and a slight dab of rouge to color her lips and cheeks) and maintained her hair in a short bob.

To settle the issue when she was blissfully alone, Ellen gave herself an honest appraisal of her attributes as she gazed at her reflection in the full-length mirror. She conducted her critique in her usual self-deprecating manner—curly red hair, freckles, amber-colored eyes, and a slender frame. She turned from side to side but couldn't understand why anyone considered her attractive.

She assumed her friends, including the kindly detective, took pity on her and tried to be kind. Although Ellen was currently working as a nanny, she didn't consider this her real calling. Her life would be spent in a convent, diminishing her guilty conscience in daily prayer with only a portion of her face visible, as the rest of her plain appearance disappeared in a floor-length habit and long veil. Hiding away from the pain doled out in an otherwise maudlin existence, without suffering the well-intentioned compliments of others, was the perfect solution. Now all she had to do was tell Frank.

ONCE AGAIN, FRANK woke up exhausted. He couldn't get the thought of Ellen out of his mind. He decided asking her out on a date would be a perfect solution to sleepless nights filled with images of her.

Two months after the murder, he worked up the courage and asked her to attend the blockbuster hit, *Gone with the Wind.* Thrilled and shocked, Ellen did her best to casually accept the invitation.

"I don't have any plans this Saturday, if—"

Before she finished her sentence, Frank jumped right in saying, "That would be perfect, and if the weather isn't too cold, we can start with a walk around your neighborhood before we leave for the show." Frank stopped when he realized he cut Ellen off mid-sentence and didn't allow her the courtesy of completing her response.

"All right, Frank. Would you be able to pick me up at six?"

Frank nodded, and with plans now in the works, he spent his free time for the remainder of the week, minimal at best after working eleven-hour shifts, thinking about Ellen and getting ready for their date. He selected what he hoped was an appropriate outfit of black slacks, white shirt, and a gabardine jacket ribbed at the waist. The rest of the time was spent waxing his car until he could see his reflection.

On the big day, Frank forced himself to relax. Although experienced in dating lovely ladies, Frank was clueless about his nervousness. Ellen should've been like any other twenty-three year old, so what made her so different? Despite attempts to build up his confidence, Frank stumbled throughout his routine in a daze as he prepared for his date.

His trusted jalopy, gleaming like polished silver, didn't start until the fifth try. When he arrived at the O'Malley residence, Ellen came out of the house, and unfortunately, her younger sister, Veronica, trailed behind. In true Irish fashion, Ellen's mother was overly protective and made certain someone would tag along if one of her daughters went for a walk with a young man—a strict rule imposed on all the O'Malley girls who ventured out with a boy. And it usually worked. After one date, the potential suitor gave up. Anyone willing to withstand the scrutiny deserved a second chance.

But Frank would not be deterred. "Ellen, you look beautiful." He kept sneaking glances at this vision before him, sporting a stylish below-the-knee scotch plaid skirt, short-sleeve white button-down shirt with matching epaulets, and a tri-cornered hat surrounded by her curls. Frank knew he was the luckiest guy in the world.

"Thank you, Frank, for the lovely compliment. It's kind of you to say so, even if it isn't true," Ellen said with a hint of sadness.

Frank gaped open-mouthed at Ellen's statement. He detected no guile on her part and was amazed that she truly believed herself to be plain.

With the weather turning chilly, they cut their stroll short as Frank devised a plan to lose their young chaperone. "Veronica, you're shivering. Why don't I take you home?"

"Th-th-thank you, but I th-think I'm supposed to go with you to the s-show," she said through chattering teeth.

Frank escorted Veronica to their front door and diplomatically said, "Wouldn't you be more comfortable inside your nice warm home?" Sensing Veronica was still reluctant, Frank decided bribery was in order. "If you do go inside, I promise to give you a ride in my patrol car."

Torn between her mother's directive but eager to capitalize on a situation, she added, "Can we use the lights and siren?"

Frank laughed and readily agreed.

With one dollar to spend on their long-awaited date, he recalculated their expenditures to now include carfare when his car refused to start—fifty cents for two movie tickets, thirty cents for the streetcar, and twenty cents for ice cream sundaes to cap off their first night on the town.

Although Ellen fully intended to tell Frank about her pending religious vocation, the words never passed her lips. Instead, she focused on her date.

"Frank, why did you become a detective?"

"As an only child born to older parents set in their ways, I sought refuge at the Carnegie West Public Library. Books transported me to new places and fed my imagination as I became a swashbuckling pirate one minute or a space explorer the next. But my favorite books involved detective stories, and I decided to pursue an exciting career of solving mysteries. After I applied to the CPD, I continued research on my own time and discovered the CPD was one of the most progressive local law enforcement agencies under the direction of Elliott Ness."

"Who's that?"

"He earned his popularity in Chicago waging a war against organized crime, and his force earned the name of the

Untouchables."

"What's he doing in Cleveland?"

"He was hired as the safety director in 1935 and completely reorganized the CPD to increase efficiency and reduce traffic mortalities. He has the backing of Cleveland's 'Secret Six'—an anonymous group of prominent businessmen—in response to escalating crime. Why, he even . . ." Frank paused his narration and said, "I'm sorry, I get carried away."

Ellen smiled. "It's okay. I enjoy your enthusiasm." Ellen couldn't believe how comfortable she felt with Frank. It was something she could easily become accustomed to.

The following Saturday, they decided to double-date with Ellen's sister, Marge, and new beau, Lou DuChez. Frank drove his jalopy over to the O'Malley home, once again sporting a polished sheen after another day of waxing.

But this time, Michael answered the door. "Me daughter's not quite ready. I would like to be havin a little chat with ye. Shall we sit in the parlor and talk?"

Instantly, Frank's hands felt clammy as a thin layer of sweat beaded his forehead.

"Feelin a wee bit hot, young man?" Michael played his part to perfection, thoroughly enjoying the young man's discomfiture.

"I, um, well . . . no sir. I mean, maybe a little." Sounding like a babbling idiot as his voice squeaked, much to his chagrin, he managed to say, "Any idea when your daughter will be ready?"

"Me darlin' Ellen's known fer bein' late. But the good news is we can spend more time talkin' so's I can get to know ye better."

Unfortunately for Michael, his daughter came running

down the stairs as she ran to rescue Frank from her father's inspection.

Frank escorted Ellen, Marge, and Lou out to his car but it was sitting at a lopsided angle. A quick inspection revealed a flat tire that was soon good-naturedly replaced by Frank and Lou as the ladies waited inside. Once they were on their way, they stopped for mugs of hot chocolate and toured the countryside while loudly singing the most popular songs of the day.

However, as they drove home a light flurry began, and by the time Frank pulled up to Ellen's home, the sidewalks were heavily laden with snow. As she looked out at the dreary weather, Ellen wanted to prevent Frank's car from getting stuck in the snow if he parked.

"Thank you, Frank, for the lovely evening." She shook his hand and said, "With the snow so deep, there's no need for you to get wet. I can walk myself to the door with Marge and Lou, but I *really* had a wonderful time."

Frank sat in a stupor as his date gave him the brush-off, his long anticipated good-night kiss now a distant memory.

For Ellen, weeks turned into months before she knew with certainty a third date with Frank remained a foolish dream. She couldn't figure out why Frank didn't contact her. She'd gone out of her way to be considerate. At least she had a backup plan as she pictured herself as a nun.

Meanwhile, Frank decided there were other women in the neighborhood. He called a Swedish girl from his graduating class and they went out on a few dates. However, he soon came to realize she did not compare to Ellen's quick wit, kind, vivacious spirit, and natural beauty.

FIFTY-ONE

IN THE SUMMER of 1940, Frank and Ellen became reacquainted on a streetcar ride.

"Ellen O'Malley?"

Turning her head at a familiar voice, Ellen laughed as she nodded. "Where are you going, Frank?"

Frank, enchanted by Ellen's laughter, responded, "I have several stops to make. How about you?" Afraid to mention his real destination and risk exiting the streetcar before Ellen, he decided to keep his options open.

"Heading home from work." Ellen remembered his gorgeous blue eyes that now looked at her admiringly. His blond wavy hair blew in the breeze during their conversation and once again, she was smitten with this handsome man. She could feel a red flush creep into her cheeks and hoped Frank didn't notice.

Although Frank's destination was uptown, he was surprised when he blurted out, "I'm heading in the same direction." He knew this was the best response when Ellen smiled. "Do you like to dance, Ellen?"

"On the streetcar? Can't say I've ever tried it."

Her dazzling smile reiterated the wonderful sense of humor

he missed.

"Well, I thought perhaps we could attend the Hotel Statler Ballroom next Saturday. We could dance until our feet fall off," Frank joked.

"Why, Frank, I thought you'd never ask."

ELLEN SELECTED A dress her sister Mayme purchased for her at Lampl's Clothing Store where Mayme worked part-time, when she wasn't on the stage, and received the latest fashions at a discount price.

Once again, Michael O'Malley waited for the knock on the door and answered with a devilish grin. "So, Frank, what have ye been up to?"

Luckily, Frank fared better than his initial meeting with Ellen's father.

When Ellen appeared in a classic, form-fitting, kelly-green dress belted at the waist and wearing a cocktail hat dipped low over one eye, he blurted out, "You look gorgeous." After those three words, he was incapable of further speech and his feet refused to move. This time, Michael took pity on the young man and guided them out the front door.

The evening sparkled with magic and laughter as they danced until the stars came out and the night whispered a lovely tune meant for young lovers.

As the end of their enchanted evening approached, Frank became nervous. He wasn't sure if he should kiss Ellen, shake her hand, or pat her on the back. The suspense grew as they neared her front door, but when the time came, he knew the right answer. He hugged Ellen and tilted her chin upward to kiss her softly on the lips as they lingered in a world filled with moonbeams as their hearts raced in anticipation. They reveled in a kiss unlike anything either of them experienced before as they pulled away, breathless and filled with euphoria.

After Frank said good night, he got into his car and drove home. When he arrived in his driveway, he wondered how he got there. He still felt the softness of Ellen's lips and sat transfixed in his car, unable to move. He stared out the window, without a care in the world.

No matter how hard she tried, Ellen couldn't keep a silly grin off her face. She floated on a cloud, and her entire body tingled, coming alive. Unaware her siblings had watched from their post at the living room window with noses pressed against the pane, she walked into the house. Ellen didn't notice they were out of breath from trying to imitate the prolonged kiss. And it didn't faze her one bit when they dished out teasing remarks until Ellen was safely ensconced behind her closed bedroom door. Her lips still tingled from the kiss and her heart galloped at a pace quick enough to win the Kentucky Derby—she never dreamed a kiss could be that good.

FIFTY-TWO

ALTHOUGH FRANK CONTINUED to work the Sheridan homicide, he found it difficult to concentrate due to his romance with Ellen. However, Frank's determination to succeed at his first investigation became his driving force. During the initial months of the investigation, Frank received piecemeal lists from his small suspect pool.

"Hey Joe, has the mail arrived yet?" Frank asked at the front desk.

"Yeah, you got a few letters. I'll bring them over."

The first letter caught him off guard—a witness list provided by Joseph O'Riley, originally sent to the wrong precinct. After contacting everyone on the list who confirmed Joseph's story, Frank reluctantly eliminated him as a suspect—for now. The second correspondence, from Todd Hershberger, corroborated his whereabouts with family members on the evening of the murder. Two down, two to go.

Frank already knew the mysterious Brett Roth didn't have an alibi and a recent phone call from the overwrought Miss Gallagher confirmed she never heard back from her fiancé. And he was certain Kurt Mueller would never divulge information about his brother, Stephen. With his suspect pool reduced to Roth and Mueller, Frank checked his sources on the street for any rumors concerning their whereabouts or known accomplices. When he came up empty, Frank returned to the station. Knocking on his captain's open door, Frank asked, "Can we discuss the Sheridan case for a few minutes?"

"Sure. What's the problem?"

"I have two suspects I can't locate, and I've searched all the routine sources. Any suggestions? I'm coming up blank."

After thinking for a moment, the captain snapped his fingers and said, "Why didn't I think of this before? You should ask Lieutenant John Saccany. He's been around forever and usually comes up with unique solutions to problems like the one you're experiencing."

Frank heard of Saccany's legendary work in the department and believed he would be an excellent resource with new insights for a novice detective. He raced up two flights of stairs and somewhat breathless, knocked on Saccany's door. "Sir, can I speak to you for a moment? It's about the Sheridan murder."

Saccany looked up and after a moment, recalled the young detective's name. "Your name's Frank, right?"

"Yes, sir."

"I prefer John to sir." Sensing the young man's insecurity, he said, "What can I do for you?"

He handed the investigation folder to Saccany and explained the problem of locating his two suspects. After fifteen minutes reviewing the file, Saccany said, "You've done a very thorough job. Your best bet at this juncture is to contact the surrounding police districts for crimes matching the Sheridan heist and murder. Although it would entail an exhaustive search, given the limited description, it might uncover either a current address, possible aliases for the two suspects, or any other clues to keep your investigation alive."

Frank checked the thirty-eight CPD zones for case files involving similar robberies but couldn't find a match to his brief witness description. In addition, none of the burglaries in 1939 resulted in fatalities or any type of violence. Discouraged his comprehensive search failed to yield any clues to advance the investigation, Frank periodically checked for criminal activities involving Joseph O'Riley, but his record remained clean.

Frank's next step was to contact local pawn shops. He pulled the Dunbar list of insured items but couldn't find the handwritten list by Mrs. Sheridan. Frank was certain his former partner, Kevin Collins, had asked for this information. The list had to be somewhere. But checking the file once again, it was still missing.

Just as he was about to call Mrs. Sheridan, an officer handed him an envelope with a note from Kevin,

> Sorry about the delay in sending this information to you, Frank. After they transferred me off the case, the attached list of stolen items from Mrs. Sheridan was sent to me at the Third District and filed away before I ever saw it. I discovered it by accident and immediately dispatched to your attention. Let me know if there's anything else I can do to assist. Good luck with the investigation. We'll grab a beer when you have a chance.
>
> K

Frank was now able to combine the Dunbar itemization he

already had with Mrs. Sheridan's list of stolen, uninsured items prior to hitting the streets. He again checked with his informants to determine if any of the items appeared on the black market. He also sent a copy of the combined lists to major pawn shops in the area.

After spending the rest of the day going in and out of pawn shops, he finally received a viable lead at a local pawn shop.

"Detective, I checked my inventory, and I purchased one of the paintings on your list in December 1939 for ten thousand dollars."

"Did you say ten thousand?" Surely no painting was worth that amount of money.

"Yes, but it's true worth was over thirty thousand."

Frank asked the owner to pull the original ticket. It proved to be useless with an address in the middle of Lake Erie and a bogus name of John W. Booth. "Do you remember anything about the man who sold you this painting?"

"Oh, yes. When the man jumped at the offer of ten thousand, I thought him to be a fool. But he had a muscular build, quite tall, and his most distinctive feature involved red hair and matching beard. He was very nervous and seemed desperate. He mentioned there were additional items, and he would return with other treasures."

"Have you seen him since that time?"

"No, I haven't. But, in this business, you never know, especially someone as frantic as Mr. Booth."

"I'm sorry to inform you, but the painting is evidence in an ongoing investigation and needs to be impounded. We can write you a receipt but the painting won't be released until the case is solved."

"But that means I'm out ten thousand dollars."

"I understand your predicament, I really do. But it's police procedure."

Confiscating the painting, Frank asked the shopkeeper to call immediately if Mr. Booth returned or if he was approached with any other stolen items on the lists provided. "Your cooperation in solving this case may result in your merchandise being returned quickly."

The owner nodded his head.

Frank brought the painting into the CPD fingerprint department but there were too many prints, most of them smudged, and they were unable to come up with a match.

WITH FRANK'S DISCOVERY, the CPD issued round-the-clock surveillance of the shop but no other merchandise turned up from the Sheridan robbery. Two weeks later, CPD refused to authorize further manpower and the surveillance ended. Frank decided to stake out the place on his free time, advising the store owner to raise his shades if anyone tried to pawn items from the list.

One week later, while doing head-bobs in his car from working long hours, Frank was startled awake when he saw the shades slowly raised. Finally, the chance he'd been waiting for!

Unfortunately, the person detained at the shop proved to be an elderly gentleman—clean-shaven with gray hair and stooped over as he leaned heavily on a cane to compensate his uneven gait. Although he didn't fit the physical characteristics of the suspect, Frank decided to interrogate him.

After flashing his badge, he said, "Excuse me, sir. But I'd like to know how you came into possession of this portrait."

"My nephew gave it to me as a birthday present, but we needed the money." He spoke with a thick German accent as he slowly enunciated each word.

"What is your nephew's name?"

"Stephen Mueller."

Frank's adrenaline pumped overtime.

"What is your name, sir?"

"Andrew Mueller."

"Do you know where I might find your nephew?"

"My wife and I came to this country five years ago. We rarely see our nephews, but Kurt and Stephen are good boys."

Frank handed him a business card. "If you should hear from Stephen again, could you please call this number and ask for Detective Szabo? My name's printed on the card."

"I'll be happy to. But Stephen isn't in any trouble, is he? He's such a darling boy, I wouldn't want to cause him any unnecessary problems."

"At this point sir, we are only interested in him as a potential witness to a crime."

"All right, Detective. I'll contact you when I hear from him."

Given the fact Frank was manning the investigation alone on his own time, the meeting was fortuitous and supported Frank's initial supposition that Stephen acted as the fence for Roth's stolen goods, especially when he considered conflicting witness accounts of the murderer. Frank believed the investigation was moving forward in the right direction and knew it was crucial to locate Stephen Mueller for assistance in tracking down his elusive partner, Brett Roth. Frank checked all the usual sources for information about Stephen—Social Security, the County Recorder's Office, and Bureau of Motor Vehicles—but Stephen fell off the map after 1939. The criminal had become a ghost. On a whim, Frank returned to former source, Kurt Mueller, Stephen's older brother.

"Sorry, flatfoot, I ain't seen my brother. Got nothing better to do than bother innocent folks?"

Frank dismissed the derogatory reference to a regular patrolman and understood his options were running out. Despite his earlier feeling that the case was progressing, his inability to find either culprit became a stumbling block. But Frank would not be deterred. He personally surveilled Kurt's residence on major holidays in the hope Stephen would make an appearance but his efforts were unsuccessful. Frank assumed Kurt tipped his brother off.

Although Frank could not locate the murderer despite his best efforts, he knew the case would one day be solved. He hoped it would happen in his lifetime. With all leads exhausted and insufficient evidence to file charges against Stephen Mueller or Brett Roth, Frank's supervisor ordered him to close the case after two years.

Frank couldn't rid himself of the feeling that the missing piece of the puzzle—something already in the box of evidence gathered in the past two years—would one day be identified. Yet, each time he focused on the facts uncovered during the investigation, the elusive clue would evaporate like a bowl of water sitting on a hot radiator. But Frank vowed to pursue the matter discretely until he identified the murderer.

In the meantime, the nation's priorities changed when the Japanese attacked Pearl Harbor on December 7, 1941.

PART THREE

War and Peace

(1941-1949)

FIFTY-THREE

The Cleveland NorthShore Post

Monday Morning	December 8, 1941	Three Cents

JAPAN DECLARES WAR AGAINST UNITED STATES!

Pearl Harbor, Hawaii. Yesterday morning, Japanese planes attacked Honolulu, Pearl Harbor, and Hickam Field. Preliminary estimates of 390 casualties are thought to be inaccurate and heavy loss of life is expected by the unprovoked air and sea attacks against the Pacific Naval Base. Shortly after the cowardly invasion, the Japanese Empire declared war against the United States and Britain. Secretary of State Sam Rayburn alerted joint sessions of Congress to convene. The nation anxiously awaits the presidential address before Congress later today in the hope of subduing rumors concerning additional strikes. When Roosevelt first heard of the attack, he put the U.S. Army and Navy on alert to execute highly secret war plans.

Cleveland's defense plan, established under Safety

Director Eliot Ness, announced the enemy alien arrest policy will be implemented once they receive the FBI order. More to follow on this story as plans unfold and the nation reels from this unprovoked and dastardly act of aggression.

WHEN LT. EDWARD Sheridan first arrived at Pearl Harbor, he predicted an attack was a distinct possibility; however, no one listened to his warnings. He had recommended to his superiors, shortly after his arrival on the island, that maneuvers should be initiated for the Top Secret Rainbow Plan. Many had regarded him with astonished looks, while others willfully ignored his wise advice. Edward recalled heated debates at the Naval Academy with Professor Kelleher who revealed the nation's top secret plan. Each color of the rainbow represented hypothetical scenarios to thwart a particular adversary. War Plan Black dealt with a possible attack by Germany while War Plan Orange addressed an assault by the Japanese. Edward believed the antiquated plans, developed in the 1920s, were outdated and insufficient to meet the current threat, especially when factoring in advances to modern warfare.

Edward had not been lulled into complacency by the serene backdrop of the island beauty and routine maneuvers of the warships posted at this idyllic locale. His thought-provoking argument about Battleship Row—housing more than half the navy's ships and the majority of its warships in one location— presented a succinct target for large-scale destruction from an offensive attack, was equally dismissed. But nothing had been set in motion until the unthinkable happened.

FIFTY-FOUR

FOLLOWING A LATE Saturday night of dinner and drinks at the Royal Hawaiian Hotel on December 6, 1941, twenty-two-year-old Edward Sheridan awoke that bright Sunday morning to confusion, shouts, and fear thick enough to constrict the very air he breathed. He knew the ongoing peace talks with Japan throughout 1941 would resume on December 7. Edward assumed the negotiations resulted in a peace treaty and everyone was celebrating.

"What's happening?" he asked after donning pants and shoes while running outside.

"It's the Japs! We're under attack!" an unknown soldier shouted over his shoulder before he was gunned down. Edward ran in a zigzag line to escape the barrage of fire from low-flying planes.

Uncertainty reigned at Pearl Harbor on December 7 as the majority of officers, off-duty for the weekend, were unavailable to mount a timely response to the attack. Many became complacent in their misplaced confidence of the six mobile radar stations on Oahu that provided a false sense of security. Had the officers known the limitations regarding image interpretation, lack of skilled operators, and restricted use between 4:00 a.m. and 7:00 a.m.—the presumed hours of an expected attack—alternate plans to augment their watchdog program in addition to radar may have been implemented to reduce casualties and increase a significant counterresponse. To further complicate matters, many attributed the explosions to a nearby air station under construction, while others assumed it was a routine training exercise.

"This is no drill!" would become an oft-repeated phrase to all ships at or near Pearl Harbor by Rear Admiral Patrick Bellinger, the commander-in-chief of the Pacific fleet. He instructed radio operators to cable similar messages alerting naval stations as far as Alaska.

When tragedy struck, the colossal scale surprised even Edward, despite his skeptical view of war preparedness. Although there were others who agreed with Edward's assessment, they were also overruled by superior officers. Profoundly saddened, he witnessed the extensive casualties and loss of equipment that impeded a counteroffensive response.

FIFTY-FIVE

THE OVERPOWERING SMELL of burning flesh caused Edward to gag as he neared the dock. He saw ships in the harbor on fire and heard the agonizing screams of men injured and dying. While he continued to dodge a rain of bullets from overhead planes, he frantically searched for a machine gun. He found only one in working order—manned by a dead man.

Edward roughly pushed the corpse aside and fired into the sky filled with enemy combatants. Ignoring his scorched skin from the smoldering gun, Edward was blinded by fury. Fueled by a deep-seated rage, he launched his own response to this reprehensible act. Edward scored hits on three Japanese bombers and silently cheered when he saw the telltale flames spiraling downward into the harbor.

Unaware that tears streamed down his face at the sight of so much carnage and human sacrifice, Edward assessed the situation. At this point, rank meant nothing but gathering men together who could fight meant everything. He assembled a group of men with limited injuries and together they jumped on board the *Neosho,* a tanker in the middle of Battleship Row.

Within minutes, under the direction of Commander John Phillips, the ship headed out to the open sea with a palpable murderous intent and need for retaliation. Edward manned the machine-gun post throughout the attack and sent a hailstorm of fire at the Japanese planes until his already burnt hands could no longer bear the weight. The ship smelled heavily of fumes, remnants of the highly explosive aviation fuel removed minutes before the attack began. Every man on board knew that a direct hit would vaporize the tanker and ignite nearby fuel onshore, but they did not back down from their pursuit.

As the ship pulled away from port, Edward continued to hear the screams of men set afire as their ships exploded. Although they jumped into the water, their flesh continued to burn in water teeming with blazing fuel. But escape from their decimated vessels didn't end the danger as bullets strafed through the water, killing many who believed they were safe.

Edward stared in amazement as many Japanese planes became suicidal lethal weapons crashing into vital structures, causing irreparable damage to many key vessels. He quaked with helpless fury at the onslaught of air and sea attacks that killed or wounded so many of his fellow soldiers.

After two hours, the attack on Pearl Harbor ceased, leaving devastation in its wake. Edward later discovered the attack resulted in the loss of 2,390 men, women, and children. The onslaught was conducted in two coordinated waves. The first involved torpedoes from submarines that destroyed nineteen warships (of the total 185 ships of varying size stationed at Pearl Harbor.)

The second wave concentrated on air raids targeting naval air stations and destroying planes at Hickam Field. Unfortunately, in an effort to discourage saboteurs, the planes were parked on the tarmac close to one another. But this only served to create a concise target that further crippled the American response to the assault.

Edward waited expectantly for the Japanese Empire to commence a subsequent strike while the Americans remained vulnerable. But the attack never came. History would later prove that Japan's failure to immediately send a third strike force on the disabled Pacific base ultimately paved the way for the Allies to achieve victory over Japan.

As Edward helped to restore organization at Pearl Harbor over the next few days, he joined survivors in gathering the dead bodies on land and sea. Their fallen comrades were buried and each gravesite had a small American flag behind the headstone and a ceremonial red lei, a bleak reminder of the blood spilled on the island.

Edward's quick response and coolness on December 7 resulted in a promotion and his own ship to command, despite his young age. His coolness under pressure and accurate predictions made age irrelevant in wartime. His training instinctively took over as he negotiated his men in a series of conflicts in the Pacific Theater with skill and expertise, fully aware that any mistake or misstep could result in the loss of his crew. He believed in being at the forefront of every battle, an equal to his shipmates in their fighting spirit and courage, while orchestrating battle maneuvers and providing encouragement.

Hardened by battle with a fierce desire to protect those under his command, Edward became a strict but fair man, kind to a fault, and beloved by all who had the privilege of serving with him. The events of December 7, 1941, turned him into a committed and dedicated leader who vowed to defeat the Japanese in retribution of the destruction unleashed on the peaceful Hawaiian Islands. This driving force and strategic planning kept him alive to fight another day after Pearl Harbor. But without thought for his safety, Edward's dedication to the cause proved to be a potentially fatal flaw as wartime battles became more perilous.

FIFTY-SIX

THE O'MALLEY FAMILY crowded around the radio to hear President Roosevelt's stirring call to action in the wake of the unprovoked bombing at Pearl Harbor. Many predicted an end to the war within a year now that the United States was involved. William O'Malley, the oldest son, became restless to join the battle and feared the war would be over before he even joined.

Most of the neighborhood men signed up to serve their country within the following week. Frank promptly took a leave from the police department to get his physical at the nearest recruiting station, but a heart murmur, although asymptomatic, placed him on the inactive list. Despite his disappointment, Frank consoled himself in the knowledge he could serve his country in another way—by returning to the force.

William wrestled with his conscience as he debated the problem of serving his country or causing his mother heartache. His patriotic duty won out and William came home on February 4, 1942, wearing a naval uniform with a sailor hat set at a jaunty angle over his dark curly hair.

"Dear boy. What have ye done?" asked his mom, concern etched on her face.

"Same thing as any red-blooded American," his father replied with pride in his voice and a mist in his eyes. "William, when do ye ship out?"

"Next Monday, Da."

"Where will they send ye?"

"Somewhere in the Pacific." Too keyed up with enthusiasm and the possibility of exotic adventures, he said, "Come on, I'll take everyone out for an ice cream cone. My treat."

His siblings cheered loudly, jumping up and down. All except Ellen.

"I miss you already. Promise me that you'll write every day and come home safely." Ellen was so close to her brother, she felt the searing effects of separation anxiety as she held back a deluge of tears while her heart was breaking. Determined not to dampen his spirits or cast a pall on his proud commitment to service, Ellen smiled and feigned happiness.

"Of course. I'll probably be home by Christmas, once I've taken out all the Japs in the Pacific. Now come on, let's go."

"I'll just be goin' upstairs to fetch me hat." Mary excused herself and when she came down, she wore a beautiful smile despite red-rimmed eyes. "So, what are we waitin' for?"

William knew spending time with his loving family made everything right in his world, but the gravity of his impromptu patriotic act and a life far away from those he loved began to dawn on him. Determined not to show fear and maintain a façade of bravery especially around his parents, William contrived a devil-may-care attitude until he was shipped out, and, before they knew it, their lives were upended yet again.

FIFTY-SEVEN

UNAWARE HER LIFE was about to change in 1942, Sadie looked forward to celebrating her eighteenth birthday. She couldn't imagine a better evening than watching *Yankee Doodle Dandy* with her friends and watching the talented James Cagney with his piercing eyes. Sadie already knew the evening would be delightful as she entered the world of adulthood.

Waiting in line, as she giggled with her friends, Sadie bumped into a rude young man who blatantly gave her the once-over and whistled. Sadie decided to ignore the disrespectful man and maintained her composure. When she approached the ticket window, Sadie realized her money was sitting on the dresser. With her face turning redder by the minute as she searched her purse in vain, the same young man gallantly paid for her ticket and refused to provide his address to repay him.

"Just give me your phone number, doll."

"Why, I'll do no such thing. I don't even know you," Sadie replied.

"Friends call me Tee. There, *now* you know me. So how about that number?"

Again she refused but felt the need to pay her debt and agreed to meet him the following week outside the theater.

Although he told her it wasn't necessary to repay the money, Sadie insisted.

The next Saturday, Sadie almost changed her mind when anxiety set in. Determined to overcome her fear and make a good impression, she changed outfits several times and paid extra attention to her hair and makeup. Convinced her efforts were in vain for a young man she didn't even know, Sadie continued the painstaking beauty ritual until satisfied at her appearance and showed up at the theater fashionably late by five minutes.

"It's about time. I almost bought a ticket to the movie rather than stand out here by my lonesome."

Flustered, Sadie said, "I'm only a few minutes late. Here's the money I owe." As she gave the young man the quarter, Sadie was shocked to discover her hand trembled. The stranger accepted the money and invited her to join him for the movie.

"Don't worry. I'm harmless." He flashed a convincing smile and she cautiously accepted his offer. By the end of the movie, Sadie decided he *was* harmless and joined him afterward for an early supper.

While waiting to place their order, Sadie wanted to find out more about her new friend. "Tee. That's an unusual nickname. What's your real name?"

"Timothy Sheridan. I live—" but stopped mid-sentence when he saw Sadie's expression. "What did I say?"

"Do you live on Millionaire's Row?"

"Yes, how did you know?"

"I used to work for your family in 1939 as a cook but left two weeks before your father died."

"*You're* the magical cook I've heard about all these years?

My family still talks about the culinary delights you created. I'm only sorry I missed out on the experience."

Sadie blushed further and nodded her head.

Their friendship blossomed into romance. She would have been skeptical if anyone told her that a quarter could lead to so much happiness. But even the ecstasy of a budding romance failed to replace the emptiness in her heart from the absence of her twin. She continued to remain hopeful that, one day, she would find Gretl. Although she hadn't heard from Gretl in years, and despite hearing rumors of Jewish tragedies at the hands of Nazis, her heart would not allow her to give up on her beloved twin.

FIFTY-EIGHT

AFTER DATING SADIE for more than nine months, Timothy knew she was the one. But on this particular night, time moved in slow motion, and he was riddled with unease. Unable to look at food, no amount of pacing relaxed him before he left the house at 6:00 p.m. On the trip over to Sadie's home, which seemed to take twice as long, Timothy's hand nervously dipped in his pocket. Temporarily reassured, he continued the interminable drive until five minutes passed when he repeated the same routine as the next five minutes went by. He wondered if this drive would ever end.

When Timothy arrived at Sadie's home, he sat in the car. Unable to move, he convinced himself paralysis had set in when his legs refused to work. He concentrated on walking and slowly approached Sadie's home on rubbery legs that threatened to collapse at a moment's notice.

When she answered the door, Sadie noticed his shaking hands and unusual pallor. "Timothy, come inside. Are you all right? Would you like some water? Perhaps you need a drink?"

"No, thank you." Mortified, Timothy realized his voice was an octave higher. Sadie gave him a strange look and waited for him to explain. "What I must do . . . I mean what you need . .

. no that's not right, either."

Sadie had never seen Timothy so flustered and her initial concern inwardly turned to amusement when she guessed the reason for his peculiar behavior.

When Timothy got down on one knee, Sadie reveled in the beauty of the moment. Neither were aware that Sadie's aunt and uncle sat in the dining room together watching the touching scene that had played out for centuries.

"Will I do you the honor of becoming my wife?"

Sadie heard the words as they were meant to be delivered, got down on her knees to cup his head in her hands, and looked into his eyes. "Oh, yes, Timothy, I'd be honored to be your wife."

Tears intermingled during a passionate kiss before they helped one another rise on shaky legs. At that moment, Sadie noticed her aunt and uncle hugging one another, happiness and pride evident on their faces. It was a moment Sadie had always dreamed of—becoming a wife and having her own family. But Sadie wished she could share this happy occasion with her parents and sister. Just the thought of their absence and the possibility she might never see her sister again, or that her twin may never experience the richness of life, momentarily robbed her of the happiness in her heart.

SIX MONTHS LATER, Timothy and Sadie drove in silence to the ship that would carry him to parts unknown. One week earlier, he had signed up at the Navy Recruitment Office. Timothy's mother wanted to see him off but Bridget had a nasty flu and Marianne couldn't leave her young daughter's bedside. Although they spoke on the phone that morning, Timothy knew his mom was upset.

Stifling a sob, Sadie slowly exited the vehicle.

"Now, my love, give me your best smile and a kiss to keep me warm at night." Stoically restraining the watershed until Timothy was safely on board, Sadie gave Timothy a long passionate kiss good-bye as they stood on the dock—amidst catcalls from sailors.

Blushing, Sadie hugged Timothy and whispered fiercely, "Please come back to me in one piece, or I'll be forced to join the WAVES and retrieve you myself."

Timothy grinned at the reference to Woman Accepted for Voluntary Emergency Service, and with a bounce in his step to camouflage the internal turmoil, he walked to the gangway, where he waved to Sadie who was too far away to see the solitary tear running down his cheek.

FIFTY-NINE

ESPITE THE COUNTRY at war, love prevailed. Or, perhaps it was because of the war. Those left behind saw the fleeting moments of life and death, which made them more determined to make the most of whatever time they had before their lives were changed forever.

Frank had been dating Ellen for three years and knew they were meant for each other. On his lunch hours, Frank made many trips to different jewelers looking for that special ring that would signify his love but fit into his limited budget. He found the perfect solitaire diamond ring in a plain gold setting with tiny baguettes on either side. But now he had another problem. How would he propose?

One night, sitting in his unmarked car during a stakeout, Frank's mind wandered as he wrestled with various scenarios about the perfect proposal.

I could rent a small boat and take her out on Lake Erie and pop the question. No, I'd probably get seasick. Perhaps we could go up the Observation Deck of the Terminal Tower in downtown Cleveland. Nah, heights make me dizzy and I might pass out. We could go for a long drive and . . . my poor old car would probably break down.

While still musing, Frank came up with a unique plan, and at five o'clock that night, gathered together his courage and called Ellen.

"Ellen, I'm running a little behind. Could you catch a streetcar down to the station?"

"Sure Frank. When would you like me to leave?"

"How about thirty minutes? That way, it'll still be light outside."

"All right. See you in a little while."

Unsuspecting, Ellen left her home in a half hour and caught the streetcar heading toward the Second District. The car was crowded during rush hour and she didn't notice someone quietly approaching behind her. Glancing around, Ellen was startled to see Frank.

"Frank, what are you going here? I thought you were working late." But Ellen could see that Frank was nervous and barely able to contain his excitement. Curious, she asked, "Are you all right, Frank?"

"Oh sure. Sorry to tell you a little fib. I actually called you from home. I had special plans for tonight."

"Oh? Care to fill me in?"

"All in good time, my dear." Luckily there was a recently-vacated seat next to Ellen and Frank joined his intended.

"Did I ever tell you that the time we became reacquainted on the streetcar three years ago, I was traveling in the opposite direction?"

"Really?"

"I just wanted to spend more time with you. Not sure why I waited so long to tell you. I think I was embarrassed."

"Well, I think it's very sweet." Ellen gave Frank a peck on

the cheek as she squeezed his hand.

Somehow Frank managed to continue a normal conversation as his hand periodically checked his pocket. The ride proceeded without incident until they came to a stop near one of Cleveland's finest restaurants. The Theatrical Grill catered to celebrities and provided the best jazz music around. As a special attraction, tonight they were featuring a new singer, Dean Martin.

Before exiting the streetcar (as prearranged with the conductor to wait a few minutes at this particular stop), Frank got down on one knee, and pulling the ring from his pocket, nervously recited his rehearsed speech. "Ellen, you're the love of my life and I can't imagine my world without you. For the past three years, I've been unable to think of anything else but spending the rest of my life with you. Will you marry me?"

As Ellen hugged Frank with tears of joy streaming down her face, she said, "Oh, Frank. Of course I will."

The passengers stood and applauded. Frank's idea went according to plan. And this time, they were both going in the right direction.

SIXTY

MARIANNE OFTEN WONDERED if she would have recovered from Louis's death without the affection and distraction provided by her youngest child, especially after her sons went off to war.

Over the next four years, Ellen continued her employment as Bridget's nanny. Initially, Marianne's health declined as depression set in. Ellen took it upon herself to care for the woman she admired. With gentle affection and forceful prodding when needed, her friend and employer's health gradually returned to normal, a process expedited by Bridget's presence.

Marianne treasured Ellen for the care and love she gave in abundance at a time when she sorely needed it. Their friendship deepened into an easygoing relationship, and Marianne came to rely on Ellen's common sense and advice. However, with the passage of time, Marianne heard Ellen speak often of the handsome detective and their plans to marry. She deduced Ellen would leave their employ in the near future. That day coincided with Bridget's decision to run away from home.

The first day of summer in 1943 carried a fanciful breeze to billow the curtains of Bridget's bedroom window as sunshine sparkled through a cloudless sky. Looking outside, she decided now was the time for an adventure, and nothing could deter her from that mission. To confirm she had all the necessary objects needed, Bridget reviewed items sandwiched into her small suitcase several months ago in anticipation of a day like today. A quick inventory of items was in order to make sure she packed more grown-up things. Teddy bear? Check. Favorite book *Pokey Little Puppy?* Check. Seashells from last year's vacation? Check. Red bandana in case she ran into pirates? Check. Special sunglasses to protect her from aliens? Check. Secret decoder ring? Check.

Bridget walked out her bedroom door with the determination of a four-year-old on a mission. She carried her tiny overnight case downstairs but paused momentarily when she heard Ellen talking to her mother.

"As you know, Frank and I will be married on Thanksgiving, and I'm sure you've been expecting this." Ellen fidgeted in her chair. "My last day will probably be June fifteenth."

Bridget was shocked. Ellen can't leave. Didn't she know it was her turn to escape? After Ellen's announcement, news of Bridget's departure may not even be noticed. She sighed deeply and then trudged upstairs with her suitcase. After hiding it safely beneath her bed, she needed consolation. Ice cream should do it. Standing on a footstool to reach the icebox in the kitchen, Bridget brought her comfort food over to the table. While eating double scoops of chocolate covered in sprinkles, Bridget decided to run away next year. By then, surely she'd be missed.

SIXTY-ONE

ON THE EVE of her wedding to Frank in November 1943, Ellen and her sisters celebrated with a small party in their home. This was the second marriage in the family, since Marge had married Louis DuChez two years earlier. It was now Ellen's turn to be the bride and she couldn't wait. The siblings shared in good-hearted teasing as they bantered back and forth about the upcoming festivities.

"Ellen, what do you think about this hairstyle?" Mayme, ever the actress, inquired as she arranged her hair in an upsweep held together with clothespins.

"Simply delightful. The only thing you're missing is a washtub." The sisters giggled at their silly comments and bristled with excitement.

Ellen's youngest sister, eighteen-year-old Veronica, perused magazines until she found something to contribute. "Sis, take a look at this article. It describes a new facial mask to make your skin shine. Wanna try it?"

"Sure, I need all the help I can get." While her sisters vehemently disagreed, Ellen laughed as a pillow fight ensued. When the laughter died down, she read the article. "Looks good, Veronica. Let's try it."

Veronica ran down to the kitchen and brought up a jar of pickled beets with a bowl. She drained the juice into the container and gently spread it over Ellen's face. After waiting one hour, Ellen washed her face and felt a tingling glow. Looking in the mirror, she was amazed at the beautiful reflection staring back.

Finally, the big day arrived. But looking in the mirror, Ellen's expression turned to horror. Her face was covered in red blotchy stains. Panicking, she sought help from her sisters.

"Marge, can you—"

"Sorry, Ellen but I'm busy putting on makeup."

Running down the hall into Veronica's room, she pleaded, "Can you help—"

"No, my gown is wrinkled and I need to touch it up."

"Mayme, I need—"

"Oh, Ellen, my hair is a disaster. It will take me *forever* to get it right."

Rebuffed by all three sisters and even her own mother, the bride was on her own. After much powder, and the right amount of rouge to blend in with her new coloring, she positively glowed. Ellen gently stepped into her satin gown with rhinestones around the neckline and a fifteen-foot train. Bursting with excitement, Ellen could've run to the church. But she didn't want to risk tripping on her long train.

Her sisters wore long taffeta gowns, cinched at the waist, in a rainbow array of colors and complimentary flowers in their hair. Mary's handmade dress of light paisley with a matching hat complimented her Irish complexion and she beamed with delight as her two youngest sons, James and Thomas, escorted her to the second pew. Ellen's father, in tux and tails, proudly walked her down the aisle as everyone turned to see the alluring vision in white satin.

Standing at the altar, surrounded by his groomsmen, was her tall, handsome, soon-to-be husband. He looked at her with such love in his eyes that Ellen blushed through her beet-juice facial. But, somehow, that no longer mattered.

As dictated by the times, they held a wedding breakfast instead of an evening reception. Most frowned on nighttime galas when so many men were off fighting and suffering in foreign lands. With Ellen's brother, William, fighting in the war, she felt having a grand party at night would dishonor sacrifices made by him.

En route to the breakfast, Frank's clunker stalled on a streetcar track. Everyone in the waiting railway car hooted and hollered as Frank and his groomsmen, dressed in tux and tails, pushed the car off the tracks while Ellen laughed at the attention. After their feat of strength, Frank and party bowed to the patient riders and received a rousing burst of applause.

They honeymooned at the Commodore Perry Hotel in Toledo for five nights. The total bill of $24.95 included nightly long distance calls to Cleveland (made by Ellen, of course). Frank and Ellen didn't see too many sights in Toledo, although the city boasted fine tourist attractions. Their cozy room contained everything they needed—love and each other.

On the drive back home, with Ellen safely snuggled beside her husband, they hit a bumpy patch of road and the tire blew out, as it had on most of their prior dates. At least, this time, it wasn't in front of a streetcar and memories of their honeymoon kept them warm and content as the happy newlyweds began their new life together.

SIXTY-TWO

FRANK AND ELLEN moved into a tiny home purchased by Frank before their marriage. Shortly after they settled into married life, they invited Marge and her family to a barbecue. Arriving a few minutes after noon, Marge and Louie brought plenty of beer as the men worked their magic over the grill. Marge set up a Bouncy Chair for her one-year-old son, Buddy, and placed his toys on the tray.

"Gee, Marge, you think of everything," Ellen replied with admiration.

"You have to, when you're a parent. So, how's married life?"

Ellen blushed at her sister's question. "It's great. Frank is the best. And he loves my cooking."

"Then he must have a strong stomach."

"Oh you," Ellen replied, gently swiping her sister's arm. "Why don't we—"

Her question was cut off by Buddy's screams. He had dropped his favorite toy and pumped his little fists into the air in aggravation.

"Wait, Marge. Let me get it." After placing the toy into Buddy's outstretched arms, Ellen asked, "Can I hold him?"

"Of course. And it's great practice for you, assuming you

want children."

"We'd like at least four," Ellen said as she picked up her nephew. She danced around and held him tightly. "Why, Buddy, what a fantastic dancer you are!"

Buddy laughed in delight until he started to fall asleep in Ellen's arms.

"I'll take him now. Time for a nap."

Together they walked into Ellen's bedroom and placed a fortress of pillows around Buddy as he cooed in his sleep.

The afternoon passed quickly and Ellen thought about her sister's question. How wonderful it would be to have a family together. Ellen knew Frank's profession could be dangerous but having a child to raise would keep her mind off the fear of losing Frank to his job. When her thoughts turned to Frank's first case, the unsolved Sheridan murder, Ellen felt guilty about withholding information from her new husband. But she couldn't forget the earring left behind on her bed following her first encounter with the murderer. But now that she was married and they lived in their own home, surely her family would be safe. Frank was a policeman and he would know what to do. She decided to confide her secret with Frank the following evening.

Ellen wanted to cook Frank's favorite meal to soften the blow of the story she was about to tell. Ellen headed to the West Side Market, walking at a brisk pace. With her mind on the best way to approach Frank, Ellen bumped into a man standing in her path.

"Oh, pardon . . ." the words trailed off when she recognized the man who murdered Louis Sheridan. Unable to move or speak, Ellen stood still.

"I saw in the newspapers that you got married. Why, they were even kind enough to include your home address. So I paid you a visit the other day. What's your nephew's name again? Buddy, right? And you'd like to have at least four children? How quaint. Remember, if you ever tell your husband about me, I still know where you live. And you know what I'm capable of, so I'd advise you to keep quiet. Understand?"

Ellen nodded while fighting nausea and dizziness. *This can't be happening. Not again.*

"Good. Let's keep it that way." The murderer walked away, whistling a tune as though he didn't have a care in the world.

Ellen found a nearby bench and waited until her heart stopped pounding. Once her symptoms disappeared, she made her way back home on unbalanced legs, praying she wouldn't stumble. But her steely determination forced her to remain in control while she fought her deeply-rooted fear until she arrived home and collapsed on the couch.

Ever the protector, Ellen maintained her silence and knew the burden of carrying the secret would, once again, be hers alone to shoulder. Ellen knew fear was a paralyzer, and although it wasn't based on rational thought, it possessed the power to infect her soul and consume her with fright. But, for Ellen, it didn't matter if the danger was based on cogent thought; protecting her family at all costs remained her number one priority.

SIXTY-THREE

B Y OCTOBER 1943, *he planned his last, and best, caper to date—a crime spree to go down in the annals of illegal enterprises. With so many men overseas fighting in the Great War, women who lived in those cavernous mansions needed a man's help. They couldn't resist his handsome looks, great personality, and winning smile. He had women practically falling all over themselves when he walked into a room. During wartime, with a distinct absence of able males, they were so happy to have a male presence in their lives, he could enter their homes at will.*

Some of the old women even gave him keys, which he promptly copied, to finish repairs while they shopped with friends or joined some victory group to help the war effort. He selected a day when five of his best "customers" were out. Unfortunately, at his last stop, he decided to celebrate his victorious string of robberies with a few too many beers. When he eyed the latest invention—an RCA television—he attempted to carry the massive trophy out the front door. In a drunken stupor, he fell and the TV landed on top of him. After passing out, he found himself in the back of a squad car headed for the station.

Given the extensive evidence presented in court and his prior criminal record, he pled guilty to multiple counts of robbery. The television bandit, a moniker assigned him by police, served six months of his sentence when his luck changed. The judge called him back to court and made an offer he found impossible to refuse.

"Son," said the judge, "I'll give you a choice. You can either serve your ten-year sentence or join the armed forces. If you select the latter and receive an honorable discharge, I'll commute your sentence to time served."

He put his head down, to prevent the judge from seeing the smirk on his face and said with as much sincerity as he could muster, "Your Honor, I'd be proud to serve my country and thank you for this chance to turn my life around." He kept his head down for fear he would laugh in the judge's face.

The police escorted him down to the recruiting office where he was immediately shipped out to parts unknown.

"I'll serve all right until I find a way to escape. It's all in the planning," he thought.

SIXTY-FOUR

THE WAR FOR many provided viable employment for those unable to hold down a regular job. The armed forces offered a life of adventure, promises of three square meals a day, and a place to sleep. Never one to pass up a free meal, Lawrence Talbot followed the course of many before him. His once shining star on Broadway became tarnished in the wake of excessive partying and indiscriminant liaisons. His glory days of starring with Hollywood's elite, including 1937 performances of *Victoria Regina* with Helen Hayes, Vincent Price, and his protégé, Mayme O'Malley, became a distant memory. No longer considered for prime roles, Lawrence went in search of other occupations to maintain his current lifestyle. Unfortunately, without recognizing his basic underlying flaws, all subsequent ventures proved to be equally unsuccessful.

With no other recourse, he ended up in the navy where he discovered life on the USS *Mississippi* was a good trade-off. His shipmates looked up to him as a celebrity while he regaled them with tales of his prior escapades involving Broadway legends. Receiving notoriety in the navy proved to be an added and unexpected bonus. Still convinced Broadway sorely needed his prolific acting skills, Lawrence knew he'd eventually return to his life of fame.

The USS *Mississippi*, first launched in 1917, proved on many occasions to be combat-worthy. A few days after the attack on Pearl Harbor, the battleship left her current post in Iceland to join the conflict in the Pacific. In early 1942, she arrived in San Francisco to provide escorts for convoys prior to being retrofitted with antiaircraft machine guns. By the time Lawrence set foot on her deck, primed for battle in the Pacific Theater, he was eager to join the fray.

War set the stage as Lawrence's training ground for the birth of courage and emergence of valor under deplorable circumstances. After a year of fighting that included several battles in the Marshall Islands' campaign, Lawrence's camaraderie with his shipmates and genuine concern for their safety astonished him. This was a totally foreign concept that, to his surprise, made him stand a little taller as he gazed with affection at friends who accorded him the respect previously missing in his life.

In October 1944, Lawrence's adrenaline surged as they drew closer to their destination, the Surigao Strait. The atmosphere, already charged with electricity, grew in epic proportions when the commanding officers provided details of their mission. They cheered and hollered when advised their assignment would deliver a direct assault against the Japanese Navy. Five battleships, destroyed or sunk at Pearl Harbor, now repaired and looking for payback, accompanied the USS *Mississippi* for this historic undertaking.

In addition to other cruisers and PT boats, the strength of the U.S. Navy demonstrated its unstoppable power. Everyone wanted to inflict a little American retribution by luring the

Japanese Navy into a trap. Surigao Strait proved to be perfect the ambush site.

Lured into the strait, the Japanese maintained strict radio silence, which prevented them from communicating the fate awaiting other destroyers. The American forces formed a gauntlet through which the Japanese battleships must pass. As the Japanese attempted to survive crippling blows, they managed to get in a few of their own.

Bullets strafed across the deck of the *Mississippi* from the Japanese destroyer, *Asagumo*. Lawrence summoned the courage and mounted a counterattack that decimated the gunnery station aboard the Japanese ship.

In the heat of battle, Lawrence lost his glasses. During his search, he tripped over two unconscious young men covered in blood. He crab-walked across the bridge and in two separate trips, dodging stray bullets and exploding shrapnel, transported the wounded to sick bay. Due to excessive casualties, Lawrence left the young men on gurneys outside the infirmary before returning topside. His impulsive act of heroism later astounded him because it was the first time he ever committed a selfless deed without regard for his own safety.

When he returned to the deck, he found his spectacles kicked into a corner and miraculously intact. With clear vision, Lawrence fought with bravery and honor over the next several hours. Following a barrage of heavy gun bombardments and torpedo attacks, the majority of Japanese battleships sank.

Historians determined this would be the last campaign between battleships in the Pacific Theater, an outcome of the crippling blow to the Japanese Navy, rendering them incapable of mounting serious offensive attacks. Unaware of the historic significance, each man felt vindicated as he fought with courage in defense of his country.

SIXTY-FIVE

THROUGHOUT THE WAR, Marianne Sheridan's fear for the safety of her two sons fighting in foreign lands grew exponentially, but Bridget helped her mother maintain a sense of normalcy. Bridget grew into a fiercely independent child and quite adept at getting her own way. It merely required flashing her baby-blue eyes, batting her long lashes, and shining a dazzling smile.

Before Marianne knew it, Bridget was primed and eager to begin school in the fall of 1944. Her test scores surpassed the norm, and she entered first grade at the age of five. Bridget had it all planned out. First, she'd get straight A's and before long, would start teaching the first grade by herself.

Bridget was about to encounter her first disappointment in life. None of her engaging tactics, even approaches that worked on the most stubborn people, resulted in her teacher relinquishing the classroom over to Bridget. Perhaps the teacher didn't know how things worked in the world; Bridget would be happy to show her.

And, with this effort, she encountered her second disappointment, along with a note sent home from the teacher. Even Bridget knew this meant trouble. She promptly gave the note to her mother.

> Dear Mrs. Sheridan,
>
> Your precocious daughter has been determined to replace me as the classroom teacher. Although I applaud her enthusiasm and confidence, kindly advise her that a teaching position at age five is not possible. I've offered her the position to assist me in class, but she feels this is beneath her.
>
> I would be most appreciative if you would intervene and explain that her behavior is unacceptable. Also, she may need to see an eye doctor—she keeps blinking her eyes. Thank you.
>
> Respectfully,
> Anne Marie Drew

Marianne was grateful her daughter couldn't see her expression as she read the brief note and the effort required to suppress laughter. However, Bridget needed to be taught boundaries, so they sat down for a mother-daughter bonding conversation.

"Bridget, you do realize the teacher has a lot of responsibility in instructing her class and ensuring each student has a good understanding of the subject matter being taught, correct?"

Bridget rolled her eyes and sighed. "Yes, Mommy. I have a good idea, but Teacher said no."

She could tell her daughter was up to mischief. "Okay. Tell me your idea."

"Promote Teacher to second grade."

Unable to control herself, Marianne laughed out loud but instructed her daughter that, without a teaching certificate, she needed to remain a student for now. Reluctantly, Bridget agreed and gave up her grand scheme of taking over the class, knowing she'd have at least eleven more tries to get it right.

When Marianne looked down at her daughter, her heart overflowed with love. She thought, not for the first time, that Bridget was her link to sanity. Without her daily diversion and hugs, Marianne would have been consumed with anxiety for her two sons. Each day she prayed for Edward and Timothy to return home without injuries and with the same inner strength inherited from their father, to overcome the horrors of battle and experiences certain to scar their souls.

SIXTY-SIX

O N APRIL 1, 1945, Edward Sheridan was in command of a battleship that invaded the Japanese island of Okinawa. It became the bloodiest battle of the Pacific War and tested Edward's leadership skills and fortitude on a daily basis. Unremitting shells attacked the troops as they inched their way inward. Edward learned from the few letters he received from his mother that his brother, Timothy, also joined the navy. Edward prayed each day for his safety and hoped he was spared the bloody campaign that became a daily occurrence for Edward in Okinawa. But others faced equally challenging conflicts as they fought the enemy by land and sea.

In June 1945, William O'Malley boarded the USS *Indianapolis* that left San Francisco. The *Indianapolis*'s two aircraft landing bays had been removed to transport critical components, including uranium, for a special bomb known as "Little Boy." After delivering the crucial parts to Tinian, an island in the Western Pacific 1,400 miles off the coast of Japan, the battleship headed toward the Philippines for their next assignment.

On July 30, 1945, William was exhausted from completing a night's rotation on deck. He dropped onto his bunk, fully prepared to fall into a deep sleep, when he felt the heavy cruiser list from a torpedo. William jumped up, laced up his lifejacket, and started toward the steps when he saw a sailor who remained in his bunk snoring loudly.

"Get out of bed now and put on your life jacket! We're under attack, probably a Jap submarine." He roughly shook the young man awake and ran toward the upper deck.

Once topside, William ran along the gangway as the ship took its second torpedo hit. The freighter tilted further, and with it, William and several others slid from the deck into the sea. Those without their life preservers flailed in the water until sucked into the heavy undertow.

Others grabbed onto floating debris from the damaged ship. Several men clustered around larger segments from the ship, believing there was safety in numbers. William and the young man he rousted from sleep gripped a section from the afterdeck as they clung to life with six other men.

Those still on board the ship panicked at the sight of exploding fuel shortly before being propelled into the ocean without life preservers. Others lucky enough to find the few remaining life boats, navigated the vessels without benefit of oars toward the cries for help as they hoisted men out of the sea. Sailors without life-threatening injuries from the explosions on board did not survive the first twenty-four hours in the water because their bodies were quickly depleted from lack of nutrients and water needed to heal their wounds.

Due to the delicate nature of their mission, the USS *Indianapolis* traveled unescorted; therefore, a distress signal citing their exact position in the vast ocean would be critical for a successful rescue mission. The survivors in the water had to believe a distress signal was sent. Anything else was terrifying. However, during the twelve brief minutes before the mighty vessel sank, even Captain Charles McVay had been unable to ascertain if a message was sent prior to loss of radio communication.

Men clustered in groups floating in the open sea spanning a distance of several miles, many with only a life jacket to keep them afloat.

Those who lived through their first night, exhausted from treading water, prayed for a speedy rescue. However, as dawn approached, William saw a frightening sight that filled him with despair. Hoping his eyes were playing tricks on him, he rubbed them vigorously, trying to clear his vision. But the horrendous sight remained the same, only now it was closer.

"Oh, sweet Jesus. Look!" He choked on the word "shark," unable to voice the unthinkable. Instead, he pointed with an unsteady hand at the large school of fins heading toward them. They watched helplessly as the carnivorous creatures chomped down parts of their former shipmates dead in the water. As the swirling sea turned red, they knew it was a matter of time before the sharks, lured by blood in the water, would be attracted to them.

William and other survivors remained adrift and defenseless, while sharks circled and chose their victims indiscriminately. The men hovering in the water were unaware that constant motion of their legs acted as a beacon to hungry sharks.

Each man prayed they would be spared, but as delirium set in from exhaustion, fear, and dehydration, many wanted a quick death. While barely hanging onto his lifeline, William felt a gentle nudge against his leg followed by a searing pain strong enough for him to lose consciousness. As he dipped into oblivion, he prayed fervently for a miraculous rescue from their hopeless circumstances.

SIXTY-SEVEN

ELLEN SCREAMED. SHE tried not to but couldn't help it. Being in the early stages of labor with her first child on August 1, 1945, Ellen was amazed at the force of each painful contraction. She called her husband at work, frantic to tell him their child was ready to make an appearance.

"Frank, I need you to come home right now. The baby's on its way."

"Are you sure? It's not due until next week."

"Seems he has a mind of his own."

"*He*? Do you know something I don't?"

"No, Frank. It's a figure of speech."

"Well, maybe your stomach's upset from something you ate." Frank stalled in an effort to combat his case of the first-time-father jitters.

"No, I'm in labor."

"Are you sure he's ready to come out? Maybe he needs a little more time."

"Any more time and I'll be delivering this baby myself. Please, come home now. I've already called the doctor, and he's on his way to the hospital."

Normally it took ten minutes to drive home. Frank made it

in two with sirens blaring as he pulled up to the house. He left his car door open and raced into his home, nervous and shaking.

"Where are your bags for the hospital?"

"They're right by the front door where they've been for the past month."

"Oh, yeah. Right." Frank grabbed the bags, then raced out to the car and drove off toward the hospital. After three blocks, Frank was mortified to discover the passenger side was occupied by suitcases, not Ellen. Frank turned the car around and headed home.

Ellen stood patiently on the front porch until he returned, sirens once again jarring the neighborhood.

"Did you forget something?" she asked with a grin on her face.

Frank blushed and said, "Only the two most important people in the world. Now come on and hop in. We'll be at the hospital in no time."

"I don't think I can hop at this stage."

"Oh, right. Sorry." He jumped out of the car and eased her into the front seat as a contraction increased in severity. Frank was relieved when it passed. He hated to see his beloved Ellen in so much pain.

"Are you sure you remember where the hospital is located?" she asked, while holding on as he drove the car at a dizzying speed.

"Pretty sure, but if I head toward the veterinary hospital, let me know."

"Oh, you are a funny one."

Over the next fourteen hours, Ellen's labor grew in intensity until general anesthesia blissfully knocked her out. Frank anxiously hung around the expectant fathers' waiting room. He paced, bought coffee, looked at the newspaper, and when the inactivity became overwhelming, he paced some more. Ellen arrived in recovery one hour later and the baby was transported to the newborn ward, where Frank got a quick glimpse of their precious infant.

When Frank arrived in Ellen's room, he found his beautiful wife still unconscious from anesthesia. Grinning, he pinned a note to her gown.

> Congratulations, Mom, it's a boy! He looks just like you, except for a few extra parts. I am so proud of you. I'm returning home for some much-needed rest. I'm exhausted.
>
> Love,
> Frank

Ellen awoke to find the endearing note and smiled at his last sentence. With her newborn baby nestled next to her, she fell asleep and didn't hear the nurse as she carefully lifted James Francis from her bed and returned him to the nursery.

For the first time in months, Ellen dreamed of Patrick. Now that she had a child of her own, she thought of her sweet baby brother abducted when he was less than two years old. Ellen couldn't imagine the horrors faced by her parents. Not only was he taken from his loving home, but her parents never found out what happened to him. Ellen didn't know what she would do if her baby was harmed or kidnapped. She, once again, increased her resolve to keep her family safe, no matter what the cost.

SIXTY-EIGHT

IN A WORLD far away from happiness and the promise of a new life, Edward Sheridan was exhausted, discouraged, and depressed after more than eighty days of bloody fighting in Okinawa. As an integral part of the Pacific Theater's bloodiest battle, he found the casualty rate of more than 62,000 Americans, with an additional estimated 12,000 dead or missing, to be unacceptable. And those figures didn't include 100,000 civilian deaths with multiple suicides, and perhaps the worst type of collateral damage—countless rape allegations.

However, once atomic bombs decimated Hiroshima and Nagasaki in August 1945, the capture of Okinawa as an operations base to launch direct attacks on Japanese soil became moot. After bearing witness to the agonizing death of many men long before their time and watching countless others suffer horrendous injuries, Edward felt numb.

In the military, he was accustomed to following orders. But why did the battle for Okinawa, fought in blood and won at the cost of human sacrifice, ever happen? Months after this nightmare, Japan formally surrendered on September 2, 1945. Edward experienced conflicting emotions as he attempted to grasp the concept of amity when the ghastly vestiges of war plagued his thoughts without respite.

With victory at hand, Edward knew he should feel something. Anything. But no matter where he looked, blood and gore clouded his vision. Peace had become a concept so forlorn, it seemed impossible the war was truly over and that soon he'd be heading home. His mind failed to grasp waking up in anything but a dirty hovel, eating canned rations, or sleeping on the ground with one eye open.

How could someone with his experiences acclimate back into normal society when life's simple pleasures, formerly taken for granted, had become completely foreign? Edward's tortuous life for the past four years involved going for months at a time without changing his clothes as he trudged through muddy landscapes, rifle at the ready, while never truly relaxing. The need to protect his men, without regard for his own safety, became his mission and took precedence above all else. Now his battle experiences under deplorable conditions would recede like a nightmare that dissipates after awakening. For years, he prayed for peace. Now that it was here, Edward prayed for strength.

SIXTY-NINE

W HEN WILLIAM REGAINED consciousness in the
perilous waters of the South Pacific, he was relieved to
discover the skin around his ankle remained intact. He
discerned the etiology of pain must have been a piece of metal
striking his angle with sufficient force to break a bone. He could
deal with pain, a minor inconvenience compared to sharks. He
fervently prayed the absence of blood would keep the sharks at
bay until help arrived.

As the days dragged on, William and the other survivors
from the USS *Indianapolis* had been exposed to the sun's
relentless rays beating down upon them unmercifully. Their
skin became scorched, and they experienced a thirst so
powerful some were driven to madness and drank seawater
despite its known dangers of dehydration, hallucinations,
insanity, and death. Terror and isolation filled their days as they
clung to the hope of rescue in the face of insurmountable odds.
The cover of darkness encompassed each man like a shroud as
desolation took hold. Night terrors accompanied by screams,
born of pain and fear, escalated into despair. Surely tomorrow
would be the day—a mantra repeated each of the four nights
before falling into an exhaustive slumber.

Hanging onto the debris next to William was a young man clearly out of his mind. Despite William's attempts to provide hope and quiet his disturbing screams, William saw the madness in his eyes as he relinquished his hold on the floating wreckage sustaining the small group of men. William held on with one hand and attempted to pull the man back onto their tiny refuge. But his hand came up empty except for a fistful of water and the man's tags.

On the opposite side of William, a brief inspection of the sleeping youth he met earlier on the ship revealed minor scrapes and sun damage. "Hang on," William encouraged the man, although barely able to speak with his swollen tongue. "Help will arrive soon." Despite the words of encouragement, even the indomitable William fought despondency that threatened his own sanity.

As the young man drifted in and out of consciousness, William made certain his friend's grasp on their lifeline did not completely relax. He used the tags, pulled from the unfortunate soul headed toward the depths of an unforgiving sea, to tether his friend onto their makeshift raft. In a helpless rage, William was determined not to allow the ocean to claim another life.

Time dragged on as the men barely clung to life in a sea of death. After what seemed like an eternity, his friend spoke.

"Where are we?" he asked during a period of lucidity.

Barely able to speak, William spoke with an economy of words. "In Pacific. Japs blew up ship."

The man, barely conscious, had been blissfully unaware of the surrounding dangers. Although planes flew above the survivors during their ordeal, the widely dispersed seamen in small groups remained invisible because the distress signal had never been sent. The vast ocean made it impossible to see specks of humanity from the plane's height.

Over the next five days and four nights, survivors from the USS *Indianapolis* were catapulted into a hellish nightmare until they were accidentally discovered by a bomber pilot on August 2, 1945. The pilot radioed his base, and the USS *Cecil Doyle,* along with a seaplane piloted by Lt. R. Adrian Marks, responded to the distress call.

William and his four companions hung onto the shared debris until they were rescued the following day. He couldn't believe he had survived the grueling conditions of starvation, dehydration, and sunburn on top of already burnt skin, sharks, and utter desolation.

Among the survivors was the stranger that William had roused from sleep; however, another week would pass before the young man regained consciousness. Together they would later learn that, of the estimated 900 sailors who survived the explosion, a little more than 300 survived their perilous time in the water.

Both men were confined to the naval hospital for treatment of burns, severe dehydration, and festering wounds sustained during the attack. After William's ankle fracture was set and placed in a cast, he slowly began recuperating. The young man from the ship was placed in a bed next to William, and during the recovery process, the two survivors struck up an easy friendship.

"What happened?" the young man asked William when he was coherent.

Startled to discover details of their ordeal, he expressed gratitude to William for rescuing him. He also felt indebted to the young sailor whose dog tags saved his life.

"Do you know the man's identity so I can contact his family?"

"No, sorry. I was passed out when they took his tags, among hundreds, retrieved from the floating dead and delivered to the commanding officer for family notifications."

William reached for a pitcher of water, something he would never again take for granted, and asked the young man, "Where are you from?"

"Ohio," replied the young man.

"So am I! What's your name?"

"Name's Sheridan. Timothy Sheridan."

"My sister used to work as a nanny for a family on Millionaire's Row. Don't suppose you'd be a relation?"

"One and the same. Kinda funny we never met. Your sister was a godsend after our father was murdered. Don't know how our mother would have made it through that difficult time without her wonderful help."

"That's kind of you to say. We think she's pretty special, too. But, right now, there's only thing in the world I want—to return home."

"You said it, pal."

When sufficiently healed, both men were transferred to the nearest naval hospital stateside for additional treatment over the next two weeks. Survivors of the *Indianapolis* each received the Purple Heart for injuries sustained in battle; those killed in battle received posthumous medals.

SEVENTY

A LTHOUGH ALL ABLE-BODIED men over the age of eighteen were registered in the draft, deferments were granted to those with medical or psychological problems in addition to men who were the sole supporters of their families. Kurt and Stephen Mueller managed to avoid the draft when their physicals revealed congenital heart rhythm abnormalities. They remained in Cleveland but had dissociated from the German American Bund in early 1941 after discovering well-deserved contracts had been awarded to German-born members. Another factor was a deep resentment shared by both brothers when Eric Kaufmann was treated like a golden boy with preferential treatment. Despite Eric's vociferous pleas, Stephen and Kurt Mueller severed ties with the Bund and each went his separate way.

However, Eric, firmly entrenched in principles espoused by Nazi rhetoric, remained steadfastly loyal. Unfortunately, after December 7, 1941, the American War Department interned 25,000 members of the German American Bund in a labor camp for the war's duration. It would prove to be a humbling experience for Eric, no longer able to demand and strut, forced to wait in long lines for food and weekly showers. Mail call underscored his isolation as he received only two letters during his four-year stay, both from his cousin, written succinctly without preamble, to inform the demise of his mother followed by the death of his father six months later.

Time and distance from the Third Reich gave Eric insight into his past transgressions, especially the excessive hatred he directed at his parents. Instead of his solitary existence being a liberating experience, something he deeply wanted as a youth, it was a sad and lonely feeling for a twenty-five year old.

When released from the camp in September 1945, Eric's feeling of seclusion from the rest of the world left him disconnected as he attempted to adjust to his new reality. He recognized the civil treatment accorded those in the labor camp and assumed prisoners the world over received similar care. But newsreels about the Nazi death camps sickened him. For the first time, he was filled with shame at his blind obedience and allegiance to the crazed fanatics espousing drivel and inciting hatred. Eric became determined to atone for past mistakes.

With no home or real family, he vowed to put the Nazi ideology and intolerance behind him. Acknowledging the warped wisdom of conscripting young men, so malleable in the hands of propaganda masters, he finally understood the depth of brainwashing perpetrated upon him as a youth. In addition to the sheer genius of indoctrinating small children and filling their minds with the cancerous growth of prejudice fed by adult approval, their "accomplishments" were rewarded by meaningless medals. Eric knew this didn't absolve him of blame, but he became angry at being used like a puppet on a string.

Unfortunately, his newfound insight was short-lived as he set about the difficult task of finding a job. No one wanted to hire a German, especially one with the added stigma of residing in an American concentration camp. To ease the pain and dull his increasing panic, Eric turned to alcohol. All he needed was one drink to alleviate the heartache. And when that didn't work, surely a few more couldn't hurt. Without understanding or enlightenment, his inevitable decline left him without home or friends, begging in the streets for sustenance. Following a night of heavy drinking after finding a dollar floating in the gutter, he believed his luck was about to change.

Staggering out of the decrepit bar, Eric entered the street just as he saw a car seconds away. His last thought was the irony of being hit by a car, evoking memories of 1935.

He was dead before he hit the pavement. The long overdue debt of justice for the untimely demise of Benjamin and Rachel Leibowitz by a Hitler Youth had finally been satisfied.

SEVENTY-ONE

WITH THE END of the war, combatants returned home but faced a new challenge: acclimating to normalcy and attempting to reconcile their prior lives to the experiences that forever changed their perception of daily existence.

William returned home in mid-September 1945 to a joyous celebration of family and friends. Ellen couldn't believe how much William had changed. His gaunt frame with sunken eyes and reserved manner contrasted greatly to the young man who had left home three years prior.

Establishing a normal daily routine proved to be a difficult transition after the hell of battle and brutality he had witnessed. William rarely recounted his exploits, and his astute family waited patiently until he was able to share them. As William regained strength and put on weight, his sense of humor deflected the horrors he experienced.

James and Thomas were both upset they had missed all the action. Thomas wanted to jump out of planes, and James wanted to take them apart. William delighted in being around his brothers, but he firmly downplayed the glamour of battle. He stressed war was not a glorious undertaking but a grueling test of each man's fortitude and stamina as they faced the possibility of a painful death on a daily basis. When he told them, in detail, the problems he had faced aboard the *Indianapolis*, he put the allure of wartime conflict in its proper perspective as his brothers grasped the sobering details.

For several months after returning home, William awakened with frightening screams whenever he dared to close his eyes. He fought the rising panic induced by sleep, which transported him back to a time of abject terror akin to a living death. Once his mother discovered the horrific details of her son's ordeal, she provided comfort as only a mother could. Given time and space, William's nightmares began to subside as his spirit revived in the nurturing love from his family and comfort of being home.

EDWARD AND TIMOTHY Sheridan arrived home three weeks apart in the fall of 1945. It was good to hear them laugh when six-year-old Bridget asked if they brought her anything. Ecstatic that both sons returned home relatively unscathed, Marianne became concerned about their mental well-being. Although Edward and Timothy quickly returned to normal health, they seemed listless and lacked ambition. Fractured sleep, interrupted by moans and screams, augmented haunting memories of their shocking wartime experiences. Marianne suggested they visit wartime friends referenced in their postcards home.

Timothy never ceased to be amazed at his mother's wisdom. He paid an unexpected visit in October 1945 to his wartime buddy, William O'Malley. His brother, Edward, had heard so much about the young man who saved Timothy's life that he decided to tag along.

"Surprise, buddy!" Timothy exclaimed as William opened his front door. He heartily shook William's outstretched hand and introduced his brother as a fellow war hero.

"Wow. It's great to see you again." William, overcome with emotion and afraid to speak further lest they detect his tremulous voice, directed the brothers to sit on the front porch swing and brought out some beer. "How are you adjusting?" he asked with concern, well aware of his own problems.

Timothy responded first. "Not well. I can't stop the nightmares from returning and find myself thrust back in the ocean. But in my dreams, the sharks bite off pieces of me until I'm little more than a skeleton with no hope of rescue and forever doomed to relive agonizing moments. I can't talk about this to anyone else, and my friends are tiptoeing around me, not sure how to react."

"How 'bout you, Edward?"

Edward replied, "Days are long but nights are the worst. Can't seem to get certain images out of my head so I wake up screaming and entangled in the sheets." Edward spoke with an indisputable sadness and confusion at the air of alienation upon returning home.

The brothers discovered a mutual friend in William as they shared haunting tales with an understanding comrade. William told the brothers that helping his father, overloaded with post-war plumbing contracts, had turned out to be a great equalizer that slowly helped him adjust back into society.

"Maybe if you both return to the workforce, you can replace the bad thoughts with newer, happier memories. I know it's tough and takes time but, after a while, it'll become easier. And, you need to start dating."

Timothy laughed. "No problem in that department. I picked up where I left off with my fiancée, Sadie."

"You don't mean that skinny little girl who used to hang around our house with my sisters?"

Timothy nodded and smiled at William's recollection, thinking he should see the beauty she became.

"I haven't seen her since the swastika was painted on their home in the mid-1930s. It created a huge fuss and the entire neighborhood chipped in to help. I know she continued to see my sisters, but not me. I stayed away from girls at that age, except my sisters. Couldn't get away from them."

William smiled at his recollection and turned toward Edward. "Speaking of girlfriends, how about you?"

"Okay, so I don't have a girl. Any ideas?"

"Yes, I do. Come back Sunday, around noon, and join us for supper. There's someone I think you'd enjoy meeting."

"Great! We'll see you then."

SEVENTY-TWO

"VERONICA, YOU SHOULD wear something special for this Sunday's dinner," said William.

"Why?" she asked suspiciously.

"Because I'm having a few buddies over and want to show off my lovely sister."

"Anything for you, William. But your buddies better appreciate all my hard work."

"I have a feeling they will." He remained cryptic after that and refused to divulge any further information.

Edward and Timothy arrived promptly at noon in their dress whites. It was an impressive sight for two American heroes to wear uniforms that displayed bars of their heroic deeds following their discharge into civilian life.

Fran and Ellen arrived ten minutes later with James Francis in tow. "I'm sorry we're late but James was being fussy. I see we have guests—"

Recognizing Edward and Timothy, Ellen's complexion paled and she found it difficult to concentrate. But in the happiness of the moment, no one noticed. William made introductions to his parents, siblings, and their spouses.

He surreptitiously added, "Now, *this* is my sister Veronica."

He waited for Edward's jaw to drop when he gazed upon her. He was not disappointed.

Veronica, completely unaware of the underlying motive concerning their dinner guests, spoke animatedly throughout the meal. Edward was smitten with this adorable, petite woman. Captivated by her lovely peach dress with her dark hair decorated with flowers from the garden, she looked as refreshing as a cool breeze.

During the dinner, Ellen managed to overcome her anxiety and asked about Bridget. But Ellen's decreased attention span made it difficult to concentrate on their responses. Her thought processes felt sluggish as though her brain fought its way through a dense fog. Although her employment in the Sheridan household ended a mere two years ago, it seemed like a lifetime. Ellen's upset stomach prevented her from eating; however, she hid her unease well. Seeing the Sheridans was a reminder of a time filled with pain and turmoil. The brothers discussed an upcoming trip to Europe the following year as a welcome-home present from their mother. But, halfway through the meal, Ellen complained of a headache and left early with Frank and their baby. Edward didn't mind, not with the lovely Veronica to entertain him.

After dinner, William suggested Veronica and Edward should retire to the porch swing, and he would bring them each an ice cream cone.

Veronica immediately became suspicious of her brother's behavior until she sat on the swing alone with Edward.

As casual as possible Edward asked, "Veronica, would you like to see the movie *Caesar and Cleopatra?*"

"With you?" Somehow that didn't come out right. "I mean,

I'd love to." For the first time, she realized how handsome he looked in his dress whites, decorated with multi-colored bars and assorted medals. *Aha.* Veronica smiled at the realization of William's strange behavior.

"We could go this evening, if you're free."

"Let me grab my sweater." She raced into the house so fast, she almost bumped into William carrying two ice cream cones. "Sorry, William. You and Timothy will have to eat those. Edward and I are going to the movies." She gave him a big hug and planted a loud kiss on his cheek.

"What was that for?" William grinned and told them to have a wonderful time.

Veronica and Edward soon began seeing one another with a standard Saturday date night. He always brought her surprises—flowers, candy, phonograph records, and sentimental cards. Spending time with Veronica, Edward finally found peace and contentment that miraculously dispelled the nightmares of wartime experiences.

SEVENTY-THREE

WHEN ELLEN ARRIVED home from the family dinner, she fought back a severe bout of nausea.

"Ellen, honey, why don't you lie down?" Although Frank didn't know the source of his wife's discomfort, he assumed it was the stress of being a new mother.

"I will, Frank. I'm sorry we left early but I can feel the beginning of a migraine." After placing their son in his crib, Frank helped Ellen into bed and placed a cool cloth on her forehead before turning out the lights. "Thank you. I don't know what I'd do without you."

Ellen didn't know how much longer she could remain silent and feared she stood in the way of the Sheridan family receiving closure to Louis's premature demise.

Feeling as though her head would explode, Ellen stayed in the dark room until the migraine slowly receded. Lately, she experienced migraines with greater intensity and increased frequency; she assumed it was punishment for her past transgressions.

As a child, Ellen was taught her guardian angel was the spirit of a loved one who stood by her side to watch over and protect her. In the past, Ellen received assistance from her protector in the form of dreams or an inner voice that guided her in times of turmoil. However, this time her angel remained silent, and Ellen knew she'd have to find her own way out of this predicament as she prayed for strength. Life before the murder had been black and white. Any lie was wrong. Her conviction that the truth was irrevocable had been sorely tested. Ellen understood reality produced shades of truth molded by circumstances. In her case, choosing to protect others proved how malleable the truth could be.

As time passed and the Szabos socialized with the Sheridans while in the company of Ellen's siblings, her slight uneasiness in the presence of Edward, Timothy, and Bridget remained. Although she was bursting to reveal her secret involving their father's death and beg their forgiveness, she knew this wasn't an option. How would they react if they knew she could have prevented their father's death by providing police with the murderer's description during an almost deadly assault months before their father's demise?

Despite her ever-present companions of guilt and fear, she put a smile on her face, gave the impression all was right in her world, and hoped she was as good an actress as Mayme.

SEVENTY-FOUR

NOW THAT THE war was over and Timothy had returned home safely, Sadie tackled a daunting project very close to her heart. Despite war-torn Europe, she remained determined to find her long-lost twin, Gretl. Sadie wrote to the last known address for the Leibowitz and Goldstein families, but the letters were returned, unopened. She then obtained a phone number for a nearby family often referenced in Gretl's letters. Helen Davis gave Sadie the news that her sister's family disappeared one night in the back of a truck never to be seen again.

After she politely thanked Mrs. Davis for her time, Sadie slowly replaced the receiver, still in a daze, before crumbling onto the bed and weeping until there was nothing left. She was inconsolable when her dream of finding her sister was brutally crushed.

Timothy made federal inquiries but received the same results. Sadie slipped into a depression, lost weight, rarely smiled, never laughed, and refused to leave the house. Fearing for Sadie's sanity, Timothy asked his mother's permission for Sadie to accompany the family on their trip to Europe in 1946. Marianne readily agreed for her heart ached to see the lovely

Sadie so distraught.

In the meantime, Timothy continued to research the fate of Sadie's family. He hoped answers would assuage the burden of remorse Sadie wore like a heavy cloak. He understood Sadie's happiness would never be complete without finding the fate of her sister, and even then, her guilt at escaping the traumatic demise of so many Jews, possibly her own sister, by the Nazis continued to plague her. Timothy reached a friend in the American Liaison Department who was in the process of compiling a list of German concentration camps, extermination facilities, ghettos, and labor camps. Fortunately, the Germans were fastidious about generating lists to document their work on the Final Solution.

The Allies worked on completing an inventory of victims, supplied by the inspector of concentration camps. Although incomplete, the list provided a potential clue. Miles Leibowitz had survived the concentration camp. Sadie's cousin, and Gretl's adopted brother, may be able to provide Sadie with the answers she desperately sought. After many long-distance calls and frustrated hours of investigation, Timothy located Miles in a hospital near Berlin. Intermittent phone service resulted in weeks of aggravation until he reached Miles to confirm Gretl was his cousin and adopted sister.

The years had not been kind to Miles as he watched family and friends overworked in the camps, wearing away until death mercifully took them home. But the story he relayed to Timothy about Gretl being kidnapped in 1935 was agonizing as Miles recalled his failure to protect the petite little cousin he loved for her sweet and gentle ways. Timothy told Miles that the Sheridans, including Sadie, planned a trip to Europe in about six months and would stop in to see him. Miles cried at the thought of seeing his long-lost cousin.

After Timothy hung up, he reeled from the news. Perhaps hope still existed, but he pondered about his next step. He decided to share the news with Sadie, knowing full-well the possibility of her hopes being dashed once again might propel her further into darkness. But her radiant smile when he recounted Miles's story was worth the risk. Now all they had to do was track down Gretl.

SEVENTY-FIVE

O N JUNE 15, 1946, St. Patrick's Church witnessed an unusual event. The double wedding of Edward Sheridan to Veronica O'Malley and Timothy Sheridan to Sadie Leibowitz filled the church to maximum capacity with family and friends. At Sadie's request, Rabbi Budin concelebrated the joyous occasion with Father Kenny. No one wanted to miss the Catholic-Jewish ceremony for each group received a glimpse of religious ceremonies and rituals previously shrouded in mysticism.

Edward and Timothy escorted Marianne down the aisle before they resumed their places beside the groomsmen. Bridget Sheridan, now seven years old and ecstatic at being the flower girl, was thrilled to play dress-up in a floor-length lemon yellow dress and a matching taffeta bow in her curls, gathered at the nape of her neck. However, someone forgot to explain that her job entailed gently scattering rose petals onto the white aisle runner. Instead, she tossed the petals high into the air with careless abandon as she aimed for the vaulted ceiling. Tickled at being the center of attention and responding to the laughter, she giggled throughout her walk down the aisle and considered a repeat performance until her mother grabbed her and gave her *the look.*

The entire congregation stood in awe with murmurs of appreciation as Veronica and Sadie were escorted side-by-side down the aisle with Veronica's father and Sadie's uncle. The brides wore matching white silk dresses, embroidered with flowers, layered in beaded lace, and twenty-foot trains sprinkled with rose petals. The brides exchanged glances of delight and ecstasy on their radiant faces.

Following the weddings, a luncheon at The Cleveland Room, known for its majestic high arched windows that overlooked the hotel, provided the guests with delicious food, followed by dancing and drinking into the night. However, by 5:00 p.m., the newlyweds snuck away to their respective suites for their own private celebrations.

Their new lives would begin with a honeymoon trip the following week to Europe, initially planned as a welcome home present from Marianne after her sons returned from the war. Veronica and Sadie, both overjoyed about the upcoming trip to Europe, experienced far different emotions. Veronica reveled in the awe and excitement of traveling outside the United States; however, Sadie worried about visiting her homeland destroyed by war and concerned the search for her sister would prove to be another disappointment.

SEVENTY-SIX

SADIE SHERIDAN KNEW this was *the* day as she excitedly jumped out of bed, shaking Timothy awake. Despite being nervous about her first trip on an airplane, she believed their flight would be comfortable and enjoyable in first-class seats on the Pan American flight to Germany with her new brother- and sister-in-law. They agreed the first two days of their trip would be spent sightseeing Germany, or the ruins left behind, to give Sadie the opportunity to see her cousin and perhaps, learn the whereabouts of Gretl. From there, the group would travel by rail to Denmark, followed by a ship to Norway for the remainder of their honeymoon.

Once the plane left the ground, Sadie squeezed her husband's hand so hard it turned purple. "Hey, it's a good thing you're not nervous," said Timothy as he held up his discolored hand.

"Oh, sorry. I guess I am a little worried. Do you think we'll find her?"

Timothy knew Sadie's fragile optimism might end in disappointment but attempted to allay her fears. "We'll certainly give it our best try. But, no matter what you find out, I'll always be here for you."

Sadie kissed Timothy's hand before releasing it. As she looked out the small window of the plane, Sadie was grateful Timothy couldn't see her face filled with anxious hope. She resigned herself to the unspoken truth that her wish would probably remain an unfulfilled fantasy.

WHEN THEY ARRIVED in Berlin and settled into their hotel, Sadie asked about the hospital where Timothy had reached Miles several months earlier. The manager informed them it was two miles away and called for a taxi. Accompanied by Timothy for moral support, Sadie went to visit her cousin. When they arrived at the hospital, they spoke to Miles's physician.

"It's a good thing you arrived when you did. Miles's health is rapidly deteriorating and I believe he only lasted this long to see his lovely cousin." As she listened to the doctor, Sadie assumed he must be mistaken. After all, robust and rebellious Miles could not be dying at twenty-seven-years old.

When they reached Miles's bedside, Sadie reflexively turned away. His skeletal frame, an improbable 80 pounds covered with translucent skin, hung on his slender body like an ill-fitting suit. He was totally bald, his eyes bulged from a gaunt face, and his few remaining teeth were deeply discolored. Fighting the urge to gasp in horror, Sadie gently approached her cousin's bedside. When she softly touched her cousin's shoulder, Sadie saw a sparkle in his eyes that she remembered from her youth.

"I've been waiting for you." Miles grabbed Sadie's hand and kissed it as his body shook with the effort. After introducing her husband, Sadie recounted the Leibowitz's migration to America, events leading up to their visit, and Sadie's search for her missing sister.

"Timothy told me your brief story about Gretl being abducted in 1935. Can you recall any other details? Perhaps the name of the couple who kidnapped her?"

Miles slowly and with great effort gathered his strength before responding. "Once my father discovered being Jewish in the New Germany would bring nothing but heartache, we attended local Protestant services. After a few months, we met Harry and Hilda Alsentzer. They often remarked on Gretl's resemblance to Hilda and seemed to pay special attention to her. One Sunday, while clearing away food after a church picnic, Hilda asked Gretl to help her carry some items to their car. They quickly shut the door and drove away. We never saw Gretl after that. I remember the auto had flags on the hood that fluttered in the wind with colorful patches surrounding a cross in the center.

"Not long after, my family made inquiries about Gretl's whereabouts, a group of Nazi soldiers arrested my family. They called us subversives who spoke against the Nazi regime. I always thought the timing of our arrest and our search for Gretl were connected to conceal their actions. But, of course, I had no proof. I assumed the Alsentzers must have been Nazis or secured help from highly placed friends in the Party to facilitate our arrest. Unfortunately, the rest of my family didn't survive life in the camp, so perhaps Gretl *was* the lucky one." Miles closed his eyes from the exertion of the longest speech he'd made in more than a decade. He sobbed quietly but no tears spilled forth from his severely emaciated body.

The painful memories enveloped Miles, and he coughed with an intensity that severely shook his slender frame. The doctor intervened and said the visit needed to end and Miles must rest. Sadie gave her cousin a hug and promised to visit the next day before they departed for Denmark. However, when she arrived back at the hospital the next morning, Sadie was informed Miles had passed away during the night. When the staff told her that he died with a smile on his face, a remarkable tribute after seeing his beloved cousin one last time and knowing he was not alone, Sadie broke down.

The Sheridans remained in Germany two extra days as Sadie organized a small prayer service with her new family before her cousin's cremation. Standing next to the ruins of the Goldstein's childhood home, Sadie said a small prayer for her cousin and parents. She was grateful to the Goldsteins for taking in Gretl after the death of her parents and silently hoped her sister was still alive. Sadie then scattered the ashes in the last place where Miles roamed free to dream and hope. She closed her eyes and could hear Miles's laughter as he joined his family in a place where they would never again know fear or pain.

SEVENTY-SEVEN

MILES'S ACCOUNT GAVE Sadie hope. On the day of their scheduled departure from Germany, Sadie asked for the morning alone. The Sheridans readily agreed, understanding she needed time to grieve. Feeling guilty that she kept her destination a secret from Timothy and her new family, Sadie made other plans, fearful voicing her intentions would yield another disappointment.

From childhood trips to see the Goldsteins in Berlin, Sadie remembered the building's location that might provide much-needed answers. It was one of the few structures that remained unscathed by war, although the surrounding area had been marked by devastation. As she walked along roads reduced to rubble and decimated homes, she saw the result of bombs that rained down fury and destruction.

Entering the building, Sadie asked the woman at the front desk. "Can you please help me find something?"

"Certainly. It's rare today that anyone comes in at all. How may I help?"

Sadie described the information she needed, and the woman brought her into a large room that housed books, journals, and newspapers from around the world, a plethora of knowledge.

The kind woman closed the door behind her, leaving Sadie to look through the materials in solitude.

For the first time since finding Miles, Sadie's heart raced as she located the item she sought. She pulled a piece of paper and a pen from her purse to copy the data for future use. Sadie felt one step closer to discovering what had happened to her beloved sister.

SADIE RETURNED TO the hotel in time to pack for the next leg of their journey—railway to Denmark and, from there, a ferry to Norway.

"Are you all right, my love?" asked Timothy, concern and love etched on his face.

"Yes, my dear. I needed time to myself," Sadie replied, feeling guilty for her white lie. After all Timothy had done to assist in locating her twin, Sadie wanted to present him with what she hoped would be a happy ending. "But I do have a request, provided everyone agrees. After we visit Norway, can we take a train ride over to Sweden? I understand the scenery is breathtaking and may help dispel the tragic memories of Miles."

"I'm sure no one will have a problem and the change will be refreshing," Timothy said, eager to please his beloved Sadie. After they boarded the train to Denmark, everyone agreed wholeheartedly to Sadie's recommendation. After spending three days in Denmark visiting quaint sightseeing locales and breathtaking views, they boarded the ship to Norway.

Their trip through Norway's beautiful wilderness and charming seaside towns had a calming effect on the Sheridans. They stayed at the historic Dalen Hotel with its magnificent façade that catered to its guests like visiting royalty.

Reading from a brochure, Veronica commented, "Says here the hotel was built in 1894 with gables, galleries, towers, and turrets suggestive of a fairy-tale palace. I'd have to agree with that one. Oh, and each night, they light a fire in the hall while Mozart piano concertos are played as guests relax on the Chesterfield. Hmm, wonder what that is?"

"My dear, that's a large sofa with overstuffed arms for ultimate relaxation."

"Edward, how do you know that?"

"Some of us like to read," he replied with twinkling eyes as he dodged a playful swipe from his new bride.

"Sadie, look at the beauty surrounding us. From the mountains to the canals filled with gondolas," Timothy said as he held Sadie in his arms. "It's so peaceful, my love."

Despite her apprehension, Sadie was overcome with the splendor that encompassed her like a gentle breeze to soothe the soul. Sadie knew that soon she'd have answers to her long-awaited quest. Now she quietly prayed for the strength to accept the outcome of her pursuit, hoping for a reunion with her dear Gretl.

SEVENTY-EIGHT

WHEN THE SHERIDANS arrived in Sweden, they were enthralled by the sheer majesty of the mountains and picturesque villages. Each destination of their trip rivaled the one before with the splendors of nature and sites that captured their imagination. Although Sadie remained quiet, she did her best to participate in sightseeing and didn't want to burden the family with her apprehension.

They stayed at the countryside hotel Villa Gransholm, which was located in a national park surrounded by a lake and mountains. It became the perfect place to end their journey.

"Sadie, how in the world did you ever find this wonderful hotel?" asked Edward, inspired by the scenic atmosphere.

"You're not the only one who can read, buster."

Laughing, they checked into the hotel and booked several days of whirlwind tours involving Sweden's countryside and long walks along cobbled roads.

On their third day, Sadie could no longer stand the suspense. "I understand there's a beautiful estate not far from here. It would mean a lot to me if we could stop by. They say it's truly splendid."

"Sadie, I do believe you have another reason for this detour, but I'm game," said Timothy. "How about everyone else?"

They nodded their heads in agreement and called for a car. When it arrived, Sadie pulled the piece of paper from her purse and handed it to the driver.

They arrived at a beautiful mansion reminiscent of another fairy-tale castle. It seemed Europe had a resplendent supply of grandiose palaces. But Sadie riveted her gaze on the limousine parked in the circular driveway as she watched the magnetic flags on the hood flickering in the slight breeze. She felt a shiver run through her, as though Miles stood beside her with his description of the car that carried his sister away into the unknown. Words echoed in an endless loop as she stared in wonderment at the physical embodiment of his remarks.

After paying the driver, Sadie leaped out of the car and rang the bell before anyone else exited the vehicle. A butler answered the door and Sadie asked to see the owner while her remaining party exchanged bewildered looks.

"Yes, madam. May I say who is calling?"

"Sadie Leibowitz Sheridan."

"Very good, madam. Please wait here." Sadie was ready to jump out of her skin as they stood in the expansive vestibule. Fearful she might be wrong and wasted everyone's time in the process, she could feel her hands shaking until she heard footsteps running down the grand staircase. Sadie turned and came face-to-face with herself.

"Sadie! Oh my God, is it really you?" Gretl was overcome with emotion, crying and hugging her sister as they had so many years ago when circumstances forced their separation. Engrossed in their happy reunion, it took a moment for Gretl to notice a party of three people standing beside Sadie. "Let's go sit in the parlor where we can have something from the bar. I rarely drink, but this occasion calls for a toast."

Gretl was dressed in expensive clothes and wore her long blond hair in a fashionable updo, but the resemblance was uncanny. Flutes of champagne filled to the brim were shared by all as the sisters sat next to one another, holding hands.

"I thought I'd never see you again!" they both echoed simultaneously.

Beaming with pride and happiness, Sadie proclaimed, "This is my sister, Gretl." Realizing she stated the obvious, but not caring, the Sheridans crowded around Gretl to kiss her and welcome the newest member to their family. For Timothy, the happy reunion was sweeter for Sadie's brilliant smile had returned.

"Sadie, how in the world did you find me?"

Turning to the Sheridans, she made a quick apology. "I'm so sorry to keep you in the dark. Remember that morning in Germany when I wanted time to myself?"

Everyone nodded and Sadie continued. "After all the background work that Timothy did, it was important for me to pick up where he left off to find my sister on my own. So I went to the local library, the same one we used to attend as children when we visited our cousins. Miraculously, the building was intact and the librarian most helpful. Based on Miles's description of the diplomatic flag on the car that kidnapped Gretl, I was able to determine its country of origin. I then checked residences in Sweden with a surname of Alsentzer and copied this address in anticipation of finding Gretl. I hope you can forgive my secret, but I didn't want to burden everyone with another distressing event on our honeymoon."

Timothy knelt before his lovely Sadie and held her hands within his own while gazing into her eyes, "Your pain would be ours, Sadie. You no longer have to shoulder disappointments by yourself. You need to always remember that we're family and sharing the good along with the bad is a package deal."

Sadie nodded as tears spilled onto her lap, and she hugged Timothy, grateful for his love and support.

Once the excitement subsided, Gretl pulled a worn photograph from a nearby desk. "I've kept this picture all these years, waiting for this moment."

The picture, taken shortly before their parents died, revealed two lovely young girls with their arms around each other wearing silly grins.

"I thought this would be the last picture we took; although I treasured it, I had to keep it hidden from the Alsentzers. They told me that my adoptive family, the Goldsteins, died in Germany at the hands of the Nazis. I didn't want to believe them, but the stories of Nazi atrocities that my aunt and uncle discussed when they thought I wasn't listening supported their tale."

"What happened to you, Gretl? I just saw Miles Leibowitz and he told a strange tale of your abduction."

"That is a memory to be shared on another day. Right now I want to bask in the ecstasy of being reunited with my beautiful sister and her family. For years, I faced the possibility that you were dead."

"Oh, Sadie, I feared the same thing about you. And yet, here we are. It truly is a miracle!" Sadie and Gretl raised their glasses as everyone joined them in another toast

Sadie told Gretl about her family's relocation to America,

their own brush with intolerance, her marriage to Timothy, and the fate of the Goldsteins with the recent demise of Miles.

At the mention of Miles's name, Gretl begged her sister to relay everything she saw and heard.

"Dear Gretl, Miles was nothing more than a skeleton lying in bed. He miraculously survived the camps, unlike the rest of his family. Miles believed your abduction was related to the Goldsteins being sent to the camps shortly after they began to investigate your whereabouts. But without proof, I'm sure it was nothing more than a coincidence. I—" Sadie stopped when Gretl cried out in anguish.

"If it weren't for me, they wouldn't have begun an aggressive search after I was kidnapped and perhaps they would still be alive." Gretl's small voice filled with shame and sadness.

"But Gretl, you could not have done anything. You were a mere child. You are *not* responsible. In all likelihood, the Alsentzers saved your life because the remaining Jewish families in your town expired in the camps except for Miles. He never blamed you and knew you were innocent. In fact, I believe he endured years of hardship and pain to make certain we reunited. Earlier, I reeled from his death and gave up all hope of finding you. But he provided two clues: an accurate description of the diplomatic flags on your foster father's car and the name of the family who abducted you. Without his help, I never would have found you. Now, come here and give your *older* sister a hug."

Throughout the remainder of their luncheon, the sisters held hands, afraid to relinquish the tenuous hold of their newfound reunion.

"Where are the Alsentzers now, Gretl?"

"They died during the war while attending a diplomatic function. A bomb annihilated the building and no one survived. After the war, I made inquiries about families with the surname Leibowitz but came up with the same results. Everyone died in the camps."

Despite Gretl's sobering statement about the fate of so many Jews during the war, the Sheridans felt honored to partake in the emotional, but glorious, afternoon. Gretl made arrangements for lunch the following day before they continued their European honeymoon.

When they met at the restaurant, Gretl had a surprise for them.

"Waiter, if you could please bring your best bottle of champagne."

The Sheridans exchanged curious looks at the extravagant gesture. "I'd like to celebrate a decision I made last night."

When the champagne glasses were raised in a toast, Gretl told them of her plans. "I contacted an estate firm in Switzerland and they agreed to sell the Alsentzer property, including any furniture or items I elect to leave behind in anticipation of moving to America."

Everyone cheered and hugged Gretl at the joyous news.

Sadie took her sister's arm and led them to a private corner of the restaurant. "Pinch me."

Gretl did as she was told.

"Ouch. Well, at least I'm not dreaming. Do you know how hard I prayed for this moment? Finding you alive and knowing we will once again share our lives together is the best possible gift."

"I know exactly what you mean," said Gretl. "My heart is so

full it feels like it will burst." Placing her hands on a face she knew so well, Gretl said, "My darling sister, my other half. I finally feel whole."

The sisters hugged, overcome with pure elation and happiness. After several minutes, they joined the others to continue the celebration.

Sadie offered to stay on and help, but Gretl knew that disposing of the Alsentzer estate was something she needed to do alone. In spite of saving her life and providing her with every possible luxury, Gretl would never forgive them for the murder of her adoptive family. It was a pain that resonated throughout her time in Sweden and Gretl knew closing out their estate would be a painful, but necessary, process.

SEVENTY-NINE

WITHIN THREE MONTHS, Gretl settled the estate, packed most of her belongings, and booked passage to America.

"Sadie, is that you?" Gretl grasped the phone and held it close to her ear. With the poor connection, she faintly heard a voice she knew as well as her own.

"Yes, dear, how are you doing?" Sadie shouted into the receiver willing the long-distance call to be clear and precise.

"I've booked my trip to America and will arrive next month. I'm afraid to fly and decided to travel by boat."

"That's wonderful! I can't believe we'll be together after all this time. Send us a cable when you know your exact arrival time, and we'll meet you at the dock."

"Oh Sadie, I can't wait to see you. I'll be counting the hours."

"Me, too, sweetie. I love you, sis."

Gretl stifled a small sob as she ended the tenuous connection with Sadie.

AS THE WEEKS passed quickly, Sadie prepared their spare rooms for Gretl to use until she purchased a home of her own. Although the short time felt like an eternity, the big day finally arrived.

"Oh, Timothy, hurry. We don't want to miss her." Sadie stopped and smiled as she recalled a saying her mother often used: *You're as nervous as a long-tailed cat in a room full of rockers.*

"My love, we have hours before your sister arrives. But I'll hurry in case her ship docks early." Timothy looked at his wife and marveled at the beautiful woman standing before him. Sadie looked positively radiant as she glowed with anticipation at being reunited with her twin sister.

They drove to the dock and discovered they had two hours before the ship arrived. To fill the time, they looked for a restaurant and ate a leisurely lunch. Finally, the moment arrived and Gretl stepped onto the gangway. Sadie's heart raced as she and Timothy shouted out greetings, unaware of the curious stares from others.

Longing to embrace her sister, Sadie wanted to vault over anyone in her path but forced herself to wait in line.

When Gretl crossed the barrier and ran into her sister's arms, they screamed with delight. Gretl hugged Timothy and thanked him for meeting her.

"Don't be silly. Remember, we're family now and wouldn't miss it for the world. But I arranged for someone to help unload your baggage." He caught sight of William and motioned for him to join their party. "Gretl, I'd like you to meet a good friend of mine, William O'Malley."

"William, it's a pleasure to meet you. Any friend of Timothy and Sadie is a friend of mine." She daintily placed her hand out for William to shake but he was too busy admiring her beauty. She looked so much like Sadie, his sister-in-law. After an awkward minute, Timothy tapped him on the shoulder and startled William.

He kissed Gretl's hand as she blushed furiously and William, in an unusual, high-pitched voice, managed to say "The pleasure is all mine."

The rest of the afternoon was spent loading and unloading Gretl's voluminous trunks and suitcases.

As the weeks passed, William stopped in frequently to see his good friend, Timothy. Gradually, William worked up the courage to ask Gretl on a real date. But his plans, hours in the making, didn't work out quite as he expected.

After arranging large trunks and moving heavy furniture on a particularly hot day, William worked up a decent sweat and sat down in the kitchen with a cool glass of lemonade to catch his breath. Gretl walked into the room.

"William," Gretl said with concern, "are you all right?"

Shyness took over and William sat as still as a statue, fearful he would forever lack the courage to ask her on a date. He did the only thing his petrified body would allow. He nodded.

"William, there's a wonderful new show, *Hamlet*, playing this weekend at The Hanna Theater. I wondered if you'd like to attend as my guest. It would be my way of thanking you for all your help."

Surely he must have misunderstood. *She* was asking him out?

"Um, I think that would be fine."

"Wonderful. Why don't you pick me up at eleven and we'll catch an early lunch before the matinee."

"Sure thing," William said, inwardly appalled at his

inarticulate and inane response.

William couldn't wait for Sunday to arrive and managed to occupy his time helping his father at O'Malley Plumbing. With sweat pouring down his face and exhausted from work, William was able to keep his thoughts of the upcoming date in the back of his mind. Nighttime was another matter as he tossed and turned, equally anxious and excited at the potential prospect of spending time with Gretl.

"What's wrong with William? Sure hope I don't get whatever he has. He's acting so goofy," Thomas said to James.

James smiled at his younger brother. "One day, you'll understand."

EIGHTY

ARLIER IN THE week, Gretl spoke to her sister and expressed apprehension about her invitation to William. "What if he thinks this is a date? I'm not ready to become involved with anyone yet. I just moved here and don't even know how I feel about William. I wanted to do something nice to thank him for all the hard work."

"I think you'll find William is a wonderful friend and that's the best way to start any relationship. Take it one step at a time. You'll know when you are ready. Trust your older sister."

Despite being apart for years, Sadie still knew the right thing to say. Gretl decided to enjoy the day and whatever it brought.

The big day arrived and William dressed in his Sunday best. He stepped into his car that shown like a newly minted coin. As he drove closer to Sadie's home to pick up Gretl, his palms began to sweat and he panicked. Somehow, the car continued to drive on autopilot and in the passage of what seemed like a few minutes, he pulled into the driveway.

When Gretl answered the door, the heady scent of perfume greeted him as he gaped open-mouthed at the vision before him. Gretl's golden locks, intricately braided down her back, were offset by a bonnet that matched her knee-length dark blue dress with a starched white collar. Gretl beamed at William's reaction, and he gallantly offered his arm while escorting her to the car.

"Sadie, get away from the window before they see you," Timothy said. But, as she backed away, Sadie bumped into Timothy looking over her shoulder.

Once he got over his shyness, William had a unique talent for putting others at ease. Gretl enjoyed his company and delightful sense of humor. When they said good-bye, Gretl discovered time spent with William soothed her mind and provided peace, something missing from her life for years.

"So, did you two have a good time?" Sadie asked in what she hoped was a casual manner.

"Oh, William is wonderful. The time passed quickly and I laughed so much my side aches. The play was wonderful and the food a disaster. But somehow, it didn't matter." Gretl, aware of her nonstop chatter, was unable to stop her ramblings.

Her sister understood and gave her a big hug.

William made it a point of stopping in to see Gretl every few days after calling first. They soon became an item and whenever William was seen about town, Gretl was with him. Life became a grand adventure during their easy courtship.

To the delight of everyone, they became engaged. Together they pooled their resources and purchased lakefront property with a private beach on the shores of Lake Erie where they planned to host many family functions. Gretl furnished their new home with quaint knickknacks and comfortable furniture prior to their marriage in 1949. Two years later, with the birth of their wonderful son Michael, William's war experiences were forever put to rest as he concentrated on the bliss of family life.

EIGHTY-ONE

SADIE KNEW HER sister Gretl preferred to lock away painful memories. Therefore, Sadie waited until Gretl's world was filled with peace and happiness before she produced her childhood diary.

"Since we couldn't be together, I religiously updated my diary sharing everyday events. It also made me feel as though you were right beside me."

Touched, Gretl read the entries as laughter mingled with tears. "I hoped, in turn, you could relay the facts of your life with Uncle Asher, Aunt Elsa, Miles, and Aaron."

Sadie learned that, at the same time she underwent the rigors of moving to a new country, Gretl's life in Germany with the Goldsteins had been filled with kindness and love.

"When I first arrived at their home, I tried to make myself as small as possible—anything to avoid being a burden. But, despite poverty with the added weight of having an extra mouth to feed, they always made me feel special. Miles and Aaron grew very protective and included me in their activities. We spent many wonderful hours playing tag and roaming free in the nearby forest. I loved them all for the sacrifices made on my behalf and the affection lavished on me.

"Uncle Asher called me Liebchen, just like Grandfather used to. Although his voice boomed, he managed to speak softly in my presence. He delighted in seeing the bond I developed with his sons, and I gradually emerged from my shell. Each morning, Aunt Elsa braided my hair with colorful ribbons. She whispered, when no one else was around, that she had always wanted a daughter and made me promise not to share her secret. I always did—until now."

The memory of her kind and noble family who gave their lives to protect Gretl released a flow of unshed tears. After several minutes, Gretl continued her story.

"The Alsentzers were rich and powerful. Mr. Alsentzer was a diplomat and frequently traveled, leaving his wife, Hilda, alone much of the time. She could not have any children and I always got the feeling she paid too much attention to me, as if *she* longed to be my mother. One Sunday, Mrs. Alsentzer asked my help loading their car after a church picnic. When I hesitated, she assured me that Aunt Elsa gave her permission. But when I got closer to their car and turned around, I couldn't see my family. When I tried to back away, they grabbed me and firmly placed me in the backseat. They warned me to be quiet or they'd hurt my family. So I stifled my sobs and spent my first night crying myself to sleep.

"After they kidnapped me, the Alsentzers sold their home near Berlin and moved into the most beautiful estate I had ever seen. I convinced myself I would soon be returned to my real family. Excited about living in a palace, I pretended I was on holiday and tried to put a smile on my face. I never forgot about the family I left behind, but I told myself it was only temporarily. Soon they'd return me home. I was so naïve."

Gretl cried at the memory, and her sister remained silent as she regained composure.

"The Alsentzers lavished me with love and everything a little girl desired. They even provided a tutor for homeschooling and further English lessons. However, they did not permit any mention of the Goldsteins, except to remind me that the Goldsteins couldn't afford to keep me and wanted to get rid of me.

"In my heart, I knew they lied and thought they might take pity on me if I became an obedient daughter. Perhaps they would even bring me back home. Unfortunately, while I perfected my image as the ideal daughter, I overheard them say my behavior clearly proved I was the child they were meant to have. Despite the deception and unhappiness they caused my real family, they treated me with love and respect.

"I didn't know why the Alsentzers wouldn't return me to my parents, but I vowed to discover the truth. I thought it would bring me some measure of peace. I couldn't have been more wrong."

Gretl excused herself for a few minutes and came back with a piece of paper.

"I overheard suspicious discussions in the Alsentzer home. The first involved a phone call from Herr Richter. After he hung up, my 'father' called to his wife, Hilda, and relayed the conversation. He mentioned a couple traveled from town to town showing a picture of a little lost girl, asking if anyone had seen her. He then laughed and said their efforts were thwarted by Pro-Nazi constables. The second conversation, I overheard at a dinner party held at the Alsentzers. Herr Richter proposed a final solution to the problem. The phrase meant nothing to me but my 'parents' were satisfied they could finally relax. They hugged one another, relief evident on their faces.

"I knew Aunt and Uncle would continue searching for me until I returned home. When this didn't happen, I became suspicious and decided to find the answer for myself. I selected a day when my 'parents' were out of town and I was in the care of servants. With my heart pounding, I sneaked into the study and searched through a stack of opened mail ready to be filed away. I gasped out loud when I found correspondence from Herr Richter that confirmed my worst fears."

Gretl handed Sadie a well-worn letter, stained with tears of long ago as Sadie quietly read its dire content.

Dear Herr Alsentzer,

At your request, I've detailed the Goldstein final solution, hopefully to your satisfaction.

As you know, the Goldsteins walked to nearby villages with photos of Gretl and descriptions of you and Hilda. When it became obvious they would not stop their search, we implemented our final solution. The next week, soldiers entered the Goldstein home. They heard a woman's voice as she said, "Wake up, Asher! I hear something downstairs." When her husband went to investigate, we shot him. His wife and two children ran into the kitchen unaware of the danger awaiting them. The sight of the pitiful Jew lying on the floor, surrounded by his family, was so comical the soldiers burst out laughing. The family huddled together with no idea of their fate.

"But my father served Germany with distinction in the First World War, why are you doing this?" asked the woman. Stupid useless people didn't understand. The soldiers searched the house for food and drink as payment for a good night's work.

Everything went according to schedule until the older son—I believe they called him Miles—attempted an act of bravery as he told us to leave his father alone. "Oh, so we have a fearless Jew in our midst, have we? Guess we'll have to see how brave he is at the camps."

The soldiers laughed and pistol-whipped the boy before dragging him and his family outside to the truck. Of course, none of the neighbors attempted to help—worthless swine—and we took the family to Auschwitz. I can safely guarantee no one will ever see them again. Now that inquiries have stopped, your secret is safe.

Your friend,
Franz

"After I read the damning letter, I stuffed it into my pocket hoping one day to share it with you. Although my 'father' asked me if I'd seen a letter from Herr Richter, I shook my head and he never mentioned it again. In the bustle of relocating to America and starting my own family, I forgot about sharing this with you."

KNOWING GRETL FELT responsible for the Goldsteins' demise, an unexpected catharsis of her soul occurred when she shared the letter with Sadie.

"Gretl, my beautiful sister. You, alone, have carried the weight of this burden long enough. As a young girl, you were powerless to change their fate. By now you've seen footage of the German concentration camps and persecution of the Jews in Europe by Nazi fanatics. Entire families were led to slaughter, and there's nothing you could have done to protect the Goldsteins. Once the Nazis began their Final Solution, they were doomed. Now that we both know what happened to them, we can remember them together in our hearts. Remember what Mama used to say: 'A burden shared is half the burden, while a joy shared is twice the joy.' The greatest respect we can pay them is to revel in the beauty that life has provided and through them, continue their legacy."

Together they walked out to Gretl's back porch swing and sat, holding hands, for the rest of the afternoon as they watched the sun slowly dip into the shoreline in a blaze of color.

PART FOUR

Proof from Beyond the Grave

(1978-1986)

EIGHTY-TWO

August 1982
Cleveland, Ohio

ALTHOUGH THEIR PARENTS died over thirty years ago, each of their children paid homage to Michael and Mary by instilling values they learned into their own children.

But, despite their closeness, Ellen kept her innermost secret hidden from everyone—a pain that burdened her soul and isolated her closest confidants from providing advice.

Time passed quickly as Frank continued his successful career as a Cleveland police detective while Ellen remained at home to raise their four children. But the Sheridan secret and fate of young Patrick continued to plague her.

ST. IGNATIUS HIGH School in Cleveland was in the midst of constructing a new theater complex, and crews worked long hours to complete the project before winter. As a backhoe excavated a large mound of earth, someone called out to stop and alerted the foreman to the possible discovery of human bones. The foreman called the Cuyahoga County Coroner's office, in addition to the Cleveland Police Department, and work at the construction site ceased until the remains could be exhumed without further disturbance.

Based on the coroner's estimation, the bones belonged to a one-year-old boy. The CPD searched missing person reports for the former residential neighborhood on Carroll Avenue. The only report matching the parameters belonged to Patrick O'Malley. They asked Frank to accompany them as they delivered the sad news to his wife.

In a bittersweet moment, Ellen cried at the ill-fated turn of events suffered by her tiny brother but thanked God Patrick could finally be placed at rest with his family. Alone with her thoughts once the police left, she realized the size of her family and innate happiness presented a direct challenge to the gods of fate. They determined the family's consummate joy was a defiance of life's natural order and sought retribution to rectify the balance. Ellen knew the heartache her parents suffered and the torture they carried to their graves wondering what became of their beloved baby boy. But why Patrick? If Ellen only knew what happened . . .

THE STORY OF Patrick's abduction in 1922 and recent discovery of his remains made front-page news but, other than the O'Malley family, no one would be affected like Anna Schneider. Always punctual until a power outage threatened to make her late for work, Anna barely made it to the corner before her morning bus arrived. Armed with coffee and her newspaper, Anna settled into her seat and arranged her belongings. She sighed with deep contentment as she took her first sip of coffee, an elixir of the gods.

Settling into her morning routine, she scanned the newspaper headlines and started to turn the page when a familiar reference caught her eye. Reading further, she almost dropped her precious coffee as the impact of the story hit home. Anna tore the article from the newspaper and pocketed it before pulling the cord to signify an unscheduled stop. Anna ran to the door oblivious to the passengers' curious stares, raced down the steps and didn't stop running until she reached home. Surely it can't be . . . but that *would* explain the strange story she heard as a young child.

As she entered the front door, Anna dropped her things onto the nearest chair and dashed upstairs to check the contents of a box she had inherited when her mother died fifteen years ago. Finding the box just as she remembered it, Anna sat back on her heels. Her worst fear had been confirmed. But what should she do? Anna sat on the bed, considered her options, rechecked the article, and picked up the phone.

"Cleveland Police, Second District. Sergeant White speaking."

"Well . . ." Words momentarily failed her. "May I please talk to Detective Hanigan?"

"What's this about?"

"The newspaper article about the infant . . . I mean the bones they found." Anna couldn't prevent her voice from shaking and knew she sounded like a lunatic.

"Okay. Please hold."

After what seemed an interminable time, a kindly voice spoke. "Detective Hanigan. I understand you have some information about the O'Malley kidnapping."

At the mention of kidnapping, Anna almost severed the connection. Steeling herself with courage, she cleared her throat and said, "I'm sorry. I've never done this before and don't know how to begin—"

"Well, let's start with your name."

"My name's Anna Schneider."

"All right, Ms. Schneider. If you would prefer to do this in person, I will happily come to you."

"Thank you, Detective. It *would* be easier."

She provided her address and the detective arrived within thirty minutes. After escorting him into the living room, she sat across from him, nervously fidgeting.

"Ms. Schneider, I have some experience in these matters. Just take a deep breath and start at the beginning."

The detective's demeanor had a calming effect as she organized her thoughts. After forcing herself to calm down, Anna began her narrative. "My late mother, Ethyl Schneider, left me a box of personal belongings from her only sister, Dora Reams."

Taking a shaky breath, she launched into a description of her aunt. "My Aunt Dora had mousey brown hair, gray eyes, and a slender build. Just looking at her picture, she always looked depressed from the way she slouched. In 1906, she married George Reams, but after fifteen years, she could not conceive a child. Just the sight of another baby resulted in days spent in bed crying until she became a recluse and her weight dropped even more."

Sensing her hesitation, the detective gently encouraged, "You're doing great, Anna. Can you tell me more about her husband?"

"Well . . ." Anna stopped to assimilate her recollection of stories from her mother. "George was unable to find steady work, and my mother believed it was the result of personal hygiene or lack of it. Mother said he only bathed once a month and his greasy black hair hung down into his eyes. 'Twin pools of darkness' she used to call them."

"Sounds like your mother and George didn't get along."

"You're absolutely correct. And she didn't trust him. Said there was something underhanded about him. Anyway, despite George's demeanor, he cared deeply for Dora and became determined to eliminate her depression. Around 1921, according to family legend, George worked at the Cleveland loading docks for extra income. Given his short stature with a healthy-sized paunch, everyone was amazed at his stamina in this ill-suited occupation. After six months, he accumulated a tidy sum and quit work."

Hanigan tried to end the interview. "I'm sorry Ms. Schneider, but I really don't see—"

"Detective, when he stopped working, he bought everything for a nursery but kept it hidden from Dora."

"I don't understand. I thought she couldn't have any children."

"She couldn't. But George kidnapped a child. Or so my mother assumed to explain the strange appearance of a baby in 1922. Dora's depression lifted at the thought of finally becoming a mother."

"Didn't your aunt inquire where the child came from?"

"Of course. George said a family with too many mouths to feed asked him to raise one of their children."

"That seems pretty farfetched. Did she believe him?"

"I think Aunt Dora was suspicious but afraid to ask lest her newfound happiness disappeared. She immediately called him Little George."

Scratching his head and settling back on the couch, Detective Hanigan finally spoke. "The time frame is right, but why do you think it was the O'Malley infant?"

"Because of this." She pulled an object from her handbag and carefully handed it to the detective. He gave a slow whistle and asked Anna to wait while he made a few calls.

Nearly half an hour went by before Hanigan reappeared. "Ms. Schneider, would you mind taking a drive with me? There's someone I'd like you to meet."

"Of course. Anything I can do to help."

EIGHTY-THREE

THEY ARRIVED AT their destination twenty-five minutes later. As they walked up to the front door, it burst open as a sweet elderly woman motioned for them to enter. "I've prepared fresh coffee," she offered but both declined. "This is my husband, Detective Frank Szabo. I asked him to be here for moral support."

Frank put his arm around his wife's shoulders in a gentle hug, then held her hand while nodding to the detective.

"Mr. and Mrs. Szabo, Anna has a very interesting story to tell you about Patrick, as I mentioned on the phone."

Anna, age forty-six, recounted the events she had told Hanigan. While waiting for a barrage of questions, Anna was surprised Ellen only had one. "What happened to Patrick after he arrived at your aunt's home?"

"George didn't have access to the crib, food, or any other items for the nursery. Intending to surprise Dora, he stored them at a friend's home, but he was out of town. In the evening, my uncle went to the store for food and diapers. On his way home, walking down a dark street, he was killed by a car."

"Yes. I know," Ellen replied in a small voice.

"When Aunt Dora heard the news, she placed Little Geo—I

mean Patrick—on their bed but forgot to place protective pillows around him. While sitting in her tiny living room, despondent over her loss, Aunt Dora heard a loud noise and ran into the bedroom. Little G—Patrick—fell to the floor. After a close inspection, Aunt Dora found a small bump on his head without any other injuries. So she placed him back on the bed, this time surrounded by pillows.

"Weeks went by and Patrick became more and more listless. He refused to eat, slept most of the day, and rarely cried. Even in her despair, Aunt Dora sensed this was unnatural. She ran to a neighbor's home and called my mom for help. By the time my mother got there, the baby was nowhere to be found. Aunt Dora sat in a rocking chair—her clothing and fingernails covered in fresh dirt—and never spoke another word. She became catatonic and died shortly afterward from malnutrition caused by severe depression. But she refused to let go of this."

Anna reached into her bag and gently placed the tiny blue blanket into Ellen's hands. She caressed the carefully embroidered initials as tears fell unrestrained onto the blanket. The years of searching for Patrick were finally over. Ellen closed her eyes and felt the whisper of an angel's wing stroke her cheek in comfort. In that moment, Ellen received an answer to her prayers as her soul relinquished the burden she had carried throughout her life. By easing her conscience, Ellen was filled with an enduring peace.

After Anna dried her own eyes, she finished her unusual story.

"We never knew what happened to the baby, but my mother refused to destroy the small remembrance of the first happiness my aunt had experienced in over fifteen years."

Ellen embraced Anna and thanked her for giving closure to Patrick's mysterious disappearance. With her prayers answered and Patrick finally at peace, Ellen was infused with a tranquility, absent since her childhood, fueled by the knowledge that during Patrick's short life, he was loved. Ellen contacted her siblings and children to relay the strange tale of Patrick's life and death. She took consolation in the knowledge her family, including those who never knew him, would forever remember him in their hearts and prayers.

EIGHTY-FOUR

O N A CRISP November evening in 1985, Mayme O'Malley Staab awoke to the sound of her husband's groans. When she turned on the light, Wilbur grimaced in pain as he grabbed his chest. After more than forty years of marriage and successful Broadway careers where they played a real-life married couple, Mayme's heart raced with dread.

"Wilbur, what's wrong?" Mayme asked in alarm.

"It feels like a ton of bricks are sitting on my chest, and I'm having a hard time breathing."

Mayme immediately called an ambulance. After admission to Fairview General Hospital and initial tests, Wilbur was diagnosed with a heart attack. Once he was stabilized, Mayme returned home to get some rest. However, her fears ran rampant as she realized her darling Wilbur might not recover.

Three nights after Wilbur's admission, Mayme called Ellen for a ride to the hospital. Mayme never learned to drive because Wilbur always took her wherever she wanted or her children played chauffeur. But lately, Thanksgiving pageants involving her grandchildren occupied their time and Mayme had to fend for herself. Ellen reassured her sister that Frank would drive her since Ellen was caring for a sick grandchild.

To save time, Frank drove his squad car to Mayme's home. As he pulled into Mayme's driveway, he noticed the snow falling in thick beautiful flakes onto the ground already piled high with at least six inches of fluffy powder. Despite the beautiful sight, Frank's thoughts returned to the 1939 murder, the only case in his career still unsolved. Although computers were used by the CPD now to generate crime reports, databases were limited to traffic and parking citations. Unfortunately, they didn't link into a centralized system of tracking evidence with investigative reports tied to prisoner bookings. Murders were still investigated the old-fashioned way.

As he stared up at Mayme's home and glanced at footprints in the snow, he finally realized the missing clue that had eluded him for the past forty-five years. Deep in thought with his newly formed hypothesis, Frank didn't hear Mayme pounding on the passenger's window.

"For heaven's sake, Frank, didn't you hear me?"

"Sorry, Mayme, guess my mind was somewhere else." He dropped Mayme off at the hospital and radioed into the precinct to pull evidence from the 1939 Sheridan murder prior to his arrival in thirty minutes. He decided to call Ellen from the station to advise her he wouldn't be home for at least another hour. Excited to relay his latest theory to Ellen, Frank smiled to himself as his thoughts wandered. He knew the events of the 1939 murder still haunted her despite the passage of time.

Frank was so engrossed in the possibility of finally solving the mystery that he failed to notice a car skidding through the intersection and riding a patch of black ice. Frank was puzzled to find his car facing the opposite direction; it wasn't until he felt a searing pain as steel crushed his left leg when he became cognizant of what had happened. Just before he lost consciousness, Frank heard the distant sound of sirens and thought how worried Ellen would be when he didn't arrive home as expected.

EIGHTY-FIVE

ELLEN REMAINED AT home caring for Sean, her oldest grandchild who closely resembled Patrick. Watching in amazement as he waddled across the room in the drunken sailor walk perfected by toddlers, Ellen smiled. Nearing the end of his flu symptoms, Sean's hijinks never ceased to amaze and amuse her. When she received a phone call from Frank's fellow officers at the Second District to inform her Frank had been involved in a car accident, she pushed her apprehension aside to make arrangements for a neighbor to watch Sean. She then headed to Fairview General Hospital and prayed his injuries would not be serious.

When Ellen saw Frank lying in bed discolored, swollen, and hooked up to various machines, she lost her composure. Ellen wept as she quietly sat on a bench outside Frank's room. Despite feeling alone and vulnerable, she performed the difficult task of contacting their children. She found Frank's physician to discuss his prognosis.

"Doctor, what's wrong with Frank? Will he be all right?" Her voice seemed so small and quiet as though any volume would interrupt Frank's chances for recovery.

"Your husband suffered several broken ribs and fractures of

his left leg and right arm. His vital signs are not stable and he's developed an abnormal heart rhythm. We decided to keep him in intensive care for several days where we can appropriately monitor him. However, you can see him each afternoon between two and four."

"But I need more than two hours a day to be with my husband. Perhaps I could—"

The physician interrupted her, stating there were no exceptions for ICU hospital policies. Ellen agreed and was reassured her sixty-eight-year-old husband had maintained his strength and virility since the day they met. He still loved his job as a detective and planned to retire before he reached seventy.

Their four children visited Frank as often as possible but every visit brought fresh anguish at the toll his body suffered. They were having a difficult time assimilating the robust man who sagely dispensed wise counsel and loving advice with the person who appeared so small, lying in bed hooked up to machines. As a family, they paid a visit to the hospital's chapel where they prayed for a full recovery. They weren't ready to let him go and hoped God could wait just a little while longer for his company.

EIGHTY-SIX

As Wilbur Staab recuperated from his heart attack, he heard about Frank's accident and admission to the same hospital. Mayme took Wilbur in a wheelchair to visit their brother-in-law in the ICU, just one floor below. Shocked at the bruises and swelling over most of his body, with the myriad of tubes and lines, Mayme asked in a shaky voice, "Oh, Wilbur. Do you think Frank will be all right?"

"He's a pretty tough guy. I'm sure he'll be just fine. But he'll have a rough road ahead of him."

One week after his heart attack, Wilbur was discharged home with instructions about lifestyle and diet changes. During the next month, he took it easy and adjusted his diet but not without loudly voicing his complaints about the bland food he was forced to consume. Wilbur slowly began his rehabilitation regimen, and once a week, he and Mayme took a taxi to visit Frank where they witnessed his continued improvement

Ellen couldn't imagine Frank being in one place for too long; he'd always been so active. She smiled to herself as she thought of Frank dictating orders to hospital employees as he would junior detectives at the station.

Finally, the day of Frank's discharge arrived following a

difficult month for him *and* the staff. By the time he completed two months of arduous outpatient therapy, Frank had shed more than twenty pounds and tired easily. Despite his prior decision to keep working after age sixty-five in a profession he truly enjoyed, Frank's declining health dictated he retire from the force. In spite of his outstanding record of service, the unsolved Sheridan case continued to haunt him.

Whenever Frank thought about it, he remembered the feeling of elation on the evening of his accident. Somehow, he'd figured out the missing puzzle pieces; now they remained elusive thoughts residing in obscurity and just out of reach. Perhaps if he occupied himself with other activities, the clues would mysteriously reappear as they had before his accident.

Adjusting to retirement was a difficult transition, made slightly bearable by returning to his former childhood passion of reading. Although Frank was content to sit for hours at a time curled up with a good book in the den—mostly murder mysteries, the same type of books he enjoyed during his youth— he smiled at the symmetry of life coming full circle.

But he couldn't relinquish the prospect of solving the 1939 case, and while reading an old Ellery Queen murder mystery, Frank came up with a brilliant solution. Resolutely, he walked over to the phone.

"I'd like to speak to Kevin Collins, please."

"Who's calling?"

"Tell him it's Frank Szabo from the Second District." Within minutes, he heard a familiar voice.

"Hey, Frank, I heard you retired after a bad accident. Sorry, buddy. So, how's retirement treating you?"

"Pretty good; thanks for asking. I finally finished my rehab and I've put on some weight, thanks to Ellen's wonderful cooking."

"Hopefully not too much, or they'll have to roll you out the front door. If it makes you feel any better, I retired last year but occasionally consult if an interesting case comes up."

"Well, that's the reason I'm calling."

Kevin paused for a moment. "Okay. What's up?"

"Remember the 1939 Sheridan murder case we initially worked up but it was relegated to the closed files?"

"Of course. Why, did you find some new evidence?" Kevin couldn't hide the elation in his voice at a new adventure to break the monotony of inactivity.

"I'm not sure."

"Well, that's a start."

Both men chuckled before Frank elaborated about the sight of footprints in the snow while sitting outside his sister-in-law's home.

"I can't remember why, but those images brought me back to the 1939 murder and the missing clues crystallized right before my eyes. Heading back to the station, I had radioed ahead to pull our case notes for review but got sidetracked by my accident."

"And you're thinking together we can reconstruct our notes and solve the murder."

"See now, Kevin. That's why I enjoyed working with you— always thinking one step ahead."

"Ah, Frank. I do what I can. Here's what I propose . . ."

And with that, the two veteran detectives plotted a course of action to solve the baffling mystery. Although neither admitted it, being embroiled in their only unsolved case was an invigorating cure to fill the void of retirement.

EIGHTY-SEVEN

KEVIN TRACKED DOWN Sadie Leibowitz, the Sheridan's temporary cook in 1939, surprised to discover she had married into the Sheridan family. He called and arranged a meeting with her for the afternoon.

When Sadie opened the door, a mature, beautiful woman greeted Kevin. "Please come in. How can I help you?"

"I'm working with another retired detective, Frank Szabo, to solve the murder of Louis Sheridan. Frank tells me his family and the Sheridans have kept in touch over the years, correct?"

Sadie smiled at the long-standing friendship between the families and nodded in ascent. "Absolutely. Did you know my twin sister married Ellen's brother?" Her smile only deepened at Kevin's look of astonishment.

"Frank kinda forgot to mention that one." Kevin smiled and continued his questioning. "We're in the process of re-interviewing witnesses. We've found the passage of time can often elicit information withheld during the original investigation. Unfortunately, the housekeeper, butler, and his wife are all deceased, which limits our sources."

Sadie asked, "Do you mean Alice Webber passed away?"

"Yes, several years ago. Why?"

After hesitating for a moment, Sadie informed Kevin of an omission in her original statement. "I saw Alice Webber with a red-haired man when I left the West Side Market. It must have been around October 1939 because I remember the fall foliage in brilliant colors."

Kevin couldn't hide his shock. "Why didn't you mention this before?"

"I confronted Alice when I heard the suspect description in a radio broadcast. She said it was her cousin but never mentioned his name. Although I knew she wasn't being forthcoming, Alice was clearly frightened of someone or something. I didn't want to interfere or cause her any harm; for me, involving the police wasn't an option."

Sadie briefly recounted details about her parents' early demise in Germany and terror of the Gestapo. "I promised myself to keep Alice's secret until I could verify she was no longer in danger."

"Do you think she may have disclosed information about the new lock installed on the back door to her 'cousin'? Several experts believe the locks used for many residences on Millionaire's Row were, unfortunately, the easiest to open with the right tools and a little bit of strength."

"I couldn't say for sure, but Alice was a trusting soul and may have divulged this information, especially if someone made her feel important."

Kevin thanked Sadie for her time and updated his notes. This confirmed their long-ago assumption: the robbery was well planned and connected to others in the area. Kevin knew Frank would be surprised and became impatient to share the latest update. Looking at his watch and the late hour, Kevin decided to wait until the next morning. Perhaps the two of them would go out for breakfast and share their information. He couldn't wait to see the look on Frank's face.

EIGHTY-EIGHT

WHILE JOTTING DOWN ideas to discuss with Kevin, Frank experienced dizziness, lightheadedness, and nausea as a pain in his chest grew stronger. Already seated, he remained still, waiting for the attack to resolve. Instead, he felt his body going limp and the realization hit him. As he slipped away, two thoughts were foremost in his mind. He knew Ellen would face her remaining years without him and he failed to solve the case that had plagued her for decades.

Ellen hated to interrupt her husband, hard at work on the Sheridan murder case, but Frank needed to eat and he always lost track of time when engrossed in any project. When she stood in the archway to the study, Ellen smiled at the sight of Frank sleeping peacefully in his chair.

"Okay, Frank, time to wake up. If I heat your supper one more time, you'll be eating shoe leather. I know gravy covers many culinary mistakes, but I doubt even my homemade gravy would improve the taste of twice-reheated meatloaf."

When Frank didn't respond, Ellen approached his chair but stopped when she saw the bluish discoloration of his skin. Despite her apprehension, Ellen touched his hand to confirm her suspicion. It was cold. As Ellen unconsciously backed away, her legs buckled and she collapsed on the floor. Her beloved husband had recently celebrated his sixty-ninth birthday and seemed as strong as on ox; surely, he couldn't be dead.

Luckily, her son Tom arrived to pick up some tools. When he walked into the living room, he rushed to his mother's side. "Mom, what is it? Are you all right?"

"He can't be dead. Our plans to one day visit Ireland are gone. And his dinner is getting cold. Should I reheat it again? I don't know what to do."

Tom thought his mother must have bumped her head when she hit the floor. Then he looked at his father. After gently helping his mother into an easy chair, he called the family physician who promised to contact the medical examiner. Tom called his siblings who came over right away.

After the doctor left and the body attended to, Tom closed the door of his father's den, hiding from view the papers and folders strewn across the desk. Tom didn't want his mother to be further upset by crime scene photos from the old murder case resurrected by his father.

The next few days were a blur of activity as Frank's family realized the full impact of losing their anchor, mentor, and best friend.

EIGHTY-NINE

June 7, 1986
Ellen's Home

THE PAIN OF Frank's absence, always more acute when Ellen was alone, occurred at unexpected and often inopportune moments. Grief washed over her in waves as the culmination of memories took her breath away. When loneliness threatened to overwhelm, Ellen discovered yielding to the barrage of emotions, although painful, gradually eased the torment of loss.

As she wiped her tears away, Ellen gave thanks for her family gathered together downstairs to celebrate her birthday. Fond memories of family holiday parties over the years, as her siblings settled into their adult lives and raised their own children, were celebrated as one happy family. An added bonus involved watching the cousins play together and the serenity in knowing the bonds forged would last long after she and their parents departed. Family get-togethers also gave her time to catch up with her siblings as they swapped stories of comical events involving their own mischievous broods careening into adulthood.

While slowly reminiscing, Ellen heard a phone ringing in the distance. The sound filled her with trepidation as she recalled a conversation with a virtual stranger that had forced her to make a grueling decision shortly after Frank's untimely demise. Once again, her life took another unexpected turn triggered by an event that had occurred several years prior. The telephone call, coupled with her devastating personal loss, drained Ellen's energy. As her eyelids closed, Ellen realized the truth would often emerge when least expected, thereby making her an unwitting arbiter of its unleashed power.

NINETY

May 21, 1986
Alice Webber-Thames's Home

O VER ONE HUNDRED miles away, Jerry Webber-Thames was cleaning out his mother's home in Toledo, Ohio, before placing it on the market. Although they lived in her home since she died eight years earlier, the task at hand was equally difficult and emotional. Looking up from the boxes, Jerry noticed his daughter had approached him with a strange expression on her face.

Noticing her confusion, he asked, "What's wrong, Nancy?"

"I found this envelope for you, Dad. But I think it was written by Grandma."

"I doubt that. She's been deceased for eight years." Sensing her apprehensive manner, he took the envelope from her hands, surprised that it was written in his mother's shaky penmanship.

Jerry: Do not open until my death

Jerry opened the envelope with trepidation, and not a small amount of curiosity, to discover a second sealed envelope inside.

September 12, 1978

Jerry,

By the time you read this letter, with any luck, I will be in heaven with your father. (Yes, dear, that was a joke.)

Please make certain to deliver the enclosed envelope to Ellen O'Malley Szabo. (I believe she still lives in Ohio.) We worked together at the Sheridan residence the evening of Louis Sheridan's murder on December 23, 1939. I read in the newspaper that she married the lead detective, Frank Szabo, who worked on this case. The information in her envelope should identify the intruder and solve the decades-old mystery. Please apologize to Ellen, on my behalf, and explain that my family was threatened if I provided this information to the police.

Thank you for being a wonderful son, Jerry. Your love and support have been a mainstay during the difficult times following your father's death. Take care of your lovely family. I couldn't possibly be more proud of my son!

All my love,
Your Adoring Mother

Jerry sat down, his thoughts racing. His mother never mentioned being involved in a murder! Anxious to carry out his mother's wishes, he became determined to find some answers of his own.

Worried about her father's sudden pallor, Nancy asked with

concern, "What is it, Dad?" He handed her the letter and together they sat in stunned silence as their thoughts reeled at the silent danger taking residence in their lives. They both knew something should be done, but what?

NINETY-ONE

J ERRY AND NANCY took a break from the laborious task of packing up memories and belongings. They headed over to the local public library and asked the librarian for help researching a murder in Cleveland on December 23, 1939. She escorted them back to the archives and found the correct spool of newspaper articles covering January through December 1939 for the *The Cleveland NorthShore Post*. After inserting the spool on the reader, she provided concise instructions on its use and left them to search in private. They were astounded at the glaring headline that confirmed the facts in Alice's letter.

The Cleveland NorthShore Post

Sunday Morning	December 24, 1939-Special Edition	Two Cents

Murder on Millionaire's Row

Cleveland, Ohio. Late last evening, Cleveland lost one of its benefactors, Louis Sheridan, slain in his home on Millionaire's Row. Returning home earlier than expected from a charity benefit with his wife, Marianne, Louis was accosted by an armed burglar. Mr. Sheridan attempted to wrestle a gun away from the thief but sustained a fatal gunshot wound. Other than emotional trauma and losing consciousness, Mrs. Sheridan did not sustain any life-threatening injuries.

The housekeeper, Alice Webber, and the nanny, Ellen O'Malley, were in the house with the Sheridan's seven-month-old baby. The police conducted interviews with nearby residents, who relayed information about the escape vehicle. Police also issued an All Points Bulletin in a continuing manhunt to assure justice is served. Residents of Cleveland's premiere neighborhood will not rest easy until the apprehension of this cold-blooded murderer. Additional facts will be updated in the regular edition of today's newspaper.

With a firm resolve to investigate the mystery, Jerry again asked the librarian's assistance. She directed them to the research section where they found telephone directories for major Ohio cities. He located a current address and phone number for Ellen Szabo residing in Rocky River, then contacted AAA for directions to complete the two-hour journey.

"So, Nancy. Are you ready for an adventure?"

"You bet."

When Jerry returned home, he placed an introductory, and somewhat awkward, telephone call.

"Mrs. Szabo, you don't know me, but my name is Jerry Webber-Thames. My mother, Alice, worked with you at the Sheridan residence in 1939. Shortly before she expired eight years ago, she wrote you a letter. We recently came across it while clearing out her home. I apologize for this unorthodox call, but I'd be happy to deliver the letter to your home."

Clearly intrigued, Ellen replied, "You can stop by tomorrow afternoon around two, if that's convenient for you."

"Absolutely and I must confess, I am rather curious. If you don't mind, I'll be bringing my daughter, Nancy."

"That will be fine."

After they exchanged good-byes, Ellen's slight tremor signaled a sense of foreboding.

When Jerry and Nancy arrived the next day, Ellen invited them inside for a cup of tea with homemade cookies. "Thank you for making the trip, Jerry. And it's a pleasure to meet you, Nancy."

"I was happy to do it. I should also mention my mother composed a second letter—addressed to me—and she asked me to convey her apology for not contacting you in person. She indicated someone threatened her family if the information contained in your envelope should fall into the wrong hands." Although Jerry was bursting with questions, he wasn't sure what to do. Ellen seemed distressed by his mother's unusual request, and given her age, he didn't want to upset her further.

"I'm sorry to hear of your mother's passing. We lost touch after she married your father in 1941. Goodness, such a long time ago." It appeared Ellen's forlorn gaze into the distance transported her to a different era as the decades receded.

Jerry placed the envelope into her hands. "This is the letter my mother wanted you to have. I'm sorry it took eight years to deliver it."

Ellen opened the envelope quickly and read the contents with an ominous feeling. When she finished reading, the coloring in Ellen's face drained away. Although she read every word in the correspondence, her overtaxed brain prevented her from fully processing its content or understanding the ramifications.

"Where's your kitchen?" Jerry asked with concern. Ellen pointed the way and Jerry returned with a glass of water. Ellen gratefully accepted the cool drink.

Eager to assist, Nancy asked, "Can I get you something? Or perhaps, call someone for you?"

"Thank you both. That won't be necessary. But I feel the beginning of a migraine and need to lie down before the pain becomes unbearable."

Although disappointed, Jerry replied, "Here's my business card, Mrs. Szabo. I've written my home address and phone number on the back. Perhaps one day you can explain what happened in 1939."

"I promise I will contact you when I'm able. Thank you again for making the trip. I'm sorry to cut our visit so short."

"We understand perfectly and hope you feel better soon."

After walking them to the front door, Ellen closed it behind them and sank into the nearest chair before she collapsed.

NINETY-TWO

A LMOST ONE MONTH after Frank's death in May 1986, and a mere two weeks after she received the strange letter, Ellen's confusion muddled her thoughts. She didn't think she could handle anything else; but, once again, the phone rang—this time a condolence call from Kevin Collins.

"Ellen, I'm so sorry to hear about Frank's passing. He will be greatly missed. I'm sorry I couldn't call earlier, but my wife has been sick and she's finally on the mend."

"Thank you for your kind words about Frank." A wave of sadness enveloped her. "Working with you on the Sheridan case rekindled a spark in Frank that's been missing these past several months. It gave him so much pleasure to work with you once again."

"It gave us both something to do and the challenge of solving a mystery proved irresistible. That's the reason for my call. I wondered if I could pick up Frank's notes and the evidence box to continue the investigation."

Without thinking it through, Ellen replied, "Of course. How about tomorrow?"

Attempting to keep the excitement out of his voice and failing miserably, Kevin responded, "Tomorrow it is then. And again, you have my deepest sympathy."

After Ellen hung up the phone, a feeling of dread consumed her as she realized the case neared a conclusion and her secret would be unveiled. Of small comfort was Frank's absence when the truth revealed her deception for so many years.

KEVIN ARRIVED THE following afternoon to retrieve the materials in Frank's possession. Ellen led him to her husband's den and left Kevin alone to pack up the evidence.

When Kevin arrived home, he recalled Frank believed the key to solving the case involved snow prints outside the home of his sister-in-law.

Now all Kevin needed to do was recreate the events that triggered Frank's memory, correlate it with evidence, and establish proof of the killer's identity. The mere thought of everything he needed to do overpowered him, so he put on a fresh pot of coffee and sat down to begin the arduous task.

The evidence box contained assorted photos taken by Frank that made Kevin smile. He could still recall Frank's excitement using his new camera with a flash attachment producing credible pictures that stood the test of time. As Kevin spread the pictures out, he identified the ones concerning Frank's obsession with footprints in the snow. He looked at them sideways and upside down and, at first, didn't see the relevance.

But then, something clicked as Kevin realized the discovery Frank had made just before his accident. Kevin worked late into the night, furiously making notes from the assorted pieces of evidence collected. As the clues gelled into a potential theory, Kevin knew Frank would have solved the puzzle but time was against him. Now all Kevin had to do was find proof to catch a killer.

NINETY-THREE

PROOF. THAT WAS Ellen's gift. Alice's letter with key information to solve the Sheridan murder had been shoved into a drawer. Ellen had been mentally incapable of becoming enmeshed in a murder investigation and too emotionally fragile after Frank's demise.

With the loss of her husband and best friend, she had a deep hole in her chest where her heart used to be—one that could not be filled, despite the best efforts of family and friends. But Ellen's grief, compounded by guilt at deceiving Frank for over forty years, would remain a blight on her soul until she assisted in bringing a murderer to justice.

After more than four decades, the case would be reopened and her earlier statements would be questioned. She had always thought of the Sheridan murder frozen in time—slow-moving actions and reactions that never changed, despite the passage of time or the imposition of facts upon memories. Ellen denied herself the freedom to release the demons that held her captive most of her adult life. Defense mechanisms served Ellen well over the years—the secret that protected her culpability became buried under walls that encompassed the truth. But she now realized guilt had become her prison and she alone held the key. Now that the investigation had been reopened, it was time to set herself free and search for some measure of peace.

When Kevin appeared on her doorstep, it propelled Ellen into action. Before losing her nerve, she retrieved Alice's letter and recalled an earlier vow that one day she *would* tell the truth about events of that stark and agonizing December night. Although Ellen knew Kevin resumed work on the cold case, she needed to play an active role in the investigation to atone for withholding information from her husband. And it gave her some measure of control—an element sorely missing from Frank's precipitous demise. With a sense of purpose, Ellen reread Alice's letter with rapt attention.

09/12/1978

Ellen,

By the time you read this letter, I will be gone. First, I apologize for the delay in sending this to you, but I was afraid, not only for myself but my family as well.

As you may recall, I met a strange, but very handsome, man just a few months before the Sheridan burglary. He said his name was Brett Roth and, at his request, we kept our relationship a secret. We struck up an easy friendship and he claimed to be a construction worker who renovated several homes on Millionaire's Row, including the Sheridan estate. He asked a strange question but I wanted to impress this dashing man and didn't think too much about it at the time.

He wondered if the back door to the Sheridan estate was still a problem. I laughed and said the old lock had been replaced with a newer, fancy lock. Within a month, he ended our romance abruptly and cruelly when he stated, at the last meal we shared together, there was someone else he would rather spend time with.

I never saw him again until two nights before Mr. Sheridan's murder. In hindsight, our chance meeting was surely planned by him well in advance. He said if I ever revealed anything about him or our conversations, he would kill me and my family. When he recited their home addresses with the names and descriptions of my family members, I couldn't risk my family's safety and knew I had to keep his secret.

I awoke earlier on the evening of the burglary to the sound of the back door opening. When you came downstairs to investigate, you were fortunate that Bridget began to cry in the upstairs nursery. Her distraction surely saved your life before you found Brett hiding in the study.

After you returned upstairs, I opened my bedroom door slightly and saw Brett emerging from the study and tiptoeing around while filling a bag with silverware, select paintings, and heirlooms.

I remained in my room because I was helpless to stop the robbery and never imagined the Sheridans were in any danger. They weren't due back for several hours.

When I emerged from my bedroom after Mrs. Sheridan's scream, you were just entering the downstairs bathroom in search of smelling salts. Following the struggle, Mr. Sheridan was still holding onto the murderer's mask.

In a panic, I quickly scooped up the mask with the gun, wrapped them in a towel, and hid both items in my purse. I dropped my handbag outside my window, and after the police searched the house, retrieved it before they searched outside. Using the wash bowl in my room, I cleansed my hands before coming out to give a statement to the police. I've held onto these items for almost forty years and now that my time is near, I wish to unburden myself of the lie I carried for so long.

Enclosed is a key for a safe deposit box at National City Bank, the main branch on E. 9th Street in downtown Cleveland. The contents of the box include the crime scene items and a newspaper clipping recounting the night's events.

If you feel up to the task, please send this information to the police. It should help solve Mr. Sheridan's murder and provide his family with long-awaited answers. But the decision is up to you because it's possible Brett is still alive. If so, you could be a threat to him. So, please think carefully before you take any course of action.

I enjoyed working with you at the Sheridan residence and am so sorry to drag you into this mess. I wanted to maintain our friendship but, once you married Detective Szabo, I didn't believe that would be wise for either of us. Hopefully you will find it in your heart to see that justice is done. Thank you, Ellen.

Cordially,
Alice Webber-Thames

Before changing her mind, Ellen resolutely walked over to the phone and dialed her son's number. "Jim, I wondered if you could do me a favor."

"Sure, Mom. What do you need?"

"Can you drive me to National City Bank on East 9th Street sometime in the next week?"

"Of course, just let me check my schedule."

Ellen heard papers shuffling. "How does tomorrow at noon work for you? I have a client meeting in the area and could drop you off for about thirty minutes. Would that work?"

"Yes, my dear. I'll see you then." Luckily Jim wasn't nearby to see her flushed face and rapid respiration, or he might have refused a request causing so much anxiety. Ellen gathered a few items necessary for her trip the following day, then sat down to catch her breath. With her preparations complete, she prayed her worries were groundless.

NINETY-FOUR

June 7, 1986
Ellen's Home

WITH RECENT EVENTS culminating in today's newspaper article, Ellen knew the time had arrived to tell her family the secret she had harbored most of her adult life. Sitting in her room, Ellen contemplated past occurrences and mentally rehearsed what she would tell her family as she placed those incidents, and feelings, in perspective.

Reliving events of long ago, Ellen couldn't believe how vivid her recollections of that fateful night quickly came to the forefront. Memories long repressed were seared into her brain and forever imprinted on her subconscious as she recalled events as though only a day passed instead of more than forty years. Ellen experienced an uneasy feeling as she realized lying to the police in general, and Frank in particular, began a cascading series of lies that *became* the truth as the years turned to decades.

Ironically, losing the love of her life gave Ellen the opportunity to free herself from deceit by speaking the truth without violating trust issues in her marriage. Ellen was at a crossroads—a defining moment—not only for herself, but also for family and friends impacted by the traumatic events of 1939. Its reverberations characterized subsequent interactions with those she loved when the scales of justice balanced. Ellen prayed her decision would bring some measure of peace to all parties, including herself.

Ellen's reverie was disturbed when she heard dishes clattering followed by a knock on her door.

"I'm sorry about that, Mom. Your beautiful granddaughter, Colleen, decided to climb up on a countertop and managed to open the cabinet containing your pots and pans. Not to be outdone by her adorable counterpart, Madie quietly clambered up on the opposite countertop. When the two bumped into each other, they screamed like a couple of banshees before knocking all the pots onto the floor.

"Unfortunately, they fell on your cat, Smokey, and he howled louder than the two girls combined. Some of the pots sent a few of the casseroles careening across the kitchen, so we're prioritizing food that's edible. We figured any plastic utensils that fell into main dishes are recyclable, so they're safe. But I guess the noise kinda' woke you up, huh?" Her daughter, Mary Frances, laughed apologetically.

"Well, you could say that. But the food sure smells good. Think we might be eating sometime this century?"

"Oh sure. I'd say probably even this decade, but everything should be ready in about fifteen minutes. Do you need any help?" asked Mary Frances.

"No sweetie, but thank you."

Ten minutes later, Ellen walked downstairs and gasped when she saw the bountiful feast displayed on her dining room table. They even remembered to include chocolate ice cream, Ellen's favorite comfort food since her childhood days with her

neighborhood friend, Joseph O'Riley.

The family ate with gusto and the conversation was free-flowing interspersed with laughter. When they finished the delectable food, including dessert, the table was cleared of dishes and Ellen made an announcement.

"I know you've all seen today's paper and the headline story must come as quite a shock. I'd like to explain events of the December 1939 night mentioned in the article and how it affected my life." She pulled out the letter from Alice and took them back in time. As she relayed the story, she considered this a dress rehearsal for events to come.

LATER THAT EVENING, there was one more task to complete—a phone call Ellen had dreaded since 1939.

"Bridget, my dear. It's Ellen Szabo—I'm sorry I haven't spoken to you since your wonderful mother passed away. She was an astonishing person and someone I proudly called my friend."

"We feel the same way about you. I recently learned of your husband's death after we returned home from a trip to Europe. I planned on calling to see if you were managing all right."

"Some days are better than others. But I'm doing well for the most part. I apologize for the abruptness of this phone call, but I need to ask a favor of you."

"Sure, name it."

"Could you bring Edward and Timothy over to my home tomorrow? There's something I need to tell you about the night of your father's murder." She heard a large intake of breath.

"I don't suppose you could give me a hint now?"

"This is a conversation best held in person."

"Okay, how does one o'clock sound? The three of us were scheduled for lunch tomorrow, but this is certainly more important. Would that be all right?"

"Tomorrow sounds great." After Ellen hung up, she felt rooted to her chair. Her hands shook, her heart pounded like a jackhammer, and her throat became constricted.

Ellen knew her culpability was about to be revealed. But instead of panic, a serenity enveloped her and provided a sense of peace missing since that momentous night. Ellen knew the heavy burden of guilt was slowly lifting and awoke early the next morning, ready to face her personal demons.

NINETY-FIVE

A T PRECISELY 1:00 p.m., the Sheridan siblings arrived at Ellen's home. Before the doorbell rang, Ellen swung the door wide open.

"Thank you for coming." She gave each one a hug and took their coats. "Please be seated in the living room. I'll be right with you."

After hanging up their coats, Ellen needed to sit down for a moment while she gathered her wits and courage to face her friends—a relationship that would hopefully endure after today. She went into the kitchen and poured four cups of coffee and placed them on a tray with a plate of cookies to serve her guests.

Ellen decided to dispense with chitchat to allay their concerns. "I don't know how much you told Bridget about events surrounding your father's death, so I'll try and fill in as many blanks as I can."

After repeating the synopsis of events relayed to her own family the day before, recent receipt of Alice's letter, and divulging her secret, Ellen sat back. "In 1939, my suspicions were plagued with potential danger to my family. I wanted to unburden my soul to the authorities and provide clues to catch your father's murderer. But I lacked the strength to act, especially after witnessing firsthand the brutality dispensed on a whim by this monster. I chose the cowardly but necessary option of keeping this knowledge secret, even from my beloved Frank." At the mention of her husband's name, and relief at finally bearing her soul, Ellen sobbed uncontrollably. "Pl-pl-please forgive me," she said as she sat before them, her spirit broken.

Bridget was the first to react. She placed her arm around Ellen's slender frame and held her until her emotions were spent.

When capable of coherent speech, Ellen whispered, "It may be too little too late, but I've taken steps to ensure the police are in possession of evidence I received a few short weeks ago." She produced Alice's letter and silently waited as they read its contents. Sitting with her shoulders hunched forward and eyes cast downward, Ellen continued. "I understand my confession, forty-five years in the making, comes at the high price of losing your respect. But I hope you will consider the life lesson I learned at the expense of my *own* serenity. The past is a fabric upon which our lives are woven. Shaped by the sum total of hopes, fears, and aspirations, it molded us into the individuals we have become. But our future endeavors remain to be written by each person and we, alone, control the path it will take. I pray that you will, in time, forgive me."

Edward spoke first, after clearing his throat. "Ellen, you have suffered enough shouldering this oppression on your own. You have been, and always will be, a friend of the Sheridan family. Circumstances placed you in a dangerous predicament. I believe if the situation were reversed, the outcome would have been the same for any of us to protect our families."

Ellen looked up and was gratified to see her three guests nodding in agreement.

Tensions resolved, the rest of the afternoon passed quickly with pleasant conversation among friends. But the relief at finally baring her soul to a family she'd respected most of her adult life, and in return, receive their support and love, had an extraordinary effect on Ellen. It relinquished her self-doubt that dictated decisions throughout her adult life; for the first time, she was free. Now that answers were soon to be released, Ellen along with the Sheridans, looked forward to learning the murderer's true identity.

NINETY-SIX

The Cleveland NorthShore Post

Saturday	July 21, 1986	60¢

Exclusive Three-Part Exposé of a 50-year-old Murder

Installment #1: The Original 1939 Murder Investigation

Cleveland, Ohio. On December 23, 1939, a prominent Cleveland socialite—Louis Sheridan—was murdered in his home on Millionaire's Row. He and his wife returned home early from a charity function and interrupted a burglary. During a struggle, Mr. Sheridan suffered a fatal gunshot wound.

Neighbors heard Mrs. Sheridan's screams and contacted the police. Detectives Frank Szabo and Kevin Collins responded first to the grisly scene. They confirmed it was a burglary gone awry and the murderer, long gone, gained access by picking the lock on the rear entrance. Only three people remained in the home during the heist/murder: housekeeper, Alice Webber; nanny, Ellen O'Malley; and the Sheridan's baby.

Hearing a commotion, Ellen O'Malley emerged from the upstairs nursery and began her descent downstairs to greet the Sheridans. Midstride, she momentarily froze when she saw the Sheridans collapsed on the floor. With copious amounts of blood pooling around Mr. Sheridan, Ellen rushed forward to help them without thought for her own safety. When she heard Mrs. Sheridan moan, Ellen searched for smelling salts in the guest bathroom.

The detectives obtained witness reports, many unreliable, and elicited the following key facts: Mr. and Mrs. Sheridan attended a widely-publicized dinner in their honor but arrived home early on December 23 when Mrs. Sheridan developed a headache; the intruder was described as a young white male, approximately six feet tall, with red hair and a full beard; the murderer dashed out the front door carrying a sack of stolen property and ran to a late model Ford V-8, parked at the end of the block with 1939 license plates, numbers unknown.

Based on a neighbor's identification of the getaway car, Det. Szabo conducted a title research at the Cleveland Registrar's Office. He came up with four names, including a man whose brother had a record of prior thefts and vandalism. Det. Szabo's interviews of the remaining Ford owners inadvertently led to a fifth suspect whose description matched that of the assailant. Police theorized two men were involved in the botched robbery and murder: the man with a criminal record whose appearance was dissimilar to witness descriptions and the new suspect identified during their investigation. After Det. Szabo's partner, Kevin Collins, was reassigned to another division, Det. Szabo continued the investigation alone. He pursued his search for the two suspects but, with limited resources, could not locate either man, despite interviews and aggressive surveillance of family members. With all leads exhausted by December 1941, and insufficient evidence to initiate an arrest, the data was stored away with other unsolved cases as the nation prepared for war.

Byline: Chris Hooker

NINETY-SEVEN

The Cleveland NorthShore Post

| Saturday | July 27, 1986 | 60¢ |

Exclusive Three-Part Exposé of a 50-year-old Murder

Installment #2: Anatomy of a Killer

Cleveland, Ohio. Fingerprints lifted from the blood-stained gun matched those of Stephen Mueller [verified by an extensive criminal record]; however, mug shots were inconsistent with witness descriptions of the murderer.

Stephen and his older brother, Kurt, joined the Cleveland chapter of the German American Bund who provided jobs to local Germans, including employment as day laborers at the Sheridan estate. The majority of Bund meetings were held at their headquarters in New York. While Kurt attended rallies, Stephen enrolled in acting classes where he surfaced as Lawrence Talbot, a Broadway star in the mid-late 1930s.

With knowledge of his true identity, police postulated that Mueller/Talbot reverted to techniques learned as an actor to elude capture, specifically, changing his appearance using wigs, heel lifts, makeup, and a relatively new invention (contact lenses).

Two months before the homicide, Talbot (using the fake name of Brett Roth and disguised in a red wig with matching beard—items returned to his brother after the war), dated the Sheridan's housekeeper, Ms. Webber. Through this short-lived relationship, he confirmed the rear entrance lock, formerly broken and left unlocked, had been repaired since the Muellers last worked at the estate. Roth/Talbot quickly ended their association and threatened Ms. Webber's family if she revealed their time together.

A current search of society pages from the week before the murder revealed *The Cleveland NorthShore Post* article on December 21, 1939, indicating the Sheridan's planned attendance at a charity event in two days—itinerary used by Roth.

The Sheridan's former nanny, Ellen O'Malley Szabo, recently received a letter from the 1939 housekeeper, Alice Webber, now deceased. It contained missing information of events surrounding the murder.

Ms. Webber had opened her door slightly at the unexpected noise on December 23, 1939, but quietly closed it as she cowered in fear at the sight of Roth stuffing his pillowcase with silverware. When he heard the nanny's approach, Roth quickly hid in the downstairs study until it was safe to come out and continue pillaging. With his pillowcase nearly full, he heard the front door open and pulled out his gun. Mrs. Sheridan screamed at the sight of a man dressed in black as her husband struggled with the intruder, attempting to escape. Mr. Sheridan managed to remove the murderer's mask before he was shot. As Mr. Sheridan fell forward, his wife fainted and they collapsed together. Mr. Sheridan sustained a fatal wound but his wife was otherwise unharmed.

While Ellen searched for smelling salts, Ms. Webber slipped out of her room to collect the murder weapon and mask—items she eventually stored in a safe deposit box. Threats by Roth to her family ensured her silence.

Roth/Mueller dashed out the Sheridan's front door with the stolen items as the sound of sirens grew louder. He ran to a car borrowed from his older brother, Kurt Mueller, parked at the end of the block.

To understand the underlying motives behind Mueller's eventual life of crime, we interviewed a surviving member of the Cleveland Bund chapter. He stated the Mueller brothers were resentful that the American Dream remained out of their grasp. Stephen was also known to use his good looks to prey on beautiful women, although his attitude would often ignite hidden rage and reckless behavior. Stephen became friends with another Bund member his own age, Eric Kaufmann, a German immigrant and former Hitler Youth who idolized the Third Reich. Together they supported the

Fatherland's ideologies by painting swastikas on Jewish residences and taunting Jewish students in their youth.

Despite proudly supporting Bund activities, the Mueller brothers denounced the organization in a contract dispute almost a year before Pearl Harbor. In so doing, they escaped the fate of fellow Bund members imprisoned or deported to a labor camp for the duration of the war.

Oddly enough, the life of Roth/Talbot transected both the Sheridan and O'Malley families, at times without their direct knowledge, during the 1930s and 1940s. This will be covered in detail with the last installment.

Although Talbot had a successful career in theater, binge drinking affected his performances and forced him to find another occupation. Utilizing aliases and disguises during his criminal enterprises, Talbot's life of crime deteriorated until his arrest in 1943 when he was given the option of serving in the U.S. Navy in lieu of prison.

Men who served with Talbot during the war stated that, while on shore leave, he would drink to excess and became verbose. He unintentionally provided insights to the complex man he had become. He confided that fighting in the U.S. Navy against a common enemy provided an outlet for his rage emanating from the loss of his successful career, which pivoted him from stardom into obscurity. And the camaraderie made him feel, for the first time in his life, as though he belonged.

His shipmates also described Talbot as an affable young man, quick to ply them with tales of fortune and fame during his brief stint as a Broadway star. However, they were unaware of Talbot's criminal activities as Stephen Mueller or his affiliation with the German Bund and his anti-Semitic crime spree as a youth.

Prior to his life of crime, Talbot exhibited a life filled with enormous potential until rage at his unfulfilled sense of entitlement consumed him.

Byline: Chris Hooker

NINETY-EIGHT

The Cleveland NorthShore Post

Saturday	August 3, 1986	60¢

Exclusive Three-Part Exposé of a 50-year-old Murder

Installment #3: Cold Case Resolved but Paradox Remains

Cleveland, Ohio. The 1939 murder of Louis Sheridan remained a cold case until new evidence recently surfaced. The lead detective in the original investigation, Detective Szabo, died unexpectedly earlier this year leaving behind his widow, Ellen, who was the Sheridan's nanny and is the sole living eyewitness to the events in question. Shortly before his death, Szabo contacted his former partner, Kevin Collins, and the two veteran detectives set about the difficult task of solving the cold case. According to Collins, Szabo was close to a resolution but died before solving the mystery. Kevin decided to pick up where his partner left off and pursued two clues that plagued his former partner: unusual footprints in the snow on the night of the murder and a snowy night four decades later.

After Collins reviewed the evidence and pictures taken by Frank, including several shots of the strange footprints, he reformulated Frank's hypothesis. When Frank glimpsed snowy footprints last year while sitting outside the home of his sister-in-law, a Broadway star, he accurately surmised the man who left the strange footprints long ago had the skill of a seasoned actor to alter his appearance by wearing ill-fitting shoes with heel lifts. He completed his disguise using a red wig and matching beard. Collins realized Frank was close to solving the murder in 1939 when he identified the culprits as Brett Roth (based on eyewitness descriptions) and Stephen Mueller. (Articles stolen from the Sheridan household were found at a local pawn shop and traced back to Mueller.) Without modern technology, Szabo was unable to confirm his two suspects were actually the same person. Collins's suspicions also remained a theory because he didn't have any proof linking Mueller/Roth to the murder.

But Mrs. Szabo *was* in possession of proof—correspondence she received from the Sheridan's former housekeeper, including a safe deposit key. She retrieved the items from the safe deposit box (gun, black mask, and 1939 newspaper account) and anonymously mailed the evidence to police with a succinct handwritten note. When questioned why the items were not turned over to

Collins for handling, Mrs. Szabo stated she recently decided to become involved in the investigation as her way of atoning for withholding evidence from everyone, including her husband. As referenced in "Installment #2: Anatomy of a Killer," fingerprints lifted from the blood-stained gun matched those of Stephen Mueller. Within the closed-case materials, police found Louis Sheridan's blood-soaked shirt and sent it with the presumed murder weapon for expedited analysis to a laboratory in Baltimore, Maryland, that pioneered DNA testing still in its infancy stage [referred to as RFLP (restriction fragment length polymorphism)]. Six weeks later, DNA results (combined with bullet striations compared to the bullet removed from Sheridan) confirmed the gun in their possession was the murder weapon.

Piecing together new evidence, prior investigative reports from Detectives Szabo and Collins, and corollary interviews from additional sources, including the former cook Sadie (Leibowitz) Sheridan, and a recent interview with Mrs. Ellen (O'Malley) Szabo, we now have an accurate sequence of events leading up to the murder.

During a recent interview of the Sheridan's temporary cook, it was discovered Sadie Leibowitz (now married to the Sheridan's youngest son) also withheld information during her 1939 police interview. She witnessed the housekeeper, Alice Webber, with a tall red-haired man shortly before the murder. She confronted Ms. Webber about the stranger who matched the suspect's description. When Ms. Webber became uncontrollably frightened, Sadie elected to suppress information that incited genuine terror in her friend.

When Mrs. Szabo was asked about the meaning behind her handwritten note begging forgiveness (included in the recently received evidence materials), she revealed *her* long-kept secret. In the summer of 1939, Ellen witnessed a stranger's uncontrollable rage when he pistol-whipped a man who refused to part with his wallet. (This stranger was actually Mueller/Talbot in his Brett Roth disguise.) Ellen shouted for police and scared him away but not before he got a good look at her.

The next morning, when Ellen exited her home, the same man stood across the street casually leaning against a lamppost. As he uncrossed his arms, Ellen could see a gun. Grinning at her terror, he put his finger to pursed lips and pointed to her home. She got the message loud and clear. The mere thought of harm coming to her family sent Ellen running back into the house. It wasn't until recently when police disclosed Talbot's name that Mrs. Szabo reconciled how the stranger knew where she lived. He had driven Ellen's sister, Mayme, home after a late-night rehearsal in 1937. Two years later, this information proved useful when Roth/Talbot intimidated Ellen from providing police with details about the brutal assault.

On December 23, 1939, Ellen got a glimpse of the same man, now a murderer, as she stood frozen on the stairway after exiting the second-floor nursery. Their eyes locked and with a malicious grin he pursed his lips and whispered, "Shhh. I know where you live." His campaign of terror continued and she knew that, once again, his secret was safe.

Ellen never recovered from her failure to provide detectives with an eyewitness account of the assailant just a few short months before Louis was murdered. She kept this secret from everyone, including her husband, when the stranger threatened her family. Guilt-ridden, Ellen believed her omission of providing police with an accurate description would have led to his incarceration. Instead, Roth/Talbot was free to roam the streets, which set the stage for events of December 23, 1939. The handwritten note "Forgive Me" was directed at the Sheridan family for her culpability in Louis's untimely death.

During World War II, Talbot served on the USS *Mississippi,* unaware that William O'Malley was his shipmate. In the heat of battle, Talbot carried two men covered in blood down to sick bay. Although a witness later reported Talbot's act of heroism, Talbot didn't realize one man was Captain Edward Sheridan, and ironically, the second person was a Jewish sailor.

Talbot was aboard the USS *Indianapolis* in 1945 when it was bombed by the Japanese and quickly sank into the vast ocean. Clinging to a large section of debris, Talbot surrendered his hold on the makeshift refuge after three days in shark-infested waters and slid into his watery grave. His shipmate, William O'Malley (brother of the Sheridan's nanny), watched in horror as the man began to disappear and reached out to save him. However, given his own weakness, William could only grasp the man's tags. He used those to secure a fellow seaman, Timothy

Sheridan. They were rescued five days after their nightmare ordeal and shipped to a nearby naval hospital where the two men became lifelong friends. Although neither O'Malley nor Sheridan was aware of the man's name that unwittingly saved Timothy's life, the U.S. Navy kept a logbook of tags collected with retrieval location for family notifications.

It is ironic that Mueller/Roth/Talbot would only achieve greatness and notoriety after his death. But the posthumous recognition emanated from opposite ends of the spectrum: Purple Heart for giving his life in service to his country and an indictment in the 1939 death of Louis Sheridan.

In a paradoxical twist of fate, Talbot was culpable in the death of Louis Sheridan but instrumental in saving the lives of his two sons during the war. By achieving the latter, and without conscious awareness, he atoned for his earlier transgression.

This story, with corkscrew twists and turns, proves that truth really *is* stranger than fiction.

Byline: Chris Hooker

NINETY-NINE

S EVERAL DAYS AFTER the final newspaper installment, Ellen called her son for assistance.

"Tom, could you please make me a copy of the newspaper clippings about the Sheridan murder?"

"Sure. I'll bring them over this afternoon. Need anything else?"

"Well, after you bring over the articles, could you mail a letter for me?"

"Of course; I'll see you around three."

"Wonderful, my dear, I look forward to it."

That gave Ellen just enough time to write a letter of thanks. She looked in her desk drawer and pulled out a card to address the envelope. Knowing the recipient lived two hours away, she was uncertain if the local newspaper carried the story. Ellen wanted to personally relay her thanks and advise the outcome of a journey made possible through their efforts.

Dear Jerry,

Let me begin by thanking you for your kindness in hand-delivering your mother's correspondence. I'm sure you noticed the letter from your mother unsettled me. However, in the end, it brought me an everlasting peace.

I know this was a large exposé in Cleveland but didn't know if the story was published in Toledo. So I've enclosed the articles for your review. They will explain, in detail, the events surrounding the 1939 murder of Louis Sheridan. Without your mother's letter and key evidence that she maintained in a safe deposit box, the mystery never would have been solved. Alice was a remarkable woman, and I am truly sorry for your loss.

Again, thank you for your compassion. Please give my best to your delightful daughter, Nancy.

Cordially,
Ellen O'Malley Szabo

When Tom arrived, Ellen enclosed the articles inside her note, sealed the envelope, and gave it to her son for mailing. With that small task, Ellen took consolation in the additional closure it provided.

ONE HUNDRED

TWO MONTHS LATER, on an unusually warm fall day, Ellen developed a sudden craving for chocolate ice cream. The harder she tried to ignore it, the greater her desire. The persistent feeling was similar to the gentle nudges she experienced from her guardian angel as a child. Finally, she acquiesced and called her daughter, Mary Frances, for a ride to Heinen's Grocery Store in Rocky River. Once Ellen commandeered a motorized cart, they split up to do their respective shopping. As Ellen neared the ice cream coolers, she caught sight of a familiar face. She didn't think it was possible but had to know.

Ellen moved closer to the stranger and asked, "Excuse me, but did you live on Carroll Avenue during the 1930s?"

The face registered surprise. "Why, yes I did. And you do look familiar, Ms.—"

"Ellen Szabo, but my maiden name was O'Malley."

"I can't believe it. You haven't changed at all, Ellen. It's me, Joseph O'Riley. I can't believe you recognized me."

"Well, without your red hair I couldn't be sure. But you still have the same smile and proud bearing of fifty years ago. I remember the night you and your mother mysteriously disappeared from Carroll Avenue and we never saw or heard from you again. What happened?"

"As you may recall, when the income from my parent's bakery slowed during the Depression, my father's drinking increased, and with it, a mean temper materialized as he took out his frustrations on my mom and me. To hide her shame, my mom closed all the windows, even on the hottest days, when her husband had a few too many. He screamed and belittled us until I stood between my father's fists and my beloved mother. After my dad died, my mother went into a serious depression. I tried to work at the bakery but worried about leaving her alone. So I contacted my aunt and uncle in Columbus for assistance the day after she tried to commit suicide. I knew, from then on, I could not leave her unattended so I packed up our things in a hurry and we left that evening. I wanted to say good-bye but couldn't risk even a quick visit to your home. How strange we're saying hello decades later at a time when I can finally apologize for not saying good-bye. Funny how things worked out, isn't it? Right now, we're in town visiting our daughter."

In response to Joseph's query about Ellen's life, she briefly recounted recent updates to the Sheridan murder, her marriage to the detective involved in the investigation, and his death the year before.

"During the initial Sheridan investigation, I know Frank considered you a suspect."

"You're kidding!"

Ellen laughed at his expression and replied, "I told Frank that, although you fell in with a rough crowd around that time, you were incapable of murder."

"Thank you for that, Ellen." He filled his basket with chocolate ice cream, just as she was reaching for the same item. They both laughed. "Do you have any children?"

"I have four wonderful children. Jim is an attorney, Tom's an engineer, Eileen Marie works as a teacher, and Mary Frances is a registered nurse. In addition, three grandchildren and one great-grandchild are keeping me busy and forever on my toes. How about you, Joseph? Has life been good to you?"

"More than I deserve. In hindsight, our relocation to Columbus came at just the right time. Living in Cleveland, I fell in with a bunch of thugs and probably would have ended up in jail. After we settled in Columbus, I met and married a lovely woman. Several years after our wedding, my mother died of a stroke. We have three children, all grown up and out in the world making their own way, and four grandkids. My wife and I have wanderlust and travel extensively. We just returned from a trip to Ireland this past summer."

"How wonderful. That's always been my dream. I do have to confess something. I always knew you were one of the good ones, once you sowed your wild oats, that is."

"Thanks. God always looked out for me. My mother's depression forced me to grow up and turn my life around. Now, I don't mean to cut this short, but my daughter is waiting in the car."

"Then you best be on your way. Take care of yourself, Joseph."

"Thanks, Ellen. You, too."

And with that, another missing puzzle piece fell into place. Some may have thought it strange that something as simple as ice cream could bring together friends after being apart so long.

But, to Ellen, it was a wonderful affirmation that her guardian angel was still on the job.

EPILOGUE

WHEN ELLEN GAZED at her beloved Sheridan family portrait, she realized age brought insights into past events no longer clouded by the minutia of daily life. Ellen took solace in knowing she had fulfilled her part in Louis Sheridan's final act, and justice, long denied, was meted out.

Reliving memories long repressed and tempered with the wisdom of age, Ellen saw the myriad of webs doled out by fate as lives intersected through one tragic event. The destiny of those near and far, strangers at the outset, cast them as unwitting players in Louis Sheridan's untimely death. For many, the relevance of events in which they found themselves entwined remained a mystery for decades. Their consequential acts created ripple effects similar to the concentric circles a pebble produces when dropped into still water. Some were central to the main event, while others remained on the periphery, playing ancillary parts with varying degrees of impact.

Once again, her children were downstairs with festive preparations for another milestone—her eightieth birthday. As Ellen lay down for a nap until the big "surprise," she smiled as she imagined the interactions of her wonderful family, gathered to celebrate a life well lived. She took solace knowing her children led happy and successful lives. Throughout the years, Ellen had taught her children how to survive adversity, pursue the truth at all costs, and most importantly, cling to their core belief that God vigilantly watched over them. Unexpectedly, exhaustion overcame Ellen and she closed her eyes.

Ellen's grandchildren sneaked into her room and were amazed at the radiant smile on their nana's face. But they couldn't wake her.

"Come on Nana, it's time for your birthday surprise," said Madie, a delightful child born late in Jim's marriage.

"Maybe if we tickle her toes," suggested Colleen.

When Sean approached the room, he knew his beloved Nana was gone. Fighting back tears, he rushed downstairs for the adults to come up immediately.

Madie and Colleen dragged Christopher (the only great-grandchild) into their Nana's bedroom, but all the children stopped at the room's entrance.

"Where's that music coming from?"

"What music?" asked Jim as he turned his back to wipe away a tear.

"The pretty lullaby," replied Madie.

"I don't hear anything. Do any of you?"

Eileen Marie's siblings shook their heads in unison. "How about you, Christopher? Do you hear it?"

Being four years old and feeling important as everyone waited for his opinion, he sagely said, "Yep. But where's the magic dust? And what's the land of Nigh'?"

Astounded, the adults shook their heads. Although their mother had sung the Irish lullaby in their childhood, her voice would be filled with sadness. When asked why the lullaby caused her pain, she would reply, "It reminded me of Patrick."

By unspoken rule, Ellen's children never sang the song to their offspring because they didn't want to cause their mother any more pain. But when their own children began to hum the melody in perfect unison, Ellen's children could feel their mother smiling down as she fed their souls with laughter and a life of no regret.

ONCE ELLEN CLOSED her eyes for the last time, she was greeted by her guardian angel. It was her own sweet mother, deceased over forty years, beckoning her to join Da, Patrick, and her beloved Frank. Ellen wept with joy and happily took her mother's hand, her long journey for truth and reparations finally complete.

As mother and daughter walked side by side, her mother began to sing the sweetest lullaby, a tune that reminded Ellen of Patrick. Hearing her mother's sweet, lilting rendition bursting with happiness, Ellen's heart soared as she listened to a melody reminiscent of their happy childhood innocence, "Magic O'er the Land."

Deep in the land of Westport
On the coast of Achill Sound,
Where the greenery was lush and thick
And the air sweet all around.

The hours passed by quickly.
As the end of day drew near,
We gathered for the best to come:
Mother's lullaby of cheer.

'Tis to the land we all belong
And ne'er we shall forget.
It feeds our souls with laughter
And a life of no regret.

As she sprinkled o'er her magic dust
With a twinkle in her eye,
She lulled us off to deepest sleep
'Til we reached the Land of Nigh'.

For the place of dreams 'tis bountiful
Where wishes do come true.
Just close your eyes, me darlin'
To find a world that's new.

'Tis to the land we all belong
And ne'er we shall forget.
It feeds our souls with laughter
And a life of no regret.

As she moved forward, Ellen felt the years strip away, and as a young woman, made her final journey home into Frank's loving embrace.

The End

ACKNOWLEDGMENTS

WHEN COMPILING A list of acknowledgments, I was amazed at the number of people who provided encouragement throughout the process of writing my first novel. I've tried to make this list as comprehensive as possible, and if I have inadvertently omitted anyone, please forgive me. I should also point out that recreating a time period from the mid-1900s may be fraught with inaccuracies, no matter how diligent my research efforts. Therefore, any mistakes made are mine and mine alone.

THERE WERE SEVERAL people with the courage to read first drafts of my book and provide much-needed criticisms and recommendations: my father, Frank, whose insight into life in the 1930s and 1940s was invaluable; Louis (Buddy) DuChez, whose critiques included "one to glow, two to grow"; Veronica O'Malley Collins; Margaret O'Malley DuChez; Verna Cole Mitchell; Eileen Marie Dowd; Mary Anne McGinness; Peggy Moravek; retired agent, Susan Zeckendorf; Paul Carns, MD; and Beth Minzter, MD.

GERMAINE MOODY AND Shanda Trofe published my earliest short stories and gave me confidence to pursue my dream of writing *Paradox Forged in Blood.*

MY SON, SEAN Francis Patrick, helped to score the simple melody I wrote for the book's lullaby, "Magic O'er the Land." My wonderfully talented cousin, William Staab of WMS

MUSIC utilized his remarkable musical gift to orchestrate this lullaby, which accompanies the book trailer; vocals were provided by my amazingly gifted son.

ANOTHER EXTREMELY TALENTED cousin, Lynn Bycko, curator of Special Collections, Cleveland State University, provided a high resolution picture of the estate featured on the book's cover. She also used her considerable photographic genius to provide accurate renditions of many pictures in the time travel section of my website, www.maryfrancesfisher.com. Others who assisted in providing historical pictures for the website include: Holly Reed of the National Archive and Records Administration website (includes pictures from The United States Holocaust Memorial Museum)—she also recommended assorted public World War II photos from www.fdrlibrary.marist.edu/archives/collections/franklin; Charles Klass and Kim Boggs of the Old Oak Restaurant; and Sea Shore Trolley Museum (with special thanks to John Middleton and Sherri) for permission to use images from www.trolleymuseum.org.

ROBERT J. CERMAK gave me a personal tour of the Cleveland Police Historical Society, which proved helpful in recreating a murder investigation in the 1930s and 1940s. He also provided historical assistance about computer usage in the 1980s. For further information, refer to www.clevelandpolicemuseum.org.

MANY THANKS TO Amie C. Branham and Shelly Korpisz of BRT Laboratories, Inc. in Bethesda, MD, for their assistance in explaining RFLP (DNA precursor) and testing turnaround time in 1986.

For more information about events mentioned in the book surrounding the fate of the USS *Indianapolis*, I highly recommend the following website: www.ussindianapolis.org.

Additional friends and family members who provided inspiration from start to finish: my brother Tom, and his wife, Peg; my brother Jim, his wife, Char, and daughter, Madie; Mayme O'Malley Staab; William O'Malley who served in World War II with honor and distinction; Chris Hooker; KC Eby; Miles Sternfield; Anne Marie Drew; Neil DuChez, Esq.; Nick Fuhrman; the Doubler family; Elizabeth Cook; Hanna Dexter Photography; and last, but not least, Harry Alsentzer (a World War II American hero who graciously allowed the use of his name as a Nazi sympathizer.)

With greatest affection and friendship, my editor, Lorraine Fico White, became my mentor and took on the challenge of a first-time author with diligence, humor, and excellence. You worked magic on a raw story and helped me weave it into a work that I'm so very proud of.

Award-winning author MK McClintock and Cambron Publishing LLC, have my deepest gratitude in taking a chance on a complete unknown. They have guided me through the world of publishing and marketing with valuable input on the best way to optimize my website that now resembles a work of art. And specifically to MK McClintock: Thank you from the depths of my heart. You've earned my deepest respect from your innate talents of proficiency, kindness, and expertise.

I wish the following for everyone who shares this adventure:

May each day bring you happiness,
Every moment a wonderful memory to share,
And each second filled with possibilities.

—*Mary Frances Fisher*

DISCUSSION QUESTIONS

1. Which characters in *Paradox Forged in Blood (PFIB)* resonate within your own life and how?

2. Which *PFIB* character did you dislike and describe how they would act or behave differently if they lived in today's society.

3. At what point did you first guess who the murderer was? Which clues led you to your conclusion?

4. History repeats itself. Discuss any parallels in today's society with events in the book.

5. How did Frank Szabo's murder investigation in the 1940s differ from techniques employed today?

6. Which historical event in *PFIB* was a new discovery for you?

7. What dynamics in the 1930s and 1940s created the bond between the Mueller and Kaufman families?

8. The 1940s represent a time of simplicity. How does that differ from today's hectic pace? Which is preferable to you?

9. If you could travel back in time, which *PFIB* character would you like to meet and wh

ABOUT THE AUTHOR

Mary Frances Fisher, a lifelong resident of Cleveland OH, has spent the majority of her career as a legal nurse consultant and signed with Taxi Modeling and Talent Agency as a commercial print model in 2012. With Germaine Moody and writer contributions from over 100 countries, she co-authored her first published work in 2013, *50 Seeds of Greatness* (www.50seedsofgreatness.com).

Her additional writing experiences include several short stories published by Transcendent Publishing: "Earning My Wings" in *Touched by an Angel: A Collection of Divinely Inspired Stories and Poems*, October 2013; "Mercy's Legacy" in *Best of Spiritual Writers Network 2013*, December 2013; "Be Careful What You Wish For" in *The Best of Spiritual Writers Network 2014*, January 2015; and "The Gift" in *Finding Our Wings: A Collection of Angelic Stories and Poems*, March 2016.

She has written a screenplay based on "Mercy's Legacy" and is working on a *Paradox Forged in Blood* companion novel, *Growing Up O'Malley*. Mary Frances lives in a suburb of Cleveland with her family.

Visit the author online at www.maryfrancesfisher.com.